Heart of Skulls

Ashley Earley

Heart of Skulls

Copyright © 2023 by Ashley Earley

All rights reserved.

First Edition

Publication Date: October 3, 2023

No part of this publication may be reproduced, distributed, or transmitted in any form or by any means, including photocopying, recording, or other electronic or mechanical methods, without the prior written permission of the publisher, except as permitted by U.S. copyright law. For permissions, contact the author, Ashley Earley or Earley Literary Press.

Paperback ISBN: 979-8-9879815-0-4

Hardback ISBN: 979-8-9879815-1-1

eBook ISBN: 979-8-9879815-2-8

This is a work of fiction. The story, all names, characters, and incidents portrayed in this production are fictitious. No identification with actual persons (living or deceased), places, buildings, and products is intended or should be inferred.

Book Cover by Moonpress | *www.moonpress.co*

Formatting and Interior Art by Miss Eloquent Edits

Editing by Miss Eloquent Edits and Earley Editing, LLC

content warnings

child abuse, depictions of depression, mention of suicide via cigarettes, stalking, overdose depicted, blood/gore, death/murder, misogyny, necrophilia insinuated but not explicitly mentioned, dismemberment, cannibalism.

To the girls who thought they met their prince
but ended up falling for the villain.

I see you. Your trauma and feelings are valid.
Your villain might not be as bad as this book's main character,
but we cope in weird ways, don't we?

This book was me coping.

Except, he should've died in the end.

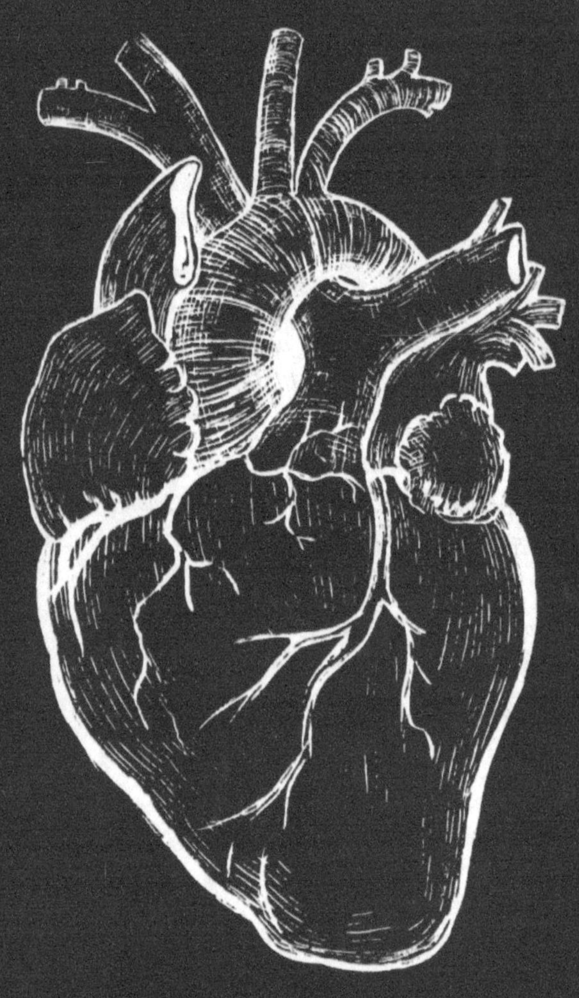

chapter one

FLICKING THE LIGHTER, I BROUGHT the flame to the tip of my cigarette, watching the white paper burn. It darkened and flaked before falling to the gravel. My mind was static, barely processing what my eyes followed. I tracked time by how many cigarettes I had burned through, only blinking from the falling ash when a train raced past. I never heard the approach. The cars just appeared, followed by a blare of a horn.

Blindly watching the sunset over the tracks, I shivered whenever the night air bit through my hoodie. When the next train sped by, stifling my cigarette, I couldn't help my shiver. I didn't bother digging into my pocket for my lighter again. The trains had stolen four cigarettes from me already.

Inhaling the smell of smoke and oil, I stood from the graffitied wall, ready to suck it up and get out of the cold.

Though my gut still twisted at the thought of going home. Being confined to chipped, dented walls made my organs gnarl, like they were trying to kill me before I could reach my front door.

I walked across the gravel until my beat-up high-tops hit pavement, the rubber scuffing the road leading to my neighborhood. Keeping my head down, I only looked up from under my brows when small one-story homes came into view on either side of the street. Barred windows, gated, locked doors, leaf-covered yards—it was like the neighbors had banded together to create one massive shitfest.

My house was halfway down the street, six houses from the corner bus stop, squished between two other trash-infested homes. I walked over uneven bricks to the front of the house, then steeled myself as I yanked open the gate to the unlocked door behind it.

It was stale inside. The air was dry the moment the world was locked outside. Smoking was forbidden, a rule Mom had made, but heavy drinking was encouraged. The TV was always on, whether for background noise or for someone watching. Usually, at least eight empty beer bottles would sit on the table beside the chair claimed by my pathetic excuse for a father. His ass was the only one allowed to slump into the crusty, stained brown leather throne.

Except he wasn't sitting in it.

"Motherfuckers, where are yeh?" came a garbled voice from the back of the house. A cabinet banged shut.

I gave myself a moment, squeezing my eyes closed before making for the kitchen.

"Who moved my goddamned crackers?" he was saying to himself when I walked in.

Pulse picking up, I quickly took in what I could. A bowl of soup was on the counter. He was still in the jeans he wore to work, his hair disheveled as he rummaged through expiring food inside our cabinets. Nearly all were open.

"Who touched my fuckin' crackers?" He spotted me. "How fuckin' hard is it not to touch my goddamned crackers?"

Before he could step toward me, I headed for the cabinet over the once-white stove caked in brown crud. When I yanked it open, he grabbed my sleeve. I swallowed, ignoring him, and reaching. He was wound tight, practically twitching for a reason to throw a punch. I was as tense, my jaw locked, teeth grinding to avoid shaking out of his grip.

A weight dropped in my stomach. I couldn't let him smell the smoke on me. I had to keep reminding myself to breathe through my nose.

I set the box of crackers on the counter before my old man could swing his free fist.

"Think yer such a smart-ass, eh?"

I stood frozen as I calculated my next move—my next words. I could do nothing right.

He probably would've trashed the kitchen in his search. He definitely would've left it for me to handle. Not having crackers to dump into his soup would've been the end of the world, but thanking me for finding them would kill him. I couldn't win.

I was silent long enough to make him scoff before snatching up his bowl, spilling soup on the counter as he reached for the box.

"Piece of shit. I haven't had that much to drink. I would've found the crackers without you. And what the fuck is that smell?"

"Yeah. Sure."

The words spewed out before I could stop them. I almost jumped back from them. He wasn't slurring too bad, but I was still playing a dangerous game. He'd already smelled the smoke on me. I couldn't push him too far without setting him off.

He stopped dead, hand crushing the box. The tension tasted metallic. Not moving, I waited for his reaction, knowing he didn't have a reasonable bone in his body and that running would only excite him. I leaned against the counter, letting the edge dig into my lower back as I stuffed my hands into my hoodie's pocket. It'd been a while since he'd bruised up my back.

He popped open the box and tossed a cracker at my feet. Fuck if I knew when the floors had been cleaned last. He barely threw out the beer bottles that piled up next to his chair, and even then, it was usual to start the week with a fresh collection to see if he could beat the previous week's record.

"Don' even think 'bout steppin' foot in this kitchen 'gain. You can go to school hungry tomorrow."

My hands clenched and unclenched in the front pocket of my hoodie, crushing everything I wanted to say. *Whatever. Go back to sitting on your ass. Not like there's anything I want to eat, anyway. Everything is expired or doesn't make sense, since you never go out for groceries. I'm not going to eat sardines straight out of a can, and I'll be damned if I ask you for a pack of crackers from that box, you fucking prick.*

My jaw was just starting to throb when he finally turned away, satisfied by my indifference. A few seconds later, the recliner creaked, and the TV's volume increased. I released the breath I'd been holding to keep my anger behind my teeth.

"Get yer ass in here and watch this."

I kicked the cracker and watched it disappear under the fridge, leaving it to rot.

When I walked into the living room, I went straight to the worn down couch and propped my back against its front. Sitting on it was not a fucking option. Not when beer stains and holes from when Dad had picked at the fake leather in his sleep covered the shitty cushions. The bastard had even smeared orange dust into the cracks.

"That survivin' competition thing is on." He waved the remote at the TV.

I glared at the person squirming about eating a tarantula on the screen.

I wanted to waterboard him with his own beer—shove the damned remote down his throat to let him choke on it.

I wanted to draw blood when he acted like everything was normal, like we had a typical father-son relationship. When he acted like he didn't beat the shit out of me every other day.

"I could make it on one of these shows. Win us a shit ton of money. Never have to work again."

He only ever worked to pay the bills and then used whatever was left on his six-pack of choice. If he didn't make enough for beer, he'd stay sober enough to make it through another shift or two.

"Don't you think I could make it on one of these shows?"

"Sure, Dad."

"Watch 'em eat that spi'er. You don't think I could do that?" I didn't get to answer. "I wouldn't build a fire. I'd build a bonfire 'n have that shit going all night. Then, if anything tried to sneak up on me, I could throw it in that fire. I would cook that son of a bitch real good."

I played along.

"The spider or the thing that snuck up on you?"

"Both."

His words drawled, almost dragging their feet as they left his mouth.

I didn't want to imagine what his breath smelled like. I didn't want him anywhere near me.

"I would cook *both!* Real good! And I would *win.*"

He would eat a tarantula in a heartbeat, but he'd be fucked if he had to build a fire or a shelter. Finally, I couldn't listen to him any longer. He was getting loud, and all I wanted was to face-plant into bed. "I can't take this anymore. I'm going to bed."

"All right, good night, son."

I didn't look back as I left the room.

"Yeah, you, too."

chapter two

THE NEXT DAY, I FORCED MYSELF to go home after school. The day before had been too much of a close call. I kept my head down as I walked along the gravel that led to the tracks. Between my itch to smoke and my hostility about going home, my lighter and Marlboros were screaming at me. Not for the taste but for knowing I would be one tobacco burn closer to blackening my lungs. Locking myself in my room was the only way to shut up the craving.

I didn't hesitate at the front door. As much as I hated it, I lived here just as much as my bastard father did.

When I stepped inside, the TV was on, like always, but Dad was propped in his stained chair, mouth gaping. I noted the number of bottles beside him, including the one in his slackened hand, before making for my room. I dumped my backpack at my desk and snatched the first notebook I laid eyes on. After flopping onto my bed, I sat up against the wall where a headboard should have been. Opening it to a blank sheet, I pulled out the black pen shoved in the back, then got to darkening the page. Pen scratched across paper as I filled it the same way I had the others, blending every written word of frustration with morbid drawings.

Dark ink turned into morphed figures, banged-up cars, deformed animals, lit up junk, or my teachers as weird cartoon characters. I sketched and scribbled whatever came to mind. Even wrote some random shit in graffiti, like a cat wearing a bucket hat while smoking a joint. I hadn't tagged a wall before, but I had cans of spray paint in my closet, waiting to be shaken and cracked open.

The first and only time I looked up was when I glanced out the window. I had no idea how long drawing had kept me zoned out, but it was already pretty dark out. Snapping the notebook shut, I threw it across my bed as I stood before walking to the living room.

My father was exactly where I had left him. It didn't look like he'd even gotten up to grab another beer. My jaw locked, tension riding up the side of my face.

I could've slipped out hours ago. Of fucking course. The one time I came straight home and I could've slipped out hours ago. I shook my head as I eased the door open. There was no helping the gated door, though. It banged shut behind me. My gut cringed, sending pins and needles to my fingertips as it sank. But I kept moving, stuffing my fists inside the pockets of my hoodie. I made for the tracks, turning the lighter over in my pocket.

Keeping my head down, I watched my shoes scrape the road until they reached gravel. My head snapped up at the sound of distant voices near the tracks. *Come freaking on.* My hand tightened around my lighter. In the weeks I had been calling it my sanctuary, no one had bothered me.

After weaving through the graveyard of abandoned cars the homeless usually slept in at night, I was met with barrels of fire pits and people I recognized from school. I stalked around the horde, keeping my head low but glaring at anyone who looked my way. Jackasses from the other high school were here, too.

They were passing each other beer cans and small bags of substances. I shook off the instinct to leave and kept moving until I reached the graffitied wall. I just needed a smoke. One cigarette. Some fresh air. One fucking hour to myself outside my stale prison.

Once my legs were dangling over the wall's edge, I snapped my lighter to bring the flame to my mouth. Wiping my sweaty palms down the length of my jeans, I tried not to look around. I didn't want anything to do with anyone or what they were doing. Staring off at nothing, I listened to the flames crackle and pop in the barrels, ignoring the muffled stutters of those hogging their heat.

This was my chance to catch my breath.

This was my chance to blacken my lungs. This was my chance to deprive my father of the satisfaction of killing me. With every box, I was paying to cut my life short, but avoiding the physical pain would be worth it in the end.

I was the one in control.

Everyone knew smoking was a slow way of committing suicide. They just didn't know that was my intention. I hated the way it tasted, how it made my skin, my clothes, my breath, and even my hair smell, but I had grown used to it. I had become addicted to the long-term effects it would have.

I closed my eyes, trying to push back the anger coiling in my chest.

I pulled one last drag before flicking the cigarette to the gravel. The rolled paper caught enough distance that it nearly bounced off the tracks. I had a new one in my mouth within seconds, but a burst of laughter made me freeze with the lighter in front of my face.

"Dumb bitch. Get the fuck out of my face!" a voice shouted over the others.

I quickly lit up before looking over.

Once the smoke cleared, I spotted a girl I'd never seen before moving through the barrels, away from the douche shouting after her.

"You have no right to tell me when I should stop drinking."

She ignored him and kept moving through the crowd, arms crossed. She stopped at one of the farthest barrels and paid no mind to those staring as she warmed her hands. The guy said something indiscernible but then turned back to the guys he'd been talking with. The girl didn't so much as look at him.

Someone went over to talk to her, but she only shook her head at whatever they said.

I turned away to stare at nothing again. I didn't have much time left. This would likely be my last cigarette before I had to go back. I wanted to enjoy it.

But I couldn't help looking at her. It wasn't hard to pick her out. Her streaked pink-and-blue hair stood out against her black T-shirt. She hadn't moved from the barrel, staring into the crackling flames. She looked indifferent to the situation and those around her.

I was about to turn away when she caught me staring, narrowing her eyes at me, before walking over.

Something in my chest sank. I quickly turned away in the hopes she would change her mind.

I didn't look over as she practically plopped down beside me, kicking her feet out from the wall. Hiding part of my face with my hair, I watched her from the corner of my eye. Without a word, she pulled a cigarette from her jean pocket and threw it in her mouth.

"Why are you watching me like a creep?" She lit the wrinkled cigarette between her teeth.

I stiffened, caught off guard by her blatant question. She had no right to sit here and call me a creep after a guy called her a bitch in front of a shit ton of people, and she'd done nothing to defend herself.

I let out a long exhale of smoke through my nose, refusing to acknowledge her outside of the occasional glance in my peripheral.

She watched the smoke drift when she blew it into the air. "Did you enjoy the show? Enjoy watching my boyfriend act like an asshole?"

"That's your boyfriend?" I asked, without an ounce of interest.

Though I gave myself permission to gauge her reaction.

She shrugged, as if the way he'd shouted was typical and didn't bother her.

"Congratulations," I grumbled, turning away from her to take another drag.

She had a small smirk on her face. "So, why are you all the way over here when everyone else is over there? You one of those lone wolves? Afraid of fire? What?"

"Why are you talking to me?" I ground out.

"Why don't you just leave if you don't want to be here?"

I turned to face her. "Why don't you just leave if your boyfriend is such a dick?"

She blew smoke straight into my face, causing my anger to spike. "Why do you care?"

"Why did you come over here?"

"I don't enjoy going around in circles, so answer my question."

"Not a chance. Wouldn't you rather join the party?"

"I'm bored." She threw her cigarette to the ground. "Enlighten me and make this shitfest bearable."

She didn't want to go back to the party. She wanted to be anywhere away from him. Eyes bore into me, and I knew it wasn't the girl next to me. A sigh left me as I turned to find her boyfriend staring at me from the barrel he'd chased her from. I didn't break eye contact. Even when the fire in the nearest barrel popped, gaining obnoxious laughs, I didn't stop staring.

"Um . . ." the girl beside me said, her voice shaky.

"He seems like a ray of sunshine," I eventually said, still keeping an eye on him from across the way.

Finally, he must've gotten tired of our staring contest because he gave in to head our way.

"Get the fuck away from—"

The girl shot to her feet. "I went up to him."

"Do I look like I give a shit?" He grabbed her wrist to yank her closer.

She gasped as she bumped into his side.

I stiffened, ready to launch to my feet. Instead, I lit another cigarette.

The boyfriend shifted her behind me, closer to him, and leaned down to me.

I didn't move. He wanted me to flinch, but I stayed planted, watching him from the corner of my eye. Every part of me was stiff, ready to throw my cigarette in his face if he so much as blinked wrong.

"You're fucked, you fucking freak," he hissed, then spit some disgusting shit next to me.

I took a long drag, refusing to let that be the moment I beat him into the ground and crushed his teeth into the pavement.

When he turned, the girl glanced at me, her eyes full of apologies.

Keeping an eye on them out of the corner of my peripheral, I took my time dragging from my cigarette. Drowning out the fire and the chatter was impossible.

But I didn't look at either of them again—I didn't look up at all—until my cigarette was nothing but charred flakes.

My eyes immediately found the boyfriend's when I stood to leave.

He held my stare, his arm firmly around the girl. She barely looked at him but didn't shrink into herself or him. He chugged a beer as I stuffed my carton and lighter into my pockets to drop down from the wall.

Before leaving, I watched him crumble a beer can like my father, glaring at me over the fire.

chapter three

PRETTY MUCH THE SECOND I got home from school, I was out the door again. Blood boiling, I was ready to burn the whole fucking world down. To relieve a fraction of what was building inside me, I slammed the door on my way out, then got far enough up the street that the bastard didn't bother trying to nab me. Lazy shit.

I rubbed the back of my neck, flinching when I grazed the spot where he'd struck me with a dirty wooden spoon.

Finding a fucking snack—finding anything to eat, really—was already impossible. Add a hungry drunk to the mix, and suddenly, I'm stealing some gourmet meal instead of an old can of Spam.

Shoving a hand into my pocket, I pulled out my lighter to flip it open, snap it on, and shut the cap over the flame. I mindlessly did this over and over as I walked down the middle of the street.

Cigarettes would just have to shut up my stomach for now.

I was going to sit out by the train tracks for a while. There was no way I was heading home before I was sure he was passed out.

The second my feet hit gravel, I grabbed my feast of cancer sticks from my back pocket.

When I looked up, I nearly stopped in my tracks.

Perched on the edge of the wall in front of the train tracks was the girl from last night's party. A surge of adrenaline shot through my body, tightening my jaw as I crossed the distance. I was not in the mood to talk to some rando. She had no reason to be in my spot.

"What the hell are you doing here?"

Her head snapped up at the sound of my voice. I had no idea how she didn't hear me coming with all the gravel. She'd been leaning over a notebook in her lap, black ink smeared on her thumb and index finger. Though her head had whipped up, she didn't look surprised to see me.

"Hello to you, too, I guess."

"What the hell are you doing here?" I bit out again, speaking each word slowly.

She set her notebook aside, then patted the concrete slab on the other side of her. "Have a seat."

I shoved my hands in my pockets, my eyes never leaving her as I stuffed my cigarettes and lighter away.

After watching the wheels in my head turn, the girl said, "Look, I just . . . I didn't like how things happened last night."

I thought back to how her boyfriend had grabbed her— how he'd crushed that beer can after chugging it empty. All emotion drained from me, the tension dropping from my jaw and hands. I sat next to her, pulled out a cigarette, and lit it. Normally, all I could think about was feeding my growing hunger and inhaling my lungs with grime. But as I dangled my legs over the edge, I felt the weight of mental fatigue.

"How long have you been waiting for me?"

She shrugged. "I really don't know. I lost track of time." She tapped her pen against her leg. "I know it's stupid, but I just wanted to thank you for last night—"

"You're not about to tell me some bullshit about how he doesn't normally treat you like that, right?"

She shook her head, looking down with a half-assed smile. "No. I'm just kind of used to it at this point."

Tightness clenched in my chest. I couldn't think of anything to say.

"So, there are bound to be awkward silences. Let's not be strangers." She stuck out her hand. "I'm Natalie. I live a few blocks over. My boyfriend is an asshole, and my hair makes everyone jumps to the clichéd conclusion that I'm an artist."

I glanced at the pen she'd been tapping against her leg, remembering the notebook. "Are you an artist?"

Her mouth twitched before a smile formed. "Maybe you should give me your name before I answer such an invasive question."

I fought not to roll my eyes. "My name is Scott."

"And?"

"And I want another cigarette."

Her eyes shot down to my hands. "Yeah, I figured."

"Don't act like you give a shit."

No one else does, that's for damn sure.

"I smoke, too, so . . ." She shrugged. "So, you snuck out?"

I shook my head. "Nah-uh. I asked you a question."

Looking down, she turned her hands over as she examined them. "I am. Though my hands don't show it right now, I just finished an abstract piece."

"Abstract?" I asked as I tossed my cigarette. Gravel put out the glowing tip.

"Yeah. I don't normally lean toward abstract, but I was angry, and splattering paint seemed like the way to go."

I felt like she wanted me to ask about her anger or the art that came from it, so I didn't. She had my full attention, though. Something about her had me on the edge of my seat, forcing me to listen. I didn't want her to go anywhere. I wanted her to stay right here. Though I'd come here to disappear into smoke, she wouldn't let me. I wasn't sure I wanted to stop talking to her.

"You snuck out. Why?" Natalie asked again, softer this time.

"Because I was angry."

Silence passed between us. I didn't feel uncomfortable. I felt nothing.

"Are you angry a lot?" she asked.

"Not as much as my dad."

She nodded. "I'm angry with myself a lot. I'm sorry for calling you a creep, by the way."

"I came here to get away from being angry last night and then my boyfriend just goes ahead and treats me like—"

"Like you're nothing."

She blinked, either surprised by my interruption or my words. "You don't know me. What if I deserve it?"

"What could you have done?" I asked, taking her in the way her eyes were begging me to.

She wanted to be seen. She wanted to be challenged. Though it had been a long time since I'd seen it on myself, I knew the look. She was desperate for someone to see her.

But I was a stranger; I didn't know what was eating at her.

I stood from the wall, the tips of my shoes hovering over the edge.

"Hey!" Natalie scrambled to her feet, too. "You can't just say shit like that and then get up to leave."

Her gaze was hard but curious, questioning, like she was trying to figure out some puzzle.

"What?"

She shook her head, hiding in her curtain of hair. "Just trust me. I deserve it."

"Your boyfriend's a dick. You shouldn't be treated like that."

Another moment of silence hung over us before she said, "Don't leave yet."

I locked eyes with her, saw how reluctant she was to leave, and slumped back to my spot on the ledge. She joined me hesitantly, kicking her beat-up shoes out from the wall.

"What now?" I asked.

I grasped for straws—an excuse not to keep talking. But I couldn't. I want to keep her talking.

Instead, I said, "What kind of . . . You said you're an artist? What kind of artist are you?"

She grinned. "The dark and twisted kind."

"But do you paint or sketch or . . ."

She pursed her lips. "Uh. Sketching isn't normally my go-to unless I'm drawing on a person. So, mostly paint, yeah."

"You draw on people?"

"Yeah, mostly flowers and butterflies and shit like that on my friends when they beg." She shrugged again, chuckling. "But, yeah, I draw on people when they let me."

A surge of adrenaline shot through my body.

"What would you do on me? If you could draw anything—anything at all—what would you draw on me?"

"Anything?" She analyzed me when I nodded. She put her hand on my shoulder, tilting it away from her to get a better look at me. "I would . . . I would do a tree. Up your arm." Her palm moved up the length of my forearm before stopping at my elbow. "No color, just black, but it would be perfect."

My eyes moved from how she was touching me to trail up from her fingers to her wrist to her arm. She was still talking, but I wasn't digesting any of it. When she glanced up at me again, her hair covered only a part of her face. The similarity it shared with my mother's fair golden hair struck me.

Blinking my thoughts away, I asked, "Why a tree?"

"That's what I see." Her blue eyes shot up to meet mine. "I don't know why I see a tree. I need to know you better before I know that."

She was too close, but I didn't want to pull away. That wasn't what I wanted; I couldn't lie to myself. Her hand dropped from my arm, but I caught her wrist. Her skin was smooth and warm despite the chill to the air. I ran a thumb over the back of her hand, amazed by the silky feel of her flesh. I could imagine her running lotion along it.

"Is this where you come to get away?" she asked.

It took a moment, but I eventually forced myself to nod.

"Meet me here tomorrow night, then." She saw my question forming and jumped to answer first. "Because I want to know you more."

Pulling her wrist from my grasp, Natalie stood, watching me get to my feet as she said, "Same time, same place?" She didn't give me a chance to respond, already slipping past the leftover barrels from the night before. She only looked over her shoulder once to say "See you then!" before she was gone.

I stood, dumbfounded by what had just happened, by who I had met, and what I had gotten myself into. Blonde with blazing streaks that perfectly demonstrated her personality, Natalie had just shoved her way into my personal space.

chapter four

I WENT TO THE TRACKS the following afternoon, but not a streak of blue or pink was in sight. It was empty. If any trains were nearby, they were silent. The sun was seconds away from dropping. Yet, Natalie was nowhere to be found.

Ignoring the pit in my stomach, I yanked the lighter from my pocket. I had snuck out again. I wouldn't let it be for nothing.

The brisk night air ran up my arms, and she never came.

When I gave up, I hurled my cigarette at the ground. Hitting the ground from jumping off the wall, I crushed the smoke into the gravel.

I left the cigarette stomped into the rocks as I made my way home, pulling all feeling back until I was detached from the cold. I was starving and didn't plan on leaving my bed for the rest of the night. If the house caught on fire for whatever fucked-up reason, I was going down with my bed.

I made for the kitchen the second I walked through the door, then grabbed a box of cereal on my way to the back bedroom. I didn't bother pushing the cupboard shut afterward. Too much noise. They squeaked shut rather than slammed when pushed.

Once I closed my bedroom door, I snatched the headphones from my desk on the way to my bed. Sprawling out on the comforter, I slid my arm elbow-deep in the box of cereal as rock blared in my ears.

I'm not sure how long I lay there, but the peace was short-lived.

I felt more than saw the door open. The creaking hinges rattled in my bones. The fresh stench of alcohol was as clear as day. His footsteps were muffled before I pulled the headphones from my ears. The edge of the bed shifted when he sat. I pulled my legs up, folding into myself as I sat up to lean against the wall.

My old man was at the edge of the bed, slouched forward, holding a bottle opener to go along with the beer in his other hand.

"Where were you?" I made out from his slurred words. I didn't get to answer before he continued, though. "You never come home after school an'more. Where do yeh go?" Again, only a short pause before he went on. "An' don't try an' act like you've joined after-school club shit or sports team or nothin'. We both know that would be the lie of the century."

He was fishing for a reason to throw a punch. He was acting like we had a normal relationship until he decided he'd had enough of the act.

I shrugged. "I just go out, hang around town for a bit."

"Not sure what 'hangin' around town' means." He narrowed his eyes. "Are yeh gettin' yourself into trouble?"

A moment of silence lingered. I burrowed into myself as I waited for the explosion.

He ground his teeth together. "Goddammit, Scott! What kind of shit are you getting yourself into?"

I didn't flinch. I kept my expression blank. It had been a long time since I shrank from his slurred shouts and spit. "I'm not doing anything. I've been going to the train tracks after school."

"To do what?"

I hesitated long enough to push his buttons further.

"To do *WHAT*?"

"I smoke at the tracks."

Because I never want to come home.

Looking down with a smile on his face, he cracked open his beer to take a gulp. Then he took another. Shouting had sobered his words. "You smoke at the train tracks." He shook his head, still smiling, when he looked up at me. For a moment, at least, before it sharply disappeared. "Your mother hated smokers. She'd be so disappointed to find you'd started such a disgustin' habit."

He narrowed his eyes when I said nothing. I could see it building in him—the resentment and the fury attached. "I can see why your mother hated you. She saw it all coming. She knew what you would turn into. No wonder she left."

Before I could blink, he had me by the back of my neck. Throwing me to the ground, he barely wasted a second to set his beer aside before hovering above me. I was numb to the first punch. I did my best to cover my face, even though he'd made it a habit to batter skin that would be covered.

"You're the whole reason," he ground out between blows.

Every punch vibrated through muscle until it reached bone.

I was trembling. I couldn't help it. He beat me harder when I folded into myself. He would kick my ribs in if I shouted or so much as wheezed. Fighting back would be suicide. It was unspoken knowledge, but I supposed it was only a matter of time before he killed me, anyway. That fact hung over me whenever I came home, like some dark cloud from a fucking cartoon.

I could only cower and hope he left my bones and teeth intact.

Ironically enough, going to the train tracks kept me breathing. The smoke from my cigarettes fought back the dark cloud, assuring me it would try to kill me before he did, promising a less painful death.

But of course this shit would happen. Had Natalie only been fucking there, I wouldn't have snuck out while the bastard was still awake. And now I was stuck in this hellhole, getting my ass handed to me.

"She hated you enough that she left!" he shouted over me. "She hated you so much that she beat you and then she left. But you walk around here like a boy. Well, you're a man, Scott! A man! You should act like one. Men don't steal their father's cereal and hide in their room. Men don't skip coming home to smoke. Men don't make their father's wives abandon them."

I was nine. Blood pooled in my mouth from holding my tongue. I was nine years old when she left us.

I closed my eyes tighter. It would be over soon. He would walk away once he needed a drink. I held onto that thought, but the urge to fight back—to shout and scream—built in my chest with each bruise he left. His words burned as harshly as his fist every time he said them, no matter how much I reminded myself of my age.

He rose to send a swift kick at my stomach. My whole body shook. I coughed, bowing into his foot when he did it again.

From my nightstand, he snatched his beer. While he took a long gulp, I swallowed the blood. It was only after he took a swig that he spit on me. I felt like I was going to explode. My chest rose and fell like my lungs were about to give out. The grip I had on my rage slipped with every struggled breath.

Teeth grinding, I kept my arms folded in front of my face. I couldn't let him see the rage building; he would take it as a challenge and then it wouldn't stop. I had challenged him once—with memories of abuse at the hands of my mother rising to the surface—when he first started drinking. That had been enough.

I lay, frozen, on the floor, like a stiff corpse balled in the fetal position.

My father—the only parent who'd ever loved me— sneered at me as he stumbled for the door. Knuckles split with blood, he held his fists taut to punch me again if I got up.

"If I catch you smoking in this house, it will be your last. I will light every cigarette you've got and watch you eat them."

I didn't move. I stayed stiff until I was sure he wasn't hovering, waiting for me to make the slightest movement to trigger his rage again. I ground my teeth when I lifted my head. My muscles were sore and bruised, making the smallest movement painful. My chest, especially. Breathing was a chore. As I pushed myself to sit up, it felt like my ribs were crushing my lungs.

My body shook harder but not from the effort it took to sit up. I was trembling from the tight grip I had on the fury coursing through me. I never flinched from his anger, but I could not help but flinch from mine. I didn't want my parents' violent tendencies.

But I couldn't stop it from boiling over.

Jaw locked, I launched to my feet to strip my bed of the covers and tore the sheets from the mattress. I unleashed my anger as quietly as I could, not wanting to give him a reason to come back. The cereal box went flying. Then I threw my single flat pillow against the wall, knocking over my flickering bedside lamp.

I stopped dead when the lamp hit the floor, disheveled hair in my eyes, hands balled into fists.

Heart pounding in my ears, I waited for him to walk back in.

I couldn't catch my breath.

After a minute, I decided he must have passed out in that fucking chair of his. I started putting everything back exactly the way I had it. My room was the cleanest in the house. No one could tell it was also my prison. No one could tell I smoked. No one could tell I was physically abused in here twice a week alone—I always washed the blood out of the carpet. No one could tell how shitty my life was or how furious I was.

Unless they knew where to look, no one could tell how much I hated life. Then again, no one ever came into this room. No one came into this house. This place was a goddamned prison. Except worse.

At least inmates got three full meals a day.

chapter five

I SNUCK OUT OF THE house when it was well and dark outside. Though the old man had passed out in his chair again with some comedy show playing on TV, I was careful sneaking by the living room. I found that comical, considering I hadn't seen him so much as crack a smile in the last few years. Before everything—before *he* turned on me.

As soon as I stepped outside, I regretted not grabbing a jacket, but I wouldn't risk going back inside for one. I ignored the cold and kept moving. Smoking wouldn't keep me warm, but I could always light a fire in a barrel by the tracks if it got too bad.

The street was dead silent. No one was out, and no cars went by, leaving me free to walk in the center of the road. A shitty block like this didn't have a sidewalk. The road curved further into the neighborhood. If you didn't turn with the pavement, gravel was straight ahead. Going that way meant dodging train cars that hadn't moved and probably never would be.

My eyes narrowed when I saw I wouldn't be alone. Someone was already standing at one of the steel drums, huddled close and staring into the flames.

I guess I would stay cold, then.

I started for the wall, already reaching for my lighter, when a vaguely familiar voice spoke up. "Do you have a thing for graffiti?"

"Where were you yesterday?" I asked after turning toward her, failing to keep the bite out of my tone.

Natalie pulled her sweatshirt around her tighter, stretching the sleeves down to her knuckles. She didn't look at me as she said, "You don't decide what I do."

My temper jumped to my throat. I could barely stop myself from yelling at her. "I thought you wanted to talk."

Rather than answering, she put a lit cigarette between her lips, staining the white paper with pink lipstick. My jaw locked, hand curling around the lighter in my pocket. My temper blazed in my chest, infuriating every breath. I hadn't even lit a one yet, and I felt like I could exhale smoke out of my nose.

She seemed different today. Off. Not as snarky as she had been the other night but more closed off. Her eyes were distant, her shoulders pulled inward as she used her hair to hide when she wasn't releasing smoke.

With closed eyes, I tried to focus on slowing my mind, but that wasn't enough. I had to pull out my lighter. After a few inhales of smoke, I calmed down.

"What's your deal?"

"My deal?" She practically huffed before turning away again, putting her cigarette back in her mouth. "You really know how to sweet-talk a woman, don't you, Scott?"

I glared at her. "It's not like you're being any nicer. Why are you here? I waited for you all fucking afternoon yesterday and then had to go back home to my shitty life."

While he was still awake.

She nodded. "So, that's why you come here to smoke. The great mystery has been solved."

Something sank in the pit of my stomach.

I couldn't look at her. I focused on breathing, inhaling, and exhaling through my nose, faster and faster, despite the sting of the cold.

"Are you going to ignore me now?" I let the silence drag on until she finally scuffed. "Fine. Then, why don't you just leave? I can't handle shit like this right now."

"I'm fucking confused. You asked me to meet you here yesterday, right?" I didn't give her the chance to answer. "But you didn't show up, and now you're here because you knew I would be, but you want me to leave?"

"Obviously, I don't know what I want."

"Obviously."

She turned to face me, glaring. "You weren't supposed to agree with me."

I shrugged. "Are you going to tell me what's going on?"

"I don't know you well enough for that."

"Whose fault is that?"

A smirk twitched at the corner of her mouth. "You've got a real attitude. I like it."

"You should stick around for when I'm actually nice."

She granted me a full smile before she looked down. "I guess you can stay."

I nodded to the wall, and she helped me pull the barrel closer so we could stay warm while we sat. "Are you sure you don't want to talk about whatever's on your mind?" I asked once we were perched on the ledge.

She shook her head. "No. I'd rather stop thinking about it."

"Well," I started after the fire snapped a few times, "here I am. What do you want to talk about?"

Clearing her throat, she discarded her cigarette into the barrel. "I want to draw on you—not today," she rushed to add when she saw my bewildered expression, "but I would like to sometime, but I need to know the real you first."

"I thought you were an artist, not a reporter. Are you really about to sit here and interview me about my life's story?"

Her mouth fell open, and she started laughing. "I knew you had a smart-ass mouth, but I wasn't aware assertiveness was included."

"It's like you said. You don't know me."

"As of right now, I'm sure I want to change that."

"Oh, you're sure now?"

"Yup. Decided just this moment."

"I guess you better start asking questions." I hid my smile by lighting another cigarette.

She glanced at me up and down. "Why the baggy clothes? Hiding tattoos? My canvas better not be vandalized already."

"No. No tattoos. Just poor."

She scuffed. "Aren't we all? You and I are a walking cliché right now." She smirked when I raised an eyebrow. "Two misfits smoking at train tracks, wearing hand-me-downs from the single thrift store in town. The guy has long dark hair and an attitude that screams 'leave me the fuck alone,' while the girl, who happens to be an artist, has streaks like she's begging for attention. We should be on the cover of an album. We're sitting on a graffitied wall, for Pete's sake!"

Taking in everything she pointed out, I couldn't help but chuckle.

"We're not part of the band, either, because we think that's lame. We're just on the cover to show how badass the album is."

My laughter cut abruptly. "I highly doubt that. There's nothing badass about what we're doing right now, not even smoking."

Her lips twitched with mischief. "Why do you smoke? How did you start?"

"That's . . ." I shook my head as I blew smoke into the air.

This snagged her attention. She swung her body toward me, pulling a leg up to cross it over the one hanging over the wall. Her eyes met mine for the second time as she waited for my answer.

"I smoke to die."

A fact. Something I hadn't spoken aloud to anyone but myself.

"Not to be disturbing or anything, but you know there are faster ways of doing that, right? I mean, smoking is a slow killer."

"That's why I smoke as many packs as I can stomach. I don't want to live forever."

"You don't have things you want to do in your life?"

"I doubt I'll live to see my mid-twenties, so . . ." I shrugged. *I'd rather have control.* "Why do you smoke? Don't you have artist aspirations?"

Something sparked in her eyes. "I want my art to be in a fancy gallery. I want to see my name on one of those cards next to it." She paused, smiling. "I don't care if it doesn't even sell. I just want one of my pieces to be good enough to be picked up like that."

Her excitement caused the pit of my stomach to flip. She talked faster, used her hands as she spoke, and didn't seem to realize it.

"Do I get to see any of your art?"

"Depends."

I waited for her to elaborate, but instead of continuing, she bit her lip as she smiled. Parts of my body felt jittery. I didn't know what else to do with my hands except curl my fingers to form fists in my lap.

"It depends on whether you like what I draw on you and if I like you enough."

"And if I hate it?" I challenged, swallowing the tease in my tone.

"Then, I guess I'll have to decide if I like you enough to keep hanging around."

"I think this is when you tell me more about yourself so I can make my own determination."

I could swear that glint in her eye faded.

"What is there to tell? I'm an artist. Am I not supposed to maintain a mysterious aura?"

"Do you want to keep being a cliché?"

"My life isn't a happy one, but then again, what famous artist had a happy life? Magic comes from tragedy."

"Save the dramatics and spill. I should know the person who's going to give me ink."

She rolled her eyes. "You act like it's permanent. Don't be a wuss."

"Spill," I said again.

She pursed her lips before spitting out everything she could think of. "My favorite thing in the world is red wine—I feel important when I drink it while I paint. I have colorful hair, but my nails are pretty much always painted black. If I could eat chunky peanut butter-and-honey sandwiches for the rest of my life, I would be the happiest woman alive. Shoving love in a corner, I despise mushrooms. Poison me with one, and I will never forgive you. I—"

"Is it the taste?"

"It's the taste, the smell. It's all of it. I can't stand them." She stuck her tongue out in disgust, as if she could taste mushrooms just by talking about them.

I couldn't help but laugh. It felt good, like a breath of fresh air but better. I couldn't remember the last time I had.

"Oh, yeah? What's something you hate?"

"Hmmm . . . the only thing coming to mind is candy corn."

"Candy corn?" She exasperated. "You hate candy corn? That's *all* I eat during the month of October. I replace the cigarettes in my pockets with bags of candy corn!"

"It's too artificial," I complained, "and it gets stuck in my teeth."

She turned serious. "I will convert you. I don't care how long it takes, Scott. I will make you fall in love with candy corn."

My heart was doing strange things in my chest at the promise—something I couldn't remember feeling before. She went on about the candy that seemed to be her devoted favorite. I half expected her to pull a bag out of her pocket and pop one in her mouth. Goose bumps rose on my arms, the chill invading my entire body. Something inside me begged for it—craved to lock eyes with her as she took a slow bite.

chapter six

NATALIE MET ME AT THE train tracks every day for the next week, talking and cracking jokes in that bubbly voice of hers. For someone who claimed not to have a happy life, she had an animated personality, peppy mixed with just enough quirkiness. I carefully noted each smile she gave me.

She was something I couldn't fathom or grasp or stop thinking about. She was always in the back of my mind. Some part of me was drawn to her. I felt it in the pit of my stomach. A yearning, but I couldn't define it. Lust, yes, but something greater—something I couldn't grab hold of.

It was our seventh or eighth-day meeting when she announced her readiness to ask me harder questions. Answers I would have to give so she could know "my soul." I would only agree if she answered mine. I watched her a lot—analyzed every word and movement—but it wasn't enough.

"Tell me your deepest, darkest secret," she demanded as she tossed a candy corn into her mouth. She'd been carrying them around just to watch my eyes narrow in disgust. "Something you've never told anyone else."

"Who is there to tell?" I scuffed. "I don't know if you've noticed, but I don't have friends."

She knocked her shoulder against mine. "You have me."

"Are we friends?"

"Getting there." She winked, tossing another candy corn in her mouth to taunt me.

I shook my head, my hair falling into my eyes. I ignore the way my mouth waters. "Are you doing that to see if I'll ask you if I can have one? Because that's not going to happen."

She pulled another candy from the bag, holding it pinched between her fingers to examine it between us. "But doesn't it look delicious? Orange, yellow, and white sugary goodness."

I shook my head. Nothing I could say would make her stop shoving the candy in my face. If anything, arguing with her would only escalate her attempts. Changing the subject was my chance to save myself.

"What or who is your muse? Don't artists talk about their muse?"

"That's a question that will change this pleasant mood entirely."

She put the candy in her mouth before sliding off the edge of the graffitied wall. She made for the train tracks and stopped only once she reached them. Grabbing my carton of cigarettes and my lighter, I jumped from the wall after her.

Arms spread wide, she walked along a track, her bag of candy corn in her grasp.

Cigarette between my teeth, I flicked my lighter on and off as I balanced beside her on the opposite rail. I waited for her to answer.

My head snapped up when her hands fell to her sides in defeat. Her steps had slowed, and she was hiding in her hair.

"My muse . . . my muse is dead." She bit her lip, staring past me before her eyes fell to her hands, chipping at the polish. "I had a brother. He died a few months ago—doing something stupid. But now my family is falling apart from grief because no one knows how to cope, so, naturally, no one gives a shit where I am. They don't even know if I'm alive or dead in a ditch somewhere right now."

Too stunned to say anything, I watched her let out a sigh that seemed to deflate her body.

"I've been painting since he died, but . . . it's not the same. My art leans toward more abstract when I'm angry, or I paint snippets of my nightmares. It's all I can think about, so I guess my muse has altered. Deformed. Maybe even experiencing a slow death, and my creativity will shrivel up and flatline. None of my work has been the same since his death."

"How . . ." I stopped, teeth grinding as my heart leaped into my throat.

I wasn't even sure it was something I could ask. I was grasping at straws, desperate to snap her out of her misery.

"A car accident. Kind of." She frowned, brows furrowed in recollection. "Stephen was high—he'd been struggling to get clean for months—and he thought he could outrun an oncoming train. A friend of his died with him."

"That's why you come to the tracks so often."

She nodded. "The party was the first time I'd been to the tracks since he died. I decided I couldn't avoid this place forever, not anymore."

"That's . . . intense."

"Yeah. It's been five months." She nodded to herself, then met my stare. "I'm going to need to know something you've never told anyone before."

I nodded, eyes on the gravel and metal rather than her, for once. It was only fair after what she'd told me.

We continued walking, and once I was even with her, I passed her my cigarette.

"I'm sure you still remember what I said at the party because you've only asked about it a few billion times—"

"You're so dramatic." Natalie rolled her eyes at me, slowly blowing smoke between pursed lips before she passed the cigarette back. "I asked once, maybe twice."

"Whatever. You asked more than once."

"We're talking about what you meant when you said about you having a shitty life at home, right? Because I'm drawing a blank on what else this could be."

"My mom straight-up abandoned my dad and me when I was nine," I rushed to answer. "No explanation—at least, not one that I know of—and not a word to me before she walked out our front door."

I had watched her from the living room, as my cheap toy cars "crashed" into each other. Our eyes had met. Dad had followed her to the front door, planted kiss after kiss on her face, but her hollow eyes stayed locked with mine until she walked out. I had become numb to memories of her but only when I was awake. I woke—paralyzed under my sheets—from nightmares of her.

"That sounds hard, but what does that have to do with being hated at home?" Her voice was quiet, gentle, but still curious. "Just because she walked out doesn't mean—"

"Because my mom was abusive. She hated her life and hated me for it. She took everything out on me." Suddenly feeling worn down, I took a long inhale of my cigarette as I stared off into the distance. I couldn't hear myself speak, but I knew my words were matter-of-fact. "My dad didn't find out about the abuse until much later. He didn't notice the bruises at first because I was a boy and was constantly getting hurt or into trouble. It wasn't until the bruises got worse that he started asking questions." I picked at my wrist, feeling the ghost of one of the worse bruises she'd left. "He didn't know what kind of mother could abuse her son, but he couldn't stop it—didn't know how to stop it." I swallowed before I continued. "But then he started abusing me once I reached my teens, years after she'd left, like he was trying to replace her and punish me for causing her to walk out."

"Oh, Scott," Natalie breathed. "You are not the reason she walked out."

Looking at the pebbles around the railing I was still balancing on, I said, "How could you know that?"

"Is that what your dad tells you? That she left because of you?" I said nothing, but that seemed to be enough confirmation from her. "It sounds like there was more going on than just that. You were nine when she left. How could you have been the reason?"

I couldn't bring myself to respond. I didn't have an answer for her. I just knew that I was. The knowledge was part of me. It was carved into my bones, stained by every bruise and rattle from forceful physical contact. My age didn't matter. She had still hated me.

"Do you remember when the abuse started?" she asked hesitantly, as if she were trying not to trigger a negative emotion.

I shook my head, finally pulling my eyes from the tracks to look at her. "A year—maybe two before she walked out?"

She nodded as if she understood, her eyes full of pity. My chest expanded at the sight, my lungs hot with sudden rage. I never wanted to see that look in anyone's eyes, let alone hers. I never wanted her to look at me like that. Ever. I wasn't pathetic. I wasn't a wounded fool. Biting the inside of my cheek, I blinked to clear the red from my vision.

"None of it's your fault, Scott. You were nine. You couldn't have been the reason she left. There had to be more you didn't know about."

I was nine. A deep part of me repeated those three words, but my mind screamed with the guilt ingrained in my mind for eight years. Dad had always accused me, even when he didn't say it outright. I had always known. I was to blame. It was my fault I was motherless.

I pulled one last drag before discarding my cigarette. "Whatever, Natalie. You don't know anything. You don't know my family or me. I don't care what you think."

I jumped down from the track, starting to walk away without looking back.

"What does this mean, then?" she called after me once I'd passed her.

Still wrestling with the flames heating my chest, I fought to suppress my anger. I couldn't even answer her, focusing on calming my breathing instead.

Natalie hopped down from the railroad track to come up behind me. "I like you, Scott. Your bullshit attitude and all." She narrowed her eyes. "But that does not mean I will let you treat me like trash."

Her words shot right through me. I still couldn't answer but not because of my boiling anger. "Then, don't fucking look at me like that. I don't want your pity."

I didn't look back at her, but I could tell it had caught her off guard from the way she stammered. "O-Okay." She cleared her throat. "Okay, Scott. You can walk away and deal with everything in your life exactly the same way, but that will get you nowhere—"

I turned to face her. "And where do you think I'm going, Natalie? Where? I'm poor. My father hates me, and I have no way to get out of this goddamned neighborhood, let alone this town."

"That's the best part. You have every reason to get out. What I meant was that, if you keep storming off, you'll have no one else but your dad."

"After all this, do you really want to be friends with me?" I bit out.

Though it felt like my heart stopped as I waited for her answer.

"Yeah." Her shy smile tugged at her lips. "I think I do. I want to keep being a walking cliché with you." I shook my head, dumbfounded by her. She merely shrugged. "We both have our own shit. I want to know more about it, and maybe I'll tell you more about my own shit."

"You'll reveal all your artistic mysteries?"

"If you want to see my art, you'll have to understand my tragedies." She stuffed her bag of candy corn into her pocket. "Speaking of which, I need to get going. There is a blank canvas calling my name."

"Fine. I'll go be a moody teen by myself."

I couldn't stop myself from watching her walk away.

"We can reform the cliché tomorrow," she called over her shoulder.

"If I'm up to the challenge of putting up with you," I muttered, starting for my house.

Everything in me knew those words were lies.

"I heard that!"

I looked back at her once before I sped down the opposite street. Her colorful hair whirled as she whipped her head forward, bouncing against her shoulders. It had only been a split second, but I could've sworn her blue eyes had been full of laughter. Whenever I caught her looking at me, they always seemed to glean she knew something I didn't. She was confident in whatever it was.

Back at the house, I was focused on what it could be—what she thought she knew—as I swung open the front door. There was a loud shatter against the wall beside me, instantly snapping me back to reality as the bottle exploded.

I flinched back before his fist could connect with my face, catching myself in time to fall into the wall instead of hitting the floor. That was where my control ended. I was trapped against it with no hope of reaching the front door again.

Dad stood over me, chest rising and falling, fueling his anger. His eyes glazed over. "Where yeh been? Smokin'?"

I said nothing, my body suddenly feeling drained of blood and sensation, leaving me empty.

"Answer me, boy."

The alcohol on his breath wafted into my face.

I swallowed to keep my voice even. I wouldn't let my response be weak. "Yes. Yes, I was smoking."

He didn't need to know about anything else. That was the only bit of power I had.

I didn't have the chance to brace myself before his fist connected with my gut. My knees buckled, but I refused to fall. He grabbed me by the collar of my T-shirt, sending a punch to the side of my face. My ears burst, the ringing blaring in my head. I locked my jaw to avoid yelling.

He dropped me, and I didn't move. "If yeh mother hated yeh before . . . I would hate to think what she'd say 'bout yeh now."

He took a moment to stand at his full height and squared his shoulders before stumbling into the living room. "Get me another beer. Cold. Out the fridge."

I heard him collapse into his chair. I waited a minute longer, reaching for the thoughts I'd had about Natalie before walking through the door and holding on to them. Standing, I ignored the impulse to look at my face in the mirror above the shoe stand. My ears had stopped ringing, but the side of my head pounded with the promise of another bruise.

chapter seven

I HID THE BRUISE AS best I could with my long hair, brushing it directly over the purple splotch rimmed with yellow and flinching every time. No one at school noticed—or, at least, no one said anything about it. Pretending bruises were invisible was an unspoken rule between the guys I smoked with—both lived in homes with either a righteous father or a crazy mom. But no one's focus lingered. Maybe everyone thought it went well with my reputation, or maybe nothing looked out of place.

Being given such a visible bruise was rare. My mom hadn't cared much, but my dad was more careful about where he executed his rage.

I knew I could've walked away with much more than a bruise by admitting that I hadn't quit smoking.

But I made it through the day. Barely above the surface of my hazy mind, but I made it.

The moment the last bell sounded, the hallway flooded. I was in the center of it, fiddling with the lighter in my pocket as I shouldered my way through a sea of bodies.

Everything was a distant muffle, almost like static on a TV or like wearing a headset without playing music.

I didn't bother riding the bus. I wasn't going to wait to sneak out. No one would stop me from going to the tracks. I hiked my backpack over my shoulders and started down the road that led straight to my shitty part of town.

Dad always complained about how our town played favorites and liked to segregate people. The moment our family had nothing, no one wanted anything to do with us. Where was the loyalty? What happened to neighbors being friendly and helpful? Once Mom left, we had nothing. No one cared about our struggle.

I might've believed that back when we moved to the opposite side of town, but I wasn't a kid anymore. I hadn't been in a long time. No one wanted to associate with us after we moved because my dad had become an alcoholic douche after my mom left. They must've been relieved when we finally left, relieved not to live next to that anymore, even though they would still run into us at the grocery store or the gas station he worked at now. When he was sober enough to get off his ass to make a shift. I was sure he only had his job because his boss was one of the few who still pitied him.

I messaged Natalie on the way, letting her know that I'd be at the tracks earlier if she wanted to bother meeting me.

I was sick of it. I was sick of going home and being used as a fucking punching bag to make my dad feel like he was doing some good in our broken, fucked-up thing he called a family.

I walked faster, hands shaking with the urge to punch through something. I shoved my fists in the pockets of my hoodie, but they only shook harder. My body was fidgeting for a smoke, my carton of Marlboros burning a hole in my back pocket, mocking my craving.

I never got a response from Natalie but found her already perched on the wall when I got there.

Sticking a cigarette between her lips, she lit another and wordlessly passed it to me as I dropped beside her.

"Everything good? You're storming around like a man with his hair on fire."

I snatched the cigarette from her.

"Whoa, testosterone, relax. What's your—"

"I'm fine, Natalie." I blew smoke, feeling like a dragon releasing flames.

Her necklace dangled forward, taunting me, inviting me. It would be easy to yank—

My eyes shifted to the T-shirt she wore, black and stretched to where it hung loosely around her collarbone and left shoulder. My mouth went dry, and the same churning from before rose. I couldn't tell if she was wearing a bra, but the likelihood she wasn't was distracting enough. I wanted to lean in and find out.

I wanted to know her, to taste her.

"You don't look fine," she pressed. "You actually look kinda pissed. Did I do something?"

I blinked, straightening to lean away from her. "No. No, why would you ask that?"

She shrugged. "Most people have been upset with me lately. It's the only way I'm noticed."

She almost always said something that left me clueless about what to say. She was so blunt. She wore everything on her shoulder around me. She always said things as if she accepted the reality of her life, but then she said others that showed her refusal to accept those things as her future.

"What the hell happened to your face?" Her tone was more matter-of-fact than shocked.

Biting my tongue to avoid snapping at her, I brushed my hair back over the bruise I'd almost forgotten about. "Don't worry about it. I'm fine."

"That looks bad, Scott. It's already yellow."

"I know, okay? It is what it is."

"You don't have to accept that—"

"What else am I supposed to do? He's my father, and I still live there. I have nowhere else to go. I have nothing."

There was no way of fighting back when there was no escape.

"Not yet, but we're seniors. College is right around the corner."

"Yeah," I said bleakly.

Not for me. I thought for a moment, watching the smoke move through the cold air. Fading with distance, the smoke reached the far walls at the end of the station, whirling against the graffiti before it was gone.

"You're an artist," I said to catch her attention, my voice distant from my own ears. "Have you ever tried graffiti?"

When I came back, I dropped the bag of spray paint in front of Natalie. With a bag of candy corn in her lap, she was sitting on the ground. She had chosen a mostly blank wall while I'd been gone, nodding to the spot she'd picked out.

"I've never tried spray paint before," she said as she jolted to her feet, careful not to spill her candy when she snatched it up with her. "I've always wanted to get one of those massive canvases to make a mess like this, but I could never afford it."

"This wall is your massive canvas. I can just watch so you can do your thing if—"

"Not a chance! I want to see what you've got. I'm not going to let you get away with sitting on the sidelines." She unzipped the bag and threw a black can at me. "Letting your butt get sore in the gravel is hella the wrong way to go. You're doing this with me."

I couldn't help my laughter as I shook the can and popped the lid. "Did you seriously just say 'hella'? Maybe you should've picked a better seat. I'm sure that gravel put a few dents in your butt."

A smile tugged on her lips. Pushing buttons, distancing from things I didn't want to talk about, she gave it all right back. As I had become addicted to the long-term effects of cigarettes, I had become addicted to giving people a reason to walk away—or even hate me.

But Natalie was different.

I didn't want to give her a reason.

"Oh, shut up." She was still smiling when she pulled a purple can from the bag. She strutted right up to the wall and sprayed a splattered purple circle in one of the blank spots. "I'm going to have to go over someone else's work a bit," she said under her breath.

I could see the wheels turning in her mind as she stared at what little blank space she had. Every movement raised her shirt, exposing the curve of her hips. I wanted to see more. I got to work on the wall before she could catch me watching her. The rest of the graffiti was colorful with bold words like *SLAP!* And *WYLD STYLE*—typical high-school crap—while mine was a blob of black.

"So, you hoard spray cans but don't use them?"

"I figured I might use them some day, but I've only ever done this on paper."

"Graffiti-style drawing?"

"Yeah. This is harder than leaving something dirty for a teacher in the corner of my test."

"What would you have thought if I'd brought my boom box to play Elvis?" She smirked. "Can your ears handle anything other than Eminem or your broody music, or do they bleed?"

"My music might be white-boy basic, but at least I don't say shit like 'hella.' What are you gonna say next, 'peeps'?"

She laughed hard enough that she had to pause. Once she calmed down, she asked for my black spray can. I threw it to her and pulled another black one from the hoard in the bag. I focused on what I was doing, turning back to the wall stained with the black figure.

The next time I looked up, Natalie had a massive owl outlined in black and was spraying it with the purple can she had started with.

"Holy shit, Natalie." I stared, dumbfounded by her art. She paused her spraying, whipping around to look at me. "All right, I'll let you do whatever the hell you want to my arm."

She nodded to my black blob. "Um, what's yours?"

I wished I could cover up my mess. She clearly had talent, while I clearly didn't.

"It's, uh, supposed to be just a guy wearing a cloak, but . . . I fucked it up pretty bad, I guess, if you're asking me what it is."

"No, I—"

"What're you doing here, Natalie?"

She went rigid before she turned to face the two guys who had walked out from behind a train car. It took me a few moments to recognize one: her boyfriend from the party. They must have heard us from over by the barrels.

"Nothing, really" was all she said once she pushed back her surprise. She stood stiffly, as if braced with her arms crossed in front of her chest.

Eyes bouncing between us, he looked furious. Of course, he was blonde and blue-eyed, so he could be only be taken so seriously. The next time he spoke to Natalie, it was as he stared me down.

"What're you doing?"

His words came out slurred.

I bit my tongue to avoid responding for her.

His friend stumbled forward, pushing past Natalie's puny boyfriend. His eyes were lazily scanning our bag. It laid unzipped, but the flaps had caved in, hiding the spray cans. "Have any alcohol I could borrow?"

"No" was all I said.

"A cigarette I could borrow?"

I shoved down the impulse to wrap my hand around the lighter and Marlboro pack in my pocket. "No."

He grinned, blinking longer every time he closed his eyes. "Have a girlfriend I could borrow?"

"Fuck you," Natalie said, but not nearly loud enough for them to hear her.

My fists were balled in my pockets, almost trembling with the force. "Fuck you and fuck off."

"Have a problem?" Natalie's boyfriend asked.

"Yeah, don't fucking say that."

"I didn't." Her boyfriend smirked, nodding to his friend. "He did. How am I supposed to control what other people say about you?"

"You could *defend me*, dickface!"

The friend stormed up to us. But instead of getting in Natalie's face, he headed straight for me. I braced myself but kept my hands inside my hoodie, never breaking eye contact. Not even when he shoved his shoulder into mine. I set my jaw, ready to free one of my fists if he tried to take the first swing. He was too drunk to know it, but that would be a massive mistake.

Refusing to meet his eyes, I exhaled a long breath.

I didn't know why they were here or what they thought they would do. I just knew they weren't getting anywhere fucking near us.

"Hey. Hey, man," the guy said, the alcohol on his breath an all too familiar smell. Cheap. A worthless smell. "What's your deal?"

I didn't acknowledge him. My eyes were on Natalie as her boyfriend made for her. He was only a little steadier on his feet than his friend. I half hoped he'd keel over before reaching her, scuff up his fucking face, bust an eye out in the gravel . . .

"Don't, Jackson," Natalie warned, pressing her fists into her chest as if to compose or defend herself. "Don't start something. Take Nathan and get out of here. This is over. Us—No, listen to me! This is done, so don't touch me. Walk away."

His friend Nathan wedged his shoulder into me again. I exhaled another long breath before kneeing him in the thigh hard enough to send him on his drunk ass. I barely looked down at him.

I kept my hands in my pockets, doing my best to stifle the full force of everything boiling and threatening to explode. I'd spent years of holding it all in, and my emotions had been building. Natalie's boyfriend stared at me, not surprised but like he was trying to comprehend what had just happened. Once he seemed to decide, he shoved Natalie away.

"Have something to say?" he shouted as he made his way toward me. When I didn't answer right away, he kept at it. "I said. Do. You. Have. Something. To. Say?"

I hated his preppy Slim Shady look. It didn't fucking fit in this part of town.

"Lay off" was all I said, keeping my tone even.

Jackson searched my face for any sign of fight or flight and seemed confused when he found nothing. "What was that? I'm sorry. I don't speak punk bitch."

Nathan had taken a few steps back, his drunk smirk laughing at my expense.

Jackson went to send a fist straight for my face. I let him have the satisfaction of that first strike across my cheek, but I had his wrist trapped before he could pull away. I pulled him down with me, breathing through the pain of the stabbing gravel, just so I could throw him on the ground next to me. He gasped for breath at the impact, and that was when he really felt my first punch. Then my second. Third.

Everything became a blur.

He fought his way on top of me, using both fists to get in as many punches as he could. It was sloppy, and I would only let him get in a few more hits. But Natalie stepped in before I could turn the table. Pulling Jackson away from me by the neck of his shirt, she practically flung him from my grip. She'd been shouting at us since our scuffle began, but it sounded like she was just getting started.

"Jackson! Go the fuck home before I drag your mother out here!"

"Shit, Natalie, fine!" He spat blood at her feet.

I hoped I had chipped one of his teeth.

They stumbled away, Nathan stumbling on the gravel enough that he had to push himself up before he ate shit.

My left shoulder and wrist hurt, but the hand I'd used to punch him with was aching.

Once they were out of sight, I strode over to Natalie, needing to touch her and know she was okay. I was cold—so cold, despite the anger that had nearly overtaken me.

"Are you—"

Natalie threw herself against me, wrapping her arms around my neck.

She was shaking.

Another wave of adrenaline crashed into me, and I wanted—

"I was scared for myself and then I was scared for you."

"You don't need to worry about me."

She pulled away, and I went cold again when she stepped back. "I know you can take care of yourself, Scott, but that's beside the point."

I didn't look at her; I focused on my breathing. She didn't understand. She didn't know about the rage bristling in my genes. Certain situations begged it to be unleashed.

"I'm not upset with you, Scott. I'm just . . . anxious. It scared me, and I'm anxious, and I could just really use some comforting right now."

I finally looked at her. She was staring at her hands, but I saw the tear resting on her cheek before she hid in her hair. My heart dropped like a brick. I gathered her in my arms, and she buried her face in my chest. She had to hear how fast my heart was beating, but she probably thought it was because of the fight.

When she wound her arms around my waist, I knew things would be different from now on.

She was okay. Here, she was okay.

I buried my nose in her colorful hair. Only for a moment.

chapter eight

WEEKS PASSED. I STOPPED WEARING hoodies, and her jean jacket eventually disappeared. I still wore baggy T-shirts, but Natalie started wearing loose tank tops. Her chest, shoulders, and arms were usually covered in flecks of paint, like she only cared to scrub it off her hands. Whether she showed up bubbly or closed off was a coin toss every day. I found myself boiling most days until I was with her.

We poked fun at each other, compared music, smoked, and complained together. She reached into me and prodded at the things I'd buried deep. I did the same. I wanted to know her, and the more I knew, the more she pulled me in—the more I watched and craved her. She had to feel it; I couldn't be the only one unable to shake it.

Something deep inside me prowled awake whenever I watched her.

I still caught her watching me with that knowing glint in her eye. I asked about it once, but she was quick to deny that she looked at me in any way.

Whenever I would ask about her plans to draw on my arm, she'd only say she would do it once I forgot about it. I loved the smirk that followed. It had grown less shy and more confident. She was growing comfortable around me. After laying out the darkness in our lives, nothing was held back or off-limits. When I talked about those things with her, it washed away the numbness. I was usually pissed about my own situation, looking to get away during the hours we spent together. Though, I couldn't ignore the passive details about how her family was treating her without feeling a surge of anger. She was grieving, too—but alone because of their neglect. And when they weren't neglecting her, it was straight-up abuse.

Our day-to-day lives strung us tight and brought us together. We met at the tracks nearly every day and messaged the other if we were desperate to get out of the house on our off days.

Like today. Natalie had texted me the second school ended, telling me to meet her, insisting she wouldn't take no for an answer.

Not bothering with the bus, I walked to the tracks and hadn't been waiting for more than five minutes when I heard panting and the crunch of gravel underfoot.

My heart shot into my throat, my hands tightening to fists.

"All right, today's the day." Natalie dropped herself beside me. Pulling her backpack into her lap, she met my eyes with excitement as her navy-blue nails tapped along the front.

I'd seen her carry around a carton of cigarettes, bags of candy, and magically pull dark polish out of her pockets to do her nails, but I'd never seen her with a backpack.

"For what? What's going on?" I asked with feigned hesitancy. I curled my hand closer to my side.

Seeing her excitement did nothing to intimidate me. It only made it harder for me to look away.

"Well, Scott," she said as she flopped the backpack down to open it, "you forgot, and I've finally come up with a design for your tree."

My eyebrows shot up. "You're actually going to draw a tree on my arm?"

"Oh, I was one hundred thousand percent serious about that." Natalie pulled cases of ink pens out of her backpack. She unzipped a smaller case, opened it, and set it on the wall between us. It was packed with black pens.

Pausing, she looked up at me before nodding at my arm expectedly. *The one day I wore a shirt with sleeves.* I rolled up my right sleeve. I felt a spike of nervous tension. It wasn't permanent, but she was going to draw something on me, for me. What if I hated it? What if I loved it? What would it expose? What would she reveal in ink?

"I want to ask about your intentions for my arm, but I know you'll just shoot me down."

"Damn straight, I will." She winked before picking one of the many black pens.

I had no clue what the difference was between them all. Maybe there wasn't one, and she collected dozens of the same pen. I wouldn't know. She was the artist. She knew about . . . pens and paintbrushes and shit.

"What?" she asked with a small, singular laugh.

I blinked, coming back into myself. "What?"

"That's what I asked you. You were shaking your head."

"Oh." I frowned. "I was?"

"Mm-hmm. I've noticed that you tend to space out. A lot. You just—stare off into the distance or zero in on something while you're lost in that head of yours." Natalie uncapped her pen, pulling my arm into her lap with my forearm facing her. She glanced up at me, pen poised above my arm. "Ready?" She wiggled her eyebrows. "Don't look so nervous. What if you like it?"

I nodded. "You're the artist. I trust you. Ready, set, go!"

The tip of the pen touched my skin on "go." She started at my wrist, putting down sharp and squiggled lines. They looked like nothing, but she had a lot of confidence. All of it was clear in the way her mouth was set, eyebrows pulled together in concentration. My eyes dropped from her face to watch her work.

Eventually, my mind must have drifted because the next thing I knew, I didn't feel the pen on my wrist, and Natalie was saying, "Hello, earth to Scott. Come back to us."

My head snapped up. Blinking, I came back from the haze. "Sorry."

That knowing look appeared again. "I told you you tend to zone out."

"Sorry."

"Apologizing is unnecessary. You zone out. I don't mind. Actually," she said, bending forward to get back to work on my arm, "I kind of like it."

"What? Why?" I blurted before I could process her words.

"Because"—she shrugged—"the face you make while you're zoned out is pretty cute."

Something inside me dropped. I had no fucking clue what to say to that. My tongue felt glued to the roof of my mouth. I couldn't swallow. I couldn't think. I couldn't respond.

Natalie seemed indifferent to my silence, her focus never wavering from the lines on my arm. I shook my head. She couldn't possibly have meant it that way. I'd misunderstood. Her face was blank.

I was fucked with my defective genes. She knew how shitty my life was and knew that my mom had been abusive before my dad stepped in to fill the role she'd abandoned. It was a miracle Natalie was sitting here with me at all.

I could hardly believe she felt safe enough to touch me like she was. She didn't know my mind—what I was thinking about when I was around her. She didn't know how often I swallowed my anger or that she was what quieted everything seething in me when we were together.

"You're not going to say anything?"

My heart dropped. "I—"

"Before you panic, I'm talking about what I've done to your arm so far."

I could have sworn sweat collected on my brow. Every tense part of me suddenly released. I gulped back my relief.

Looking at my forearm, I saw the tree was outlined on it, but the black designs only filled half. A large gap was in the center of the trunk. The bark was black against my unmarked skin. Some branches trailed down to the middle of my arm, but they were leafless. I did not know what she was going to do with the rest of it, how she would fill in the blank spot, and how it would relate to me.

"It's . . ." I shook my head. "Shit, Natalie. It's amazing."

She glanced down as if she were shy. "Isn't it? You really like it? I'm obsessed with it, but that's me—"

I covered her hand with mine, catching the pen. "It's seriously fucking awesome."

Her smile grew wider. "Okay." She nodded. "Okay." Sliding her hand out of mine, she got right back to work.

She was buzzing with excitement, and a burning sensation filled my chest. My mind hazed over as I watched her pen trail across my arm, "zoning out," as Natalie had just called it. All I felt was the light pinch of her pen at work. I was seeing the ink but not processing what was happening. I felt like my arm was shaking, and she could feel it under her hand.

Silence filled the space for a long time.

I tried to be still but felt like everything inside me was shuddering out of control. It was like a punch to the gut—the connection my mind made between Natalie, my mother, and my family genes.

I stayed like that—everything festering inside me, gnarling in my blood, as I watched Natalie work to finish my arm. My mind was a haze, thoughts distant to where I couldn't make sense of them all. The thought burning in my mind was how Natalie's emotions dripped from her while mine festered to the point of exploding.

"Have you thought about college?"

Natalie's voice broke through the haze, and the world slowly came back, my sight coming into focus, my hearing becoming less distant.

I shook my head, mostly to answer her question but also to clear my head.

"How are you going to get out of here, then?"

"I'll probably just pack up my dad's car and leave. I'll be lucky if I get out of here at all."

"Where would you go?"

I shrugged. "Anywhere but here sounds good enough to me."

She looked up from her work for a moment, eyebrows furrowed. "That's a stupid idea."

"Well, it's the best I've got with my situation."

"You could go to college. I'm sure—"

"How would you suggest I do that? I might not even make it out of here alive, and you think a college is going to accept me? There's no chance of that happening."

I couldn't help my bitter tone.

"Good job. You just popped your own bubble. The bubble of positivity I made for you." A beat of silence hung, where neither of us broke eye contact. "Aren't you desperate to leave this shitty place? We could run away together, tackle the world, if we went together."

My pulse quickened, threatening to burst out of control.

I closed my eyes, forcing myself to unclench my teeth to speak. "I don't have the money for that, Natalie."

"There are ways. Debt is a common catastrophe." She sounded as if she were trying to convince herself that going was worth it. "We could get out, graduate together, get jobs—ones that aren't fast-food related. We could start a whole new life. We could do it. I know we could. Don't burst that bubble, Scott."

I couldn't respond. Everything she said restricted my chest, carving a hole. I wanted it—the freedom I saw when she spoke. I wanted a life where I could try again, be somewhere else as someone else—someone who wasn't hated. I wanted to live somewhere where I felt safe.

I wanted to leave this worthless life in the dust, put it miles behind me.

"Finally," she said, sitting up and capping her pen as she stared at her work. "It's perfect."

The ink started at the base of my palm.

The ground was pitch black before it faded in dots of speckled dirt that grew smaller the closer they got to my palm. Roots began above my wrist, set under the surface and the sturdy, thick trunk. The branches spread out like veins on my arm. In the center, where the gap had been, was a heart with the tree trunk winding through it like a valve or something.

She ran a finger along the trunk on my arm. "See the missing pieces? The missing chunks of bark? The bumps? It's the scars no one sees. It's everything that's happened and will happen."

"It really is amazing, Nat. I don't have words."

I never wanted it to wash away. I couldn't tear my eyes from its every detail. I wanted it on my arm forever.

"And then"—her purple nail tapped the heart, the core connecting all the branches around it and the trunk winding through it—"that's what you need to reach for. That's your way out of here, Scott, as long as you listen to it."

A tenseness dropped in my stomach. "Why are you bringing this up now? You can get out any way you want. Why are you bringing this up now and judging me for—"

"Because I'm thinking about going, Scott, and I want to know if there's a chance you'd come with me."

Suddenly, the wall didn't feel sturdy. We hadn't known each other more than a few weeks. It was a struggle to make her feel comfortable around me. And as much as I wanted to, I couldn't force that. That feeling had to come over her on her own.

She didn't break eye contact.

I couldn't get enough.

"I—I see something in you, Scott. You're here. You listen. You have your own shit to deal with. I think we can get out of here together and just . . . be normal people without all the baggage."

It sounded like a distant idea, one that caused me to shake my head. "You really think that's possible?"

"I know it is. No matter what you say, I'm getting out of here as soon as I graduate. I don't know where I'm going, but I've already filled out some college applications." She shrugged. "It's the easiest way for me to get out."

I was willing to bet there wasn't an easy way out for me.

"So, are you going to think about preserving the bubble I've made you?"

chapter nine

I COULDN'T STOP THINKING ABOUT the future Natalie had suggested as she'd drawn on my arm. I'd never thought of myself as the college type. I couldn't picture it. Yet, she wanted me to run away with her, put our shitty lives behind us, and plan for something of our own.

Fuck. We knew each other, but we hadn't been friends for long. I was sure she had details I didn't know or I hadn't noticed about her. There had to be things we were keeping from the other without meaning to. Some would come up. Small habits that would annoy the other. Insecurities that would piss us off once they were out in the open. Harmless words or actions that would send the other spiraling.

I stormed up my driveway and refused to let myself hesitate when opening the front door.

He was inside. He was always inside, and right now, I didn't give a shit what kind of state he was in. I'd welcome a swing right now.

It would quiet my thoughts, halt them from dealing with the impossible Natalie had presented. It wasn't fair of her. She didn't know. She didn't know how much I'd welcome an escape. But there were risks hovering over me.

I never thought I would live to see eighteen. But I had always thought that, if I did, I would shove my things into a bag. While my drunk of a father was passed out, I'd walk out to save myself from one last brutal beating and leave the threats behind. The last thing I wanted was for him to kill me on my way out the door, steps away from freedom.

Snoring, he was passed out now, one leg propped up on the reclined chair.

Disappointment washed over me when I realized he wasn't awake to replace my thoughts with pain. A bruise would have cured everything. I couldn't stop them myself; it was impossible when Natalie's smile kept popping into my mind.

College had never crossed my mind, never came up whenever I thought about leaving.

"You zone out, I don't mind. Actually," she had said, *"I kind of like it. The face you make while you're zoned out is pretty cute."*

What if she wanted me to be . . . more? More than the guy who would pack up his shit the second he turned eighteen and left tire marks on the asphalt when he left everything else behind. She didn't want to be one of the things I left behind without looking back.

Staring at my snoring, worthless father, I felt heat rise from deep within my chest—anger I had pushed down again and again. I might not ever have a shot at an ordinary life because of him. My parents had fucked everything up beyond repair. If they—hell, or even just my dad— had been normal, given me a goddamned chance, they would push me to send out applications right now. Maybe

I would even *want* to go to college. In a perfect reality, my dad would give me a playful punch to the shoulder when I got my acceptance, and my mom would cry. And then cry again when they finished moving me into my dorm.

But I would never have that.

My mom had walked out years ago, abandoning her husband and leaving her child traumatized. My dad could barely pay the bills and drank so excessively he probably wouldn't even notice once I was gone. He wouldn't give a shit unless he caught me walking out with my stuff. My leaving would set him off. I could hear him shouting that I would never amount to anything, that leaving would be a massive mistake, and that he wouldn't help me once I walked out the door. He would never want to see my face again.

I flexed my fingers, balling my hands at my sides after cracking my knuckles.

I was his punching bag. The one person he had left, the one thing he could use to make himself feel relevant, like he was doing something important.

He didn't want me to have a meaningful life. He wanted me to stay in the pit with him, and that made my teeth grind as my chest heaved.

He didn't care enough. He never did—not when Mom was covering me with bruises and sure as hell not now. I wouldn't stay here. I wouldn't take much more of this. I wouldn't turn out like him—someone unreliable and worthless. Whether I left to find a job to help me get by or ran away with a girl I was just getting to know and understand, I would get out.

I just had to be stealthy enough not to get killed on my way out.

Maybe he'd die from alcohol poisoning before I graduated. I could only be so lucky.

With the way he was snoring, he would be oblivious if I smashed one of the many bottles beside him over his head. It would all be over in one forceful action, and I would be free, with nothing left to worry about. My life would never be on the line for any misstep. I could be more and leave this hellhole behind to become everything he wasn't—everything he didn't want me to be. He stood in the way of it all.

The only problem—with him asleep, I wouldn't be able to claim self-defense. I wouldn't be able to run away with Natalie because I would be thrown into a six-by-eight cell.

I released one last deep breath before forcing my fists to unclench.

College would put me more in debt, but wouldn't it be worth it if it meant I could escape and, more importantly, flee with Natalie? The greater the risk, the greater the reward.

Heading down the hall before he could wake up and threaten to give me a black eye for staring, I shuffled my feet to my room. I fell back onto my bed, gaze locked on the ceiling as I took in deep breath after deep breath. Raising my arm in front of my face, I admired the trunk and branches on my arm, mesmerized by the details. Eventually, every detail Natalie had left would extinguish my temper. Releasing one final, long breath, I gave myself permission to accept what I really wanted.

Being beaten within an inch of my life was something I'd risk if it meant I could get as far away from here as possible, especially with Natalie.

chapter ten

Two nights after graduation, Natalie pulled her chipped, dented red Volkswagen Beetle into my driveway. She switched the headlights off right before turning in and cut the engine the second she was parked. I'd been packed and ready for Nat's word since the last day of school. She'd been waiting for a sign—for her mom to blow up at her one more time so she wouldn't feel bad walking out on her family.

While we'd spent the last month of school and most of our graduation ceremony talking about where we would go and how we would leave, it hadn't taken Natalie's mom long to blow up.

When she called to tell me she was on her way, she practically screamed as she threw something into her car before she even said a word to me. I knew better than to ask if she was okay. If she'd hit the point where she was ready to bail, I knew she wasn't okay. I knew she'd been hoping to make it at least another week. Her family had disappointed her again.

I waited by my window to pick up the pieces, touching the sleeve where Natalie had drawn the tree for me. Though I had done everything I could to keep the ink out of the shower, it had disappeared long before graduation.

It'd been dark for a few hours now. My things were piled on the bed. All my shit fit in two bags. A few wouldn't fit, but two bags were all I had. I had packed the essentials and a few items I knew I would regret leaving behind, making sure my notebooks were wedged between my clothes. Good riddance to everything else.

When I saw her climb out of the car, leaving the door open for our quick getaway, I met at the end of the hallway. I had checked on Dad to make sure the coast was clear after hanging up with Natalie, and I could still hear him snoring. She eased the front door shut but only left it open a hair.

Natalie walked into my house with confidence, believing my father wouldn't lay a hand on me with her here. She was wrong. He was snoring, but something still sank into the pit of my stomach. She knew what my home life was like; she just didn't know she wasn't safe here, either.

When I motioned to her, she tiptoed down the hallway, peeking into the living room to take in the snoring ass molded to the chair. It'd been a few days since I'd picked up the littered bottles. Trying not to let my embarrassment show, I gripped the doorframe. My knuckles whitened and twitched.

She smiled when she reached me, putting a hand in the center of my chest as she brushed past me and into my bedroom for the first time.

Over the last few months, there had been several nights where I had almost reached for my phone to see if she would sneak out to climb in through my window. Just to have her here. Just so she could be in my space. I had wanted to see her room, too. It had always been in the back of my mind since our rooms were our havens—secondary to the train tracks—when forced to be home.

"The rest of this can't fit?" she asked as she took in the clothes on my bed.

"I decided I'd rather carry a pile of clothes than a pile of books."

She nodded and looked back at the bed before reaching for the zipper of one bag. She folded up a few shirts and tried to stuff them in what little space was on the top. "Most of my art supplies are shoved in the back of my Bug. Not a lot of room."

"I can just hold whatever doesn't fit."

She nodded. "Okay. Okay, that'll work."

I could see she was trying to convince herself we would be okay.

Stepping toward her, I reached out. I could never help myself. "Hey, we'll—"

"Are you sure about this?" she whispered.

"More sure than I can tell you."

"Classes don't start for months."

"Natalie." She whirled to face me. I could've sworn she looked happy to hear me say her name. "I'm sure. I'm really, really sure."

I was planning to leave before we'd even met, but she had set the decision in stone. Wherever Natalie went, I would follow. Things had been changing between us these last few weeks, but neither of us had crossed that line yet. We were waiting to see if the other one would.

She nodded and then smiled as she reached to zip up the bag. "Then, let's get the hell out of here and never look back."

We grabbed the last of my bags and started down the hall for the front door. Distracted about leaving, I hadn't taken one last look into my room, but I realized my old man wasn't snoring anymore.

I heard him jump up from his chair when Natalie reached the opening of the living room. I grabbed her arm to rush her down the hall a few steps before shoving her ahead of me. She looked stunned as my dad stomped from his chair toward us.

Putting myself between them wouldn't be enough to keep her out of the line of fire.

Once I let her go, I didn't have the chance to brace myself for the first punch.

But at least she was closer to the exit.

"Whe—yeh goin', son?"

His words were so slurred I was sure I was the only one who understood them.

Natalie didn't scream when that first strike knocked me into the wall, my elbow leaving a gaping hole in it.

Everything was going in and out, seeming far away or way too close. I couldn't get a grip.

"Who's yer little whore? She looks like a sweet one. Yer mama would be proud."

While my first instinct was to fall to the floor to protect my ribs, hers was to force herself between us. She didn't give him the chance to get on top of me. He barely got in a second strike.

"Stop! Don't you fucking *touch him!*" she yelled until he backed up a few steps, never stopping to take a breath.

Even as she crouched beside me and I yanked my elbow from the drywall, she never stopped shouting.

I saw him scowl over her shoulder, jaw tense, and hands balled as the wheels turned in his mind. I could practically see the smoke coming out of his ears. He was having trouble keeping track of what was happening. He took an unsteady step toward us, his eyes locked on Natalie, ready to reach for her. "Where 're—"

I put an arm across Natalie, pinning her against the wall as I stood. My breath was hot; my body braced while something in my chest twisted. He wasn't going to lay a hand on her. I would do everything I could to get us to the front door, but we were getting out of here.

"Don't fucking try anything," I told him calmly over Natalie's shouts.

She paused, hand on my arm, gripping it for dear life. As we stared each other down, she didn't move an inch, the tension wired, our tempers hanging on by a thread. He wanted to grab her—use her to keep me under his control and stop me from leaving. If he made one move toward us, I was ready to fight back for the first time in my life. And he was well aware.

Natalie didn't hesitate. Grabbing our bags, she made me walk ahead of her as I glowered back at my father for the last time. My fists shook, daring him to step closer. Anger barreled through me thinking about walking away without gaining some justice. Gallons of beer and years of abuse were going unpunished. Just like my mom when she walked out.

"The only way you make it out there is if she really does whore herself out!"

After pulling the lighter from my pocket, I conjured a flame with a flick before I tossed it. The plastic square landed right in the wrinkled ass-print of the chair, and the cheap leather instantly took to the flame.

He forgot about us the second he registered what was happening. He had bigger problems to focus on now. Running into the living room, he started throwing half-empty beer bottles to put the fire out, shouting about his precious chair the whole time.

Natalie made no sound of surprise as she pushed me forward, making me walk out the front door to leave the shitfest of a house behind. Climbing higher, flames crackled, turning the living room and chair into a bonfire. I didn't look back until I reached the passenger side while waiting for her to jump in and pop the lock up.

Curtains blew back from the force of the flames as they stretched across the ceiling, snapping and hissing as they ate away at everything in their wake.

"It's okay." Natalie tried to insert the key, but her hand was shaking too hard. She couldn't still it long enough to put the key in the ignition. "Scott, you're okay. We're okay."

Tearing my eyes from the fire, I placed my hand over hers, and her hand steadied slightly. "We're okay."

She finally managed to put the key in and start the car.

Ignoring the flames, I took in the house that had been my prison since Mom left.

I couldn't believe it. Still tense and fists clenched, I gripped the edges of the seat. Natalie was backing out of the driveway, but no part of me believed it. Even with the house in the rearview mirror. I leaned back, trying to force myself to fathom it as the adrenaline came down, and my elbow started to ache from the drywall.

Natalie pulled a mason jar from the door of her car and shook it, jangling the coins against the glass. Cash was crumbled up inside, too, the whole jar full of everything we had collected or stolen from our parents over the last several few weeks. She tossed it to me, trusting me with every cent we had to start our new lives.

It ended here.

I would never have to pause before walking into a house again. I would have my own one day, and I wouldn't continue this cycle. No one would hesitate at my door, let alone my family.

That ended here.

A fire truck rushed past, lights flashing to illuminate the street, sirens blaring. The red lights snapped me from my thoughts.

"I will never look back and regret leaving this fucking town."

Natalie reached for my hand in agreement.

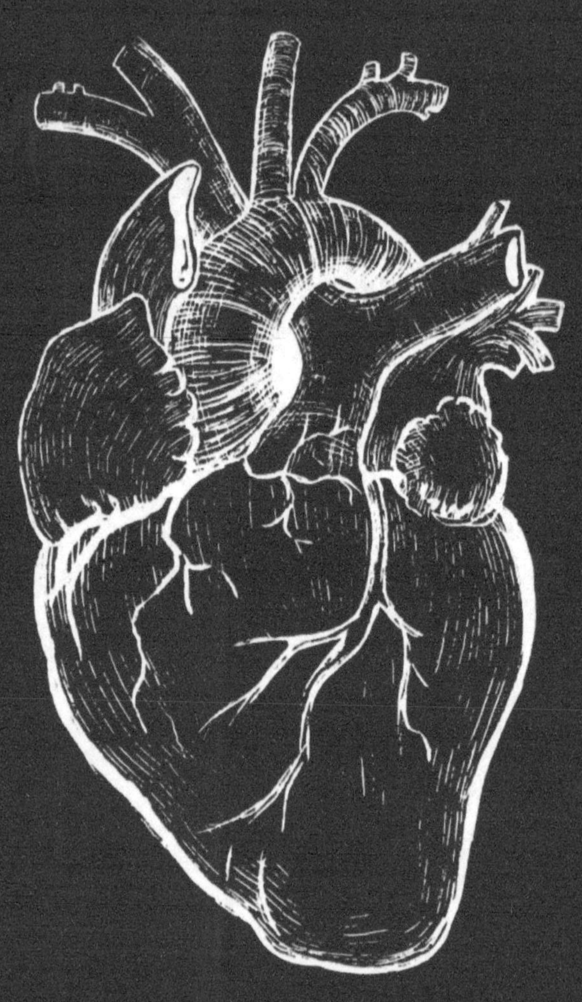

chapter eleven

2007 (Junior Year)

"AND THAT'S ALL I HAVE for you today. I hope you all have a great Thursday. I know we're all looking forward to the weekend," my anthropology professor announced as everyone packed their things to race out of the stuffy classroom.

My smile was instant as I slung my bag over my shoulder and started for the door. Except, instead of following the sea of students speeding to get the hell out of dodge of the classroom, I swung to the left and caught Natalie by the waist.

"Oh!" She laughed as I spun us both into the wall, the hem of her shirt rising enough to give me a peek at her midriff.

Thank God for low-rise jeans.

"Having a good day?" I asked her.

Her smile was wide.

"If I wasn't before, I definitely am now." She nuzzled my neck before starting down the hall, gripping my wrist as she zigzagged through students.

Completely enthralled by her, I watched her every movement. I could never get enough.

When Natalie had pulled her chipped red Volkswagen Beetle into my driveway two and a half years ago, that was when my life had started. If she hadn't come for me, I might not have gotten out of that house alive. If it wasn't for her, I would never have made a new life for myself. Without her, I wouldn't be here.

I hadn't been back since. Thanks to the amount of alcohol in my dad's system, the cops assumed he'd set fire to his own house. They never came knocking on my door. I had no idea if my dad was still alive and couldn't bring myself to care. Not when Natalie was tucked into my side as we made our way down the hallway.

Shaking the memory away, I caught up to tighten my arm around her.

We were better. Both of us were relieved to have a stable routine.

Natalie had gone back to visit her family a few times, but she put in as much as they did. We were secure in life and in each other now. We had no one else to rely on.

"Do you have free time tonight?" Nat asked me.

"For you? I always have time."

Natalie rolled her eyes and playfully shoved at the arm around her waist. "Always so sweet on me."

"Yup. That's me." I couldn't deny it. "What do you have in mind?"

"Well"—she chewed on her bottom lip—"I sent my application to the art gallery this morning, so I thought we could do a little celebrating."

She was trying to hide it, but she was glowing with excitement. For the last four months, getting into an art gallery was all she'd been fighting for. She'd been working with one of her professors night and day to reflect on her art and get it where she wanted it to be. Until she finally made a piece she felt reflected her enough.

She'd been working to find who she was in her art—to find her niche.

She was thrilled by the opportunity—the possibility of one of her pieces hanging up in an art gallery—but she was trying to rein it in, too. And while I wanted her to be excited, I wanted to protect her from rejection.

I bit back every negative thing I could say.

"Nat, that's fantastic!" I hugged her. "You finally did it. Your name is going to be on one of those little cards."

She laughed, trying to wiggle free from my hold. "I just sent in an application—"

I pulled back to smile at her, wrestling against my need to protect her, to give her the encouragement she deserved. "It's a start to getting your name out there. Don't downplay this. You've been working for this." She stared up at me with her big blue eyes. "No matter what they say, I will always be proud of you, Nat."

Her eyes glistened. "Really?"

"Of course. I will always support you, no matter what."

She shook her head in disbelief. "How did I get so lucky?"

"How did *we* get so lucky?"

Natalie was lying on her stomach on the fuzzy purple rug, her portfolio laid out before her. I was pretty sure she wasn't wearing a bra, but with her elbows propped up, it made it impossible for me to tell. She was off in her own little world while I was waiting for the *ding* to announce that our instant mac 'n cheese was ready. They weren't great, but they came in their own bowls to put in the microwave, and it was ten times better than eating pancakes and sausages on a stick.

The face I made reflected back at me from the door as the microwave beeped.

"I can't believe there's only a few more weeks in the semester, and I already finished my portfolio."

"You've been working your ass off. Of course you finished it already."

Natalie paused before turning the page, looking up at me over the counter that separated the kitchen from the living room. She dropped it and stretched out on the rug.

She definitely wasn't wearing a bra. Her eyes never left me as she fought a smile, doing nothing to cover her nipples.

"You're too sweet to me, Scott. I don't think you were this sweet before we lived together."

"I had an image to keep in high school."

She scoffed quietly. "For who? Your cigarettes?"

I swallowed my laugh, keeping my focus on stirring the mac 'n cheese. She had me there. I couldn't think of one damned thing to say. She always found a way to make me speechless. It was like she enjoyed it or something.

"Nothing?" she asked as I started toward her.

I handed her one of the small bowls. "Eat your mac 'n cheese."

She giggled quietly as I took a seat across from her. The sound made me want to throw her on the mattress and force every beautiful sound out of her. I swallowed, looking out the window, to find dark clouds rolling in. I did not want to walk to class in the rain tomorrow.

Lightning flashed in the distance, and my eyes dropped to the floor. Natalie's easel was in front of the window, left empty today, but there were droplets and splatters across the floor from when she'd dropped a brush.

She usually worked with dull colors. Yellow was out of the question, but orange and pink were allowed if they looked burnt enough and gave her the feeling she was looking for.

Not having a couch was probably a blessing in disguise because Natalie would've found a way to get paint on it, too. Somehow, though most of the floor was flecked with dried droplets, the rug was the only haven from paint.

With the smallest kitchen imaginable, a living room with creaky floorboards, and one bedroom with a mattress on the floor—our apartment wasn't much, but it was home.

This was what I had imagined for myself whenever I had thought about leaving home. I never could've predicted I would be in college or that a girl like Natalie would have picked me up in her car and pushed me to come with her.

We might be used to similar living conditions, but she deserved to live in a place better than this cramped apartment. She deserved her own art room, not the living room window.

"If it hadn't been for how we were living before," I said without taking my eyes off the window, "you probably wouldn't be able to stand living here."

Her spoon stopped, scraping against the cup. "Why are you saying that?"

I didn't answer.

"Why are you saying that? I have you. I don't need a big, fancy apartment."

"I'm going to buy us a house someday. I want you to have a backyard and an art room and a bedroom where you can jump on the bed until you're out of breath."

"We're going to lay our raggedy mattress down in such a fancy bedroom?"

I still hadn't turned away from the window.

"I'm being serious, Nat. You deserve that, and I'm going to give it to you. We're not going to be here forever. Not if I have any say about it."

Natalie moved behind me and whispered, "Oh? And what's your big plan?"

Her arms wrapped around me, one across my torso and the other across my chest. I couldn't help but close my eyes.

I needed her.

I would do whatever I had to so long as I could give her everything.

"I'm going to make it big in marketing, and I'm going to give you everything you deserve."

"You know I love you, right?" she whispered in my ear.

"I love you more." I'd never said anything more true in my life. Every time I said it, that truth was only stronger. "I wouldn't be here if it wasn't for you."

chapter twelve

COFFEE GRINDERS AND SOME OTHER spinning contraption were in full swing. Worse than that, The Roasted Bean was bustling with students.

Natalie had snatched the last open table before I got here, but it was smack-dab in the middle of everything. Anyone who tried to squeeze by us and the table beside us knocked me with an elbow, backpack, or purse. It was getting on my fucking nerves. I got extra pissed when the corner of a textbook jabbed me. I was fidgeting to stay focused and was struggling to think of an ad for the presentation I had next week.

Whenever I caught myself clenching my jaw or gripping the edge of the table, on the verge of snapping, I looked at Natalie across from me. She snapped me back from the ledge. She calmed me without ever realizing it.

Natalie bought the same drink every day. She seemed to need an iced matcha for her survival. She played with the straw as she studied, quietly staring down at her pages as it scraped and screeched against the hole in the lid, the sole reason I didn't let her study at the library.

"Oh, sorry!" a voice said. "Natalie? Hi! Scott, darn, I hit you. I'm sorry!"

Natalie's head snapped up from her textbook. "Olivia, hi! What're you up to?"

Olivia and Nat had met our first semester here, in Natalie's first class. They'd been paired for a project and had been inseparable since. If they went a few weeks without seeing each other, they would pick things right back up like they'd never left each other's sides. She was nice, but I was tired of her dragging Natalie and me on double dates with her and her dumb-ass fuck of the week.

"You're fine, Olivia," I told her, forcing myself to relax the grip on my pencil. "Don't worry about it."

She flashed an apologetic smile at me. "Just here to finish up a paper before I head out tonight. Anthony's here, too, just grabbing a coffee first."

Natalie nodded. "Where you headed tonight?"

"One of Anthony's friends is having a party at one of those little houses up the street." Olivia looked between us. "Why don't you guys come with?"

Someone bumped their cup on my shoulder. "Hey, Scott."

I closed my eyes for a moment while Olivia and Natalie were distracted.

"Anthony." I nodded at him. "How's the semester treating you?"

He came around to stand beside Olivia, the tips of his curly brown hair sticking to the corner of his lips. He brushed the strands back. "I am so sick of my accounting professor. She throws a quiz at us every chance she gets."

Like I gave a shit. We all have problems. I'd take a quiz over acting like I cared about the dentist advertisement I was bullshitting.

I gestured to the spread of papers before me. "I have to come up with a billboard ad for a dentist's office, and I hate just about every tag line I can think of."

"Do dentists even advertise on billboards?"

I wasn't sure I liked we were on the same page.

"You got me."

"Just be sure you get a cartoon tooth in there, saying someth—"

"Since they're being Chatty Cathys," Natalie said, "I think we'll accept your invitation."

Olivia smiled. "Perfect. Then, we'll see you two later. Maybe we'll all finish up here around the same time, and we can just climb into one car?"

My eyes had snapped to Natalie since she'd spoken up. I watched her nod.

Anthony brushed the back of his neck, his signature nervous tic. "Uh. Then, I guess we'll see you guys later. Draw that tooth, Scott."

I nodded to him. "I'll get right on that."

Olivia was nice enough and had become our friend, in a way. Anthony, on the other hand, would invite me to strip clubs and shit that would make Natalie uncomfortable, so I always had to turn him down when he asked me to hang out. I couldn't tell if he was just oblivious or if he was asking me so he could tell Natalie to drive a wedge between us.

"It's fine that I did that, right?" Nat asked me once they had wandered off to find an empty table. "I thought we could use the time to get out."

She was facing me again, her wavy blonde hair clinging to her shoulders, her blue eyes looking worried she had upset me. Her hair had lost their blue-and-pink streaks a few months after we moved here, and she had never dyed it back. "I don't want to look the same," she'd told me once they'd first faded. "We're starting new. I think the streaks need to stay where I left them."

"Scott?"

I blinked. "Sorry. I—sorry." I leaned back in my chair as Natalie mouthed, *Zoned out*. I shook my head at her. I never needed to explain or apologize when my mind drifted. She knew what to expect. "No, no, I'm glad we're going tonight. It'll take my mind off this crap." I gestured to the half-assed tooth I had outlined.

"And I won't be moping around after checking the mail for something from the art gallery?"

Dropping my pencil, I held my hands up in surrender. "I didn't say it."

She smiled as she shook her head. "Such a goober. You sure you're okay with going tonight?"

I reached across our papers and textbooks to take her hand. "I think it's a great idea. Stop stressing and get to work so we can go."

I was addicted to the smile she gave me. It made me squeeze her hand harder before I reluctantly released her. I would do anything for her, so long as she kept looking at me the way she did.

The Roasted Bean closed behind us, the chimes dinging near the shut door as the girl slid the lock.

"Only one thing to do now that we shut down the place," Natalie said.

"Hope everyone finished their homework 'cause it's time to party," Olivia announced. "Climb into my car!"

Olivia insisted Nat and I sit in the back, but that left Anthony free to control the radio. He cranked it up so he couldn't hear Olivia's protests. That didn't stop her from rolling her eyes every time he looked over. Between songs, she opened her mouth, but Anthony belted along to the next song.

We had no choice but to sit quietly and wait for our ears to bleed.

Eventually, a song Anthony didn't like started, and he turned the hip-hop down to a bearable level to crack open the window. I had taken to watching the lights outside mine when Natalie took my hand from her thigh and wound it with hers in her lap. My whole body relaxed.

Needing her touch, I braced our hands against the inside of her thigh and used it to slide her closer to me.

When a streetlight peeked into the car, redness bloomed on her cheeks. Her smile was bright and all for me. At that moment, I wished we were alone.

"Do either of you smoke?" Anthony asked us around the cigarette in his teeth.

There went that moment, shattered.

"Not anymore," I replied the same time Natalie said, "No, but I don't remember you being a smoker, either."

"Only at parties," he said as the cigarette in his mouth met his lighter.

"We haven't smoked since high school—"

"We're here!" Olivia announced. "Anthony, if you lay a finger on that radio, I swear I will bite it off."

"Is that a promise?"

She rolled her eyes, and we all climbed out of the car like it was seconds away from exploding.

"Is it just me, or did that car ride feel longer than seven minutes?" Natalie asked me when she came around to take my arm.

"That was only seven minutes?"

We walked up the lawn as a guitar solo started from inside. The house was small, and from the looks of the shadows in the windows, the place was packed. Olivia strutted right up to someone on the porch as she made for the front door. Anthony—not ready to part with his cigarette—went to sit with them.

A girl pushed by us on our way in, complaining into her flip phone.

"I feel bad for the guy on the other end of that," Nat said as she watched after the girl.

When we finally made it inside, we were met with a horde of people talking with red Solo cups clenched in their hands. The house was packed wall-to-wall, every girl and guy looking exactly the same in the shitty lighting.

People were even gathered on the stairs, girls leaning against banisters to show off their assets as they bit their lips for the guys who caught their eye. I couldn't imagine Natalie doing something so ridiculous. Not unless it was ironically—to make fun of them. I was the only one allowed to see Natalie in such a vulnerable way. I had every higher power to thank for that.

"I am one lucky man," I whispered into Natalie's ear.

"Why do you say that?"

"Because you're mine. You're not out here, partying and winking at guys to get them interested in your panties."

"No, babe. These panties are yours." Natalie winked before walking off. She only looked back when she reached the drink table and snatched up two beers. One was for her, the other for Olivia.

In very few instances, I drank, and when I did, I leaned toward cocktails and wine. I never touched beer or anything very strong. It was too close to everything I had spent my life hating. I didn't want reminders. I didn't want my parents' violent tendencies or their weaknesses. I wanted nothing associated with them.

Natalie handed a beer to Olivia, who was leaning against the wall, surveying everything as if to figure out what she would do first. They made small talk for a minute or so.

I couldn't hear—everything they said was muffled. The beat of the music was barely audible to me. I lost track of time.

My eyes eventually found Natalie again, my rock, as I tried to swallow against the pit in my stomach.

"Are you okay?" Natalie asked when she returned.

No. I needed a minute alone.

"Yeah, why?"

"Your eyes—they don't get that look very often anymore."

"Nah." Anthony suddenly appeared, slapping me on the back. "Our guy just needs a way to relax if he ain't gonna drink. This place isn't going to have anything but cheap-ass beer, so I think you're out of luck, Mr. Fancy Wine-Drinker."

The corny jokes that came out of Anthony's mouth only made me feel sicker.

I swallowed everything turning over in my stomach and plastered a smile on my face. "I'm fine." I stared into Natalie's eyes, hoping she would believe me.

"Then," she eventually said with a shrug, "go find yourself a handful of chips or something."

Anthony patted me on the back again. "C'mon, let's leave them to their girly business, and I'll introduce you to some friends."

He led me away just as Olivia was trying to pull Natalie into the horde. She gave me a faint smile before disappearing. Anthony didn't stop until we'd turned the corner into the kitchen.

"All right, we're away from the ladies. How are you really feeling? Do you need to upchuck in a sink? Can I get you a beer or a soda or something?"

"Not great." My eyes struggled to focus. "But not bad enough to upchuck anything. I didn't want to scare her."

"I get it. I won't rat you out. I just thought you might want to tell someone how you're actually doing. What came over you?"

Anthony might be annoying most of the time, but he had his qualities.

I ran a hand through my hair. "I think it was just the stress from earlier."

He nodded. "It caught up with you. Totally understand. Did you draw that tooth?"

I couldn't help but laugh. "Yeah. Yeah, I drew a fucking tooth. I have it tied to a dentist's chair and saying 'Rescue me from plaque!' I got the dentist wearing a cape and everything, too. It's like a comic on a billboard. I couldn't take the assignment seriously after you brought up that damned cartoon tooth."

"My god!" He laughed. "Please tell me you're going to present this billboard to me before you make a fool of yourself in front of your entire class."

"Not a chance. I don't even think Natalie could keep a straight face if I practiced in front of her. I'd rather take my chances."

"Fair enough. Don't want to lose your chances with Natalie." He nodded, taking a swig of beer. "Not tonight, with her drinking like that."

The same feeling from before seethed in my stomach. It boiled in my throat, made my eyes burn. I forced myself to take a deep breath, but my hands clenched at my sides. Anthony was no different from every other guy on campus or any campus in the country, really. He always had a one-track mind, but that—

"I think I just need a minute," I said, slipping past to head for the stairs.

If he said anything, I didn't hear it. The thump of the music drowned everything out, but things were also growing farther away.

Too far. Fuck him for even saying her name.

The second floor was hustling with people, but it wasn't as loud. Girls looked me up and down as I moved through the hallway, their eyes suggestive.

My stomach flipped at the sight.

I only ever wanted Natalie to look at me like that.

I slipped into the first empty bathroom I came across, shutting the door before heading straight for the sink. Yanking the faucet handle on hot, I braced myself on the edge as I waited for the water to warm. My anger and temptation were visible in the bulging veins of my arm. When the water turned steamy, I splashed my face, running my palms over my eyes. Fuck Anthony. I gripped the front of my hair. I knew the kind of guy Anthony was. Fuck him for saying Natalie's name. Fuck this feeling—

The door burst open, a guy stumbling inside, nearly knocking me into the shower. My teeth clamped together when I caught myself and turned to glare at the bastard, the vein in my arm pulsing again.

Pathetic bastard looked like he was tripping.

"Sorry, man," he gurgled out before he barfed. He clung to the toilet, weak and barely conscious.

I blinked water from my eyes. He was pale as a fucking ghost, but his lips were blue, eyes wide and dilated, looking like he was about to fall over. The man looked like a paranoid maniac.

"Oh, f-f-f-f-f-fuck." His hands fell from the toilet, and he dropped to the floor like a rock. Lying stiff, his body was frozen for a second before he seized.

If he hadn't been jerking around, his skin would've been a perfect match against the tile.

Braced against the sink, the faucet still running, I barely processed what was happening. The music was thumping through the floor, pounding in my head. I couldn't move— couldn't speak. Everything felt dizzy and distant. I could do nothing but watch the guy convulse and gasp like a fish out of water.

He was flopping on his back, gagging on the bile in his throat.

Everything echoed—off the tiles, in my ears. His choking was watery and gargled as the puke leaked from his mouth. Paranoia leaving his eyes and replacing with desperation to breathe, he clawed at his throat.

I didn't yell for help.

He'd been the one to burst in here. He must have known this was coming.

I watched until his body stopped jerking.

Warmth sped through my veins as vomit oozed down the sides of his face. His eyes were still wide but completely blank. The room grew silent now that his choking had cut off, puke plastered all over his blue mouth.

I backed away, practically tripping into the door.

The movement made him farther away, but I wasn't sure that was what I wanted.

I couldn't look away. He wasn't moving. He wasn't breathing. It was like a scene from a show or a clip from one of those "beware of drugs" videos they drilled into us in high school.

I could almost imagine a fly landing on his eye without him blinking.

He'd come out of fucking nowhere, and it had happened so fast, but every choke had played out in slow motion. Every convulsion and cough of puke—down to the moment it drowned him.

The adrenaline it caused—I couldn't look away. I didn't yell for help.

My ears were ringing as my shaky hand involuntarily reached for the handle. I felt isolated—everything warped with distance as I shut the door behind me.

chapter thirteen

WHEN I FOUND NATALIE, SHE was all smiles. Everything was so far away still, but she didn't seem to notice as she and Olivia danced and wound around each other. I felt the thrum more than heard it, with my heart beating in sync with it, thumping through my body, rattling inside my skull.

I clenched my hands to hide the sweat, but I could feel it already on my forehead.

Nothing would come into focus. Everything felt rushed, edges blurred.

All I could think was that there were too many people, all too close.

Natalie eventually broke away from Olivia, snagging my attention. Behind my girl, a blurry Anthony pulled Olivia into him to keep dancing. My eyes were on Nat as she made her way toward me, everything else far away. She was my rock. She never let me be in my head for too long. She always drew me back from my mind before I went too far.

She leaned into me, placing her hand on my chest as she stared up at me. "Let's go home."

"It's like you can read my mind."

My voice came out hoarse.

"It's your eyes." She winked before stumbling into me. "They tell all."

It started raining on the ride home. Olivia had dropped us at the curb in front of our complex, and we ran for the door to fight with the keys that didn't always work. By the time we reached our apartment, Natalie had sobered up, but I could tell she was exhausted. She didn't even make it to the doorway of our bedroom before she unbuttoned and shoved her pants to the ground. Stepping out of them, she headed straight for bed and flopped down onto the covers in just a shirt and panties.

God, she was a mess, but she was my mess.

"That must have felt good," I pointed out. "You know the floor is four inches under that, right? Not a whole lot of cushion."

Whatever she said was muffled by the mattress.

I shut off the lights before stripping down to my boxers to lie next to her. Rain pelted the windows. When I closed my eyes, I could almost ignore the weird twisting in my stomach.

"Did you have fun?" Natalie asked before burying her face back into the covers. "How was talking to Anthony? I know he gets on your nerves sometimes."

All I saw were the cloudy, blank, paranoid eyes and a pale form, lifeless on cold tile.

And I couldn't stop—didn't want to stop seeing flashes. My mind was spiraling.

I gripped the sheets. "Yeah. Yeah, it was fine."

Puke around blue lips.

I shuddered, feeling the hair rise on my arms and the nape of my neck.

Natalie lifted her head from the covers to meet my eyes. "Hmm. What was that?" She wiggled closer until she could rest her head on my chest.

The guy had overdosed right in front of me. I had only watched. I had *watched*. I shook my head, closing my eyes tighter as I dragged a hand down the length of my leg. No one had peeked in to check on the poor bastard upchucking in the bathroom. He'd given up his own life when he lit the spoon.

I wasn't responsible.

The arm wrapped around Natalie tightened.

I didn't know him. I had no attachments. How was I supposed to give a shit? He was just some guy who had bumped into me on his way to puking his guts up in the bathroom I'd been standing in.

He wasn't my responsibility.

The girl resting across my chest was.

"Do you want to know why women like to place their hands on men's chests?"

Natalie was my rock, and I was desperate for her to bring me back from this.

I forced my eyes open and made myself smile. For her. "Why?"

"Because we can listen to your heartbeat like this." She gave me a quick kiss before snuggling back to her spot on my chest. "Yours is my lullaby."

That made my heartbeat pick up, and that's how she fell asleep.

But the second her breathing evened, I was left without a way to ground myself from my thoughts.

He did it to himself. It wasn't my fault. Just because I hadn't yelled for someone didn't mean it was my problem. I didn't kill him. He was dumb enough to overdose.

I shut my eyes, trying to block the images dragging against my brain. Pulling Natalie closer, I focused on her breathing to keep my mind off that bathroom. Between the inhale and exhale of her breath and the rain against the window, I was able to suppress those thoughts.

But every time I was close to sleep, Natalie's breathing came out ragged, struggled.

I jolted awake every time I thought she was choking.

The next time I opened my eyes, it was a little lighter outside, but it was still raining. Natalie was facing away from me, curled into herself with her head resting on my outstretched arm. I moved my fingers and clenched my jaw. My hand was definitely asleep.

I sighed, rolling into Nat to bury my face in her hair. She always smelled so sweet. "Good morning, love."

"It's gross outside," she grumbled.

Rainy days were her downfall. If it was gloomy outside, Natalie stayed home to bundle herself in comfy clothes and blankets.

Today would be my own nightmare.

"I know, so isn't now a good time to stay locked inside and paint all day?"

I just wanted to be close to her today. I wanted to watch her bite her pinky while she stared a canvas down. I wanted to see how much paint she would spill on herself.

I wanted to make her smile and spank her ass whenever she got up from that stool.

As I warded off thoughts of last night, I closed my eyes and grit my teeth. Curling an arm around Natalie, I focused on the feel of her beside me.

She hummed, and I knew there was a smile on her face. "Okay, you win—"

I exhaled a long breath before I spoke. "So long as I make you coffee?"

She pulled the sheets up, cocooning herself in the warmth underneath. "Mind reader."

"If you want that coffee, you need to free my arm."

"This arm?" She reached out and squeezed my fingers. "It's mine. It's on my side."

I couldn't help myself as I laughed in her hair. "I don't think we have sides. You just kind of end up pushing me closer to the edge so you can take the bed over for yourself."

"Lies," she said as she shoved my arm away, rolling to the far side of the bed.

I got up and made coffee in my boxers, just the way she liked it. Except she was already back to drooling on her pillow. As I poured her coffee, my grip on the pot whitened my knuckles. I swallowed as I set the pot aside, focusing up to make sure I stirred in the correct amount of sugar. I was pretty confident I could convince her to have a "no pants" day, especially since I was bringing her a mug of caffeine.

And I was right. Once she was up and the caffeine got her moving, her focus went straight to art.

In nothing more than panties and a shirt thin enough to show off her nipples, she made for her easel. She perched herself in front of the rainy window, coffee in one hand, paintbrush in the other.

She was stunning. She was mine.

Nat wasn't so focused on her work that it didn't go unnoticed when I tried to put on pants to cover my legs. She didn't even turn on her stool, telling me to get my ass back in the bedroom and not to come out until I was ready to prance around in boxers. Following her demands, I laid out on the purple rug with my textbooks in nothing but my boxers and a T-shirt. But I still felt like I was covered in puke.

We did our separate things in silence but stayed in the same room to keep close.

It was comforting to have each other close for our breaks. Nat usually needed a peck on the lips when she grew frustrated with how her work was turning out. She knew I needed a snack when I started to lose motivation or get bored with studying. It was a balance.

As the hours went by, my eyes were playing tricks on me every time I flipped through my anthropology textbook. I thought I saw puke smudged across the page or an overdosed corpse was lying in one picture instead of one of the cultural photos taken in Indonesia. My lids twitched, almost spasming, until I saw the real page.

Whenever I saw his face, recalled his lifeless gaze, I wasn't afraid or grossed out. I tried to remember exactly how he looked when he stopped breathing.

chapter fourteen

NATALIE SIGHED, STRETCHING HER ARMS up, her shirt sliding up her breasts until her belly button was visible. Paintbrush still between her fingers, she was perched on her stool in front of a half-painted canvas, her hair pulled up into a messy bun.

"I was productive today. I deserve whatever wonderful smell that is."

"Just some cheesy queso," I told her from the kitchen. Her eyes lit up. "Queso?"

"And red wine." I winked at her from the kitchen.

With me standing at the stove, she felt a million miles away. Crossing the room to slide my hands under her shirt to her chest was all I thought about, but the stovetop kept me in place.

She dropped the paintbrush into the cup beside her easel. "You know what they say. Food is the quickest way to a woman's heart."

I looked down, smiling at the bubbling cheese in the pot. "I was under the impression I'd already won yours."

"Oh, you won it." She smiled. "But you wiggle your way into it even more every time you make me queso."

"I don't make it. I open the jar and drop a glob of it on the stove."

"Hmm, I love it when you talk dirty to me."

I shook my head. She was unbelievable. Queso had a special place in her heart. That and red wine practically made her swoon.

"Get your butt to the rug so we can chow down—"

"And chug the bottle!" She plopped herself down among the purple fuzz.

Then, taking the glass I'd poured for her, she smiled and took the first sip, watching me as I brought the big bowl of queso and the bag of chips. "Red wine and queso. What's the occasion?"

"Well, it's the weekend. You and I are alone—"

"As we normally are when we're in our apartment."

"*And*," I said, sliding the bowl away from her to take the first bite for myself as penalty for cutting in, "you're waiting to hear from the gallery, and we're both hoping for good news."

"Aren't we celebrating prematurely, then? We don't know what they'll come back with."

"No. We're celebrating you and your art. You've come a long way from drawing on people's bodies and painting to lock your family out of your room."

"We both have come a long way, Scott," she said with a cheesy chip paused at her lips. "We both have. Don't forget that."

I didn't know what to say to that, so I ate chips to fill my silence.

"Did you ever think we would be where we are now?"

I was quiet for a long moment, staring down into my wine. "I thought . . ."

This was more than I could've ever imagined for myself. I wasn't dead or in jail or flipping burgers, but I still wanted more. Not for me. I already had more than I probably deserved. Natalie was the one who deserved more.

I didn't want her to wake up one day and realize I was a mistake.

I had to do everything I could to show her I wasn't.

She reached across the rug to place a hand on my knee. "What is it? Talk to me."

"I want to find a job or, at the very least, an internship in marketing."

"Really? What brought this on? You haven't said anything about it to me before."

"I told you that I wanted to give you everything you deserved."

Her eyes dropped, almost shyly, as if she were deep in thought. She ran her finger along the rim of her glass, her attention moving from the wine to me every few seconds. "Scott, I don't *need* anything more than this—"

"Don't you get it?" I asked her, desperate for her to understand but also feeling panicked thinking about her knowing my train of thought. "I want to give us a future."

"Scott . . ." She shook her head. When she met my eyes next, she looked at me like she was revealing a secret she'd been keeping from me. "Do you believe in soulmates? I wholeheartedly believe we met at those train tracks for a reason, but do you feel the same?"

From the day we climbed into her Volkswagen Bug to leave our toxic lives, I told her what I believed. "I believe we were pushed together for a reason. I was headed down a very dangerous road before I met you, Nat. If it weren't for you, I don't even know where I'd be right now. I mean, I'd probably be in prison, and you—you'd probably be a petty thief."

One of her eyebrows shot up. "A petty thief?" She nodded to herself, considering it. "You're right. I would've been caught for slipping an expensive bracelet into my cigarette box. But you. You were doomed to become an alcoholic, lose most of your hair, and would've been arrested for starting a bar fight. Our respective antics would've led us to meeting no matter what."

"You never would've fallen for me if I didn't have my hair. It's what pulled you in. You would've left me for a lead singer in a struggling band before I went completely bald, but still."

Her head tilted at the thought, biting back a smile as she plopped another queso-covered chip in her mouth. "Huh."

Setting my wine aside, I stalked across the carpet, feeling like a tiger after its prey. Natalie leaned back until she was staring up at me from the rug. I wanted to run the tip of my tongue along her entire body. I wanted to taste every inch of her. My veins were wired with thoughts of her beneath me.

"But that's not how our lives went, Scott. We're here. Together. So, get that job, but get it for you. Not for me." Her voice was quiet and like a moan when she spoke.

"I'm doing it for *our* future and nothing less," I said against the skin of her neck.

"And what do you see when it comes to our future? Where will we live?"

"In a house big enough for you to have an art room." I shook my head as I added, "I don't care where."

"Don't forget about an office for yourself." She put a hand on my chest to lightly push me up.

We went back to sitting across from each other, wine in hand, with the queso and chips between us. My need for her was only muffled.

"Will we have kids?" she asked before taking a gulp of wine, as if she needed the courage to get the question out.

"I would hope so."

"Really? You know, we're going to argue about their names every minute for nine months."

I hid my grin by taking another sip. "Oh, I know, and every minute will be hilarious because you'll want some stupid name like Wilber."

She cracked up. "Wilber? You think I'd want to name a kid Wilber?"

"It's you. Anything is possible."

"You just think that, since I'm an artist, I'm going to want to name our kid something 'unique' like Apple or Cosmo."

Our kid.

I couldn't hide my smile when she said that. It sounded too good to be true. But it was Natalie, and she was already that and more. I would do everything I could to give her the life she was imagining. I would get a good job and give her everything she wanted. I would do everything I could to keep her.

"You really want all that? With me?"

I shook my head, smile still in place. "Don't you get it? Over everyone else, I will always fucking choose you." I touched her cheek, needing to touch her if I couldn't hold her close. "I will always treat you right if you just . . . give me the chance. I don't care what it takes."

"I just want you. Us. I don't need anything extravagant if I have you and we're happy."

"Promise?"

She smiled, holding her wine out to toast me. "I swear it," she said once our glasses met, leaning forward to kiss me long and slow.

"I'll give you as many Wilbers as you want."

She laughed against my lips. "Maybe we should have this discussion at a later date."

chapter fifteen

My weekend with Natalie had been perfect, absolutely perfect. I missed having her close, touching her, and even watching her walk around in nothing but her thin shirt and panties. I felt like my mouth could water at just the thought of pressing my lips to her neck, to the inside of her thigh. This weekend, I hadn't gotten enough of her. I hadn't taken charge of her enough. Even though she had pranced throughout our apartment, challenging me to take her every time she glanced at me under those long, lowered lashes of hers.

Yes, this weekend had been perfect, removing whatever sour taste I still had in my mouth from when the junkie that had died right in front of me.

Having Natalie all to myself had given me some perspective.

I needed to start job hunting. I needed to start somewhere. By the time Natalie and I graduated, I wanted to be stable. I wanted to give her the world, but I would settle for what we had talked about. I would climb my way to the top for her.

So, when my marketing professor dismissed class, I didn't bother packing up. As people made for the door to get on with their lives, I did my best to maneuver around them all to reach the bottom of the auditorium.

I would make Natalie proud.

We had left our small town together, and I would give her every reason to stay with me.

"Sir?" I said when I reached the podium, the word heavy on my tongue.

Dr. Ortman's head snapped up as he slid his appointment book and papers into his briefcase. "Oh, Scott." Our class met in a small auditorium, even though we only filled half the seats. He had every name memorized by the second week. "How can I help you?"

"Well, uh, I was wondering if you knew if any marketing firms were hiring students right now."

"Right now?" He put his hands on his hips, scrunching his face as he thought about it. "I think a buddy of mine is looking, but you would start at the bottom. No pay."

Starting at the bottom without pay was bullshit. Money better be on the table later.

"Do you think anything I've turned in is good enough to land something?"

"You still have that presentation tomorrow, but I think a few of your ideas have some potential. You just need to take your time tweaking—brainstorming—your work." He nodded. "You could probably learn a lot working under my buddy, even though you'd probably be making coffee runs until you proved yourself useful."

Coffee runs weren't ideal, but I would take what I could get if it meant moving up.

He pulled his briefcase from the podium. "Tell you what. Why don't I put in a good word, and you work on getting an application to them, okay? Pulse Marketing."

No matter what, I wanted to step up for Natalie. Even if it meant starting at the bottom. God, I wanted to get home to her.

"Thank you, Dr. Ortman. I really appreciate it. I'll see you Wednesday."

He nodded, leaving me to go back to my seat and pack up before the next class came in. The second I reached my desk, I froze. Puke was dripping down the edge and splattering onto the floor in clumps.

"Everything all right?" Dr. Ortman called up to me.

"Y-Yeah." I shoved my things into my bag, wrinkling pages, while my pencils drew aggressive lines down the full length of my notebook paper.

Heading for the door, I forced myself to exhale, my grip on the handle of my bag strained. I barely missed bumping into the professor of the next class as I stormed out.

"I think a few of your ideas have some potential." I'd show the arrogant prick. I'd get the job and earn more than he did babysitting a bunch of twenty-something hungover potheads.

By the time I made it back to the pot, the water was boiling like crazy. I'd been so focused on not screwing up I was rushing to undo my fuck-up. I was surprised I hadn't just cut off a finger when I dropped my knife to make it to the stove. Before it boiled over, I caught it, but damn did I have way more respect for chefs now. This shit was stressful. I was actually sweating.

I just wanted one thing to go my way.

I had filled out the application and stuffed the envelope in the pocket of my favorite jeans. Finding it online was easy, but printing it was a pain in the ass. The first printer I went to at the library on campus had been jammed, so I had to walk to the one near the library's coffee shop. Over ten other students were there, either printing their last-minute assignments or just getting hard copies so they could go the fuck home. Like me. Our school needed more printers.

I hadn't decided if I would tell Natalie about it now or wait until I got the job. Either way, I felt like we both deserved pasta for dinner.

I couldn't screw it up. I had spent twenty bucks of the savings Natalie and I had from working all summer. At my last job, I had been treated like a seasonal, even though I was full time. They'd kept me for a year before cutting me off the schedule at the end of summer, just like all the other students who worked when they weren't in school. Natalie had been supporting us since, working four days out of the week as a hostess. She was there now, which was why I was cooking dinner at ten o'clock at night.

She hated being a hostess, but she sucked it up for us. I knew she enjoyed coming home to a warm meal.

I needed one thing to go right. I just wanted one thing to go my way.

I needed that marketing internship to make real money. I would do whatever was necessary to earn enough to support us. Before Nat would resent me for not having a job.

I went back to the stove when the pasta bubbled, then stopped dead before I could stir the water. Bubbling chunks of vomit oozed from the pot. Sucking in a sharp breath, I had forgotten how to blink as I stared, my thoughts going straight to the blue mouth responsible for the blobs on my stove.

I felt far away, distant from everything else other than the pot. It was all I could see, while the outer edge of my vision blurred the world.

Like most idiots who overdose, no one gave a shit. No one talked about the guy at the party, let alone who found him. Not a single student cared. It was like it didn't even happen, or the guy didn't exist. A classic nobody addict.

Tension left my body, and I felt myself smile at the lifeless eyes staring back.

The door slammed shut, snapping me back to reality. Water and pasta roiled in the vomit's wake. I hadn't heard the door open, let alone the struggle of the key, but there stood Natalie.

"Well, I have good news and bad news." She set her bag down next to the boombox on the counter. "Is that pasta? Are you listening to Eminem? Reliving the good ol' days with your rebel, poor-boy music?"

"And sausage to go on top." I looked at her expectantly when she nosed around the kitchen.

"Oh, right! So, the restaurant wants to make me a bartender." She came around to hug me in our small kitchen. "Which means I'll make more money, thanks to tips."

Hand tightening around the spoon I'd been using to stir the pasta, I stared back into the boiling water.

Tips meant every man who sat at the bar would stare at her tits. I knew Natalie, and she would wear low-cut shirts to get extra tips, too. And I'd be worried about her safety every damned night. I'd have to make sure she got to her car without some horny asshole giving her trouble.

Swallowing my every thought, I set aside the spoon to reach for her. "That's great, Nat." I hugged her tighter before she pulled away. "So, work went well, then?"

"Just another long night, but it's over. I'm ready to stuff my face with pasta and crash into bed."

I nodded, rushing to the pot, my heart sinking when nothing stared back at me but scalding water.

Nat popped up next to me to stir the sausage, taking in the countertop. "Have you checked the mail today?"

"Nope, I've been leaving that job to you."

"I'm scared to—"

I kissed her to shut her up. "Go get the mail."

Out the door within seconds, she grumbled about how there would be nothing in the box for her.

I quickly poured out the hot water to throw the pasta, sauce, and sausage together before she got back.

I had just set our bowls on the purple rug when the door burst open.

"It's here!" Natalie said in a panic. My heart jolted into my throat as I spun to face her, my need to protect her shouting through my veins. Mail was scattered at her feet, and she was gripping an envelope. "I got something from the gallery."

My heart didn't slow, my veins still calling out. She was gripping the envelope, while adrenaline shot through me, nearly causing me to go numb. I wanted to save her from whatever was in that letter.

She would be crushed if it weren't good news. She'd been working her ass off all semester, staying up late to finish a painting or just to get it to a place where she felt accomplished. After watching how she exhausted herself for her art, I understood what it meant when an artist said they put their blood, sweat, and tears into something.

Natalie looked up at me with big doe eyes as she flipped the envelope over. My heart plummeted as she tore open the back. She froze. "Maybe we should eat first? It's late. I feel bad that you've been w—"

"Open it, Nat."

The part of me was desperate to protect her, and the other that always wanted to support her was shouting back and forth. Rattling through my head, wrestling against one another. I felt like one of them would combust as I watched her open the letter.

Hesitation gone once it was opened, Nat snatched the letter out and turned it over. All I could do was watch as the envelope fell from her hand. She covered her mouth with it. I couldn't even think of breathing because I wanted to tear the world down as I watched tears well in her eyes.

"It's, um—" She cleared her throat, trying to blink the tears away. "It's a rejection."

I was up and already moving toward her. She became a puddle when I pulled her in, needing my strength to hold her up.

Gripping her to me, I held back curses as heat climbed from her, up my neck, and behind my eyes. "I'm so sorry, Nat. They don't deserve your work for how much you put into it."

"What if I graduate with nothing?" she breathed against my neck. My jaw tensed as her tears fell onto my collarbone. "No promising opportunities, without my work being out in the world, let alone outside this apartment?"

"That's not going to happen, love. You didn't choose the wrong thing to major in, so I don't even want you thinking that way. Art is part of who you are, and you wanted to share it."

"But I didn't realize that a part of me would crumble every time someone rejected my work. It's not just my art. It's my life, my soul, heart—everything. *I* feel rejected."

"I know it doesn't—"

More tears rolled down her cheek while sobs followed, her body trembling.

"What if this just doesn't happen for me, Scott? Should I just give up now? Focus on school and figure out what I'm going to do after graduation?" She shook her head. "I—just . . . giving up feels like the only option. I *actually* might go nowhere with this."

Tear-soaked hair clung to her cheeks, and I brushed it back. "I know it doesn't feel like it right now, but everything's going to be okay. This is the first time you tried to get something in a gallery. You will not give up, and you'll see one of your pieces hanging in a big, fancy gallery where they serve those tiny foods."

A laugh erupted from her through her tears. "Finger foods?"

"Yes, those! I couldn't think of what they were called. You'll get something hung up in one of those big, fancy galleries that serve finger foods." I kissed the top of her head. "That's when you'll know you made it. When people bring a tray full of glasses of champagne to you while you look at your art."

She shook her head before meeting my eyes. "I'm not so sure. It feels impossible right now."

Though I wanted to strangle whoever had sent her the rejection, I smiled. "It's only temporary. You will make it, love."

"But what if I don't?" Sniffling, she didn't give me the chance to answer. "Okay, I'm done. I cried it out, and I want to pretend it didn't happen for now, so let's eat dinner." She pulled me toward the purple rug. "Tell me about your day. Do you have any good news?"

Now wasn't the time to mention the application stuffed into the jeans I would wear tomorrow. I did not want to give her false hope about the internship when my results might be the same as hers.

"No. No, nothing to report."

She smiled through her tears, and I knew it was for my sake, so I wouldn't worry about her. I wanted to fold her into me, hold her close, and protect her from the world. She worked hard. She didn't deserve a copy-and-paste rejection. It was a slap in the face after all the late nights she'd spent at her easel. They saw what she was capable of and denied her. They had rejected a brilliant, dedicated mind. They were fucking morons. They had made a big mistake—one they would regret. A huge fucking mistake.

chapter sixteen

NATALIE WAS ASLEEP AT MY side, facing away from me but tucked in tight. I, on the other hand, was wide awake. Propped up in our pitch-black room, I couldn't ignore the hole in my stomach—couldn't shake whatever was festering inside me. Natalie's rejection burned in my mind. Her tears, the way she practically collapsed into my arms, all the hard work she'd put into her art—was ingrained in my head, gnarling in my blood. When I shut my eyes, it only got worse. The loud echo of my heartbeat made it impossible to sleep.

I sucked in a sharp breath through clenched teeth.

Natalie was a pretty heavy sleeper, but I was still careful as I gently untangled my legs from Nat's and rolled out of bed.

She didn't stir as I made for the door. But her sadness and my anger were all I could think about.

People were going to get in Nat's way. I could see that now. Others would try to corrupt her art—muffle her voice until she felt like she wasn't good enough. Until she gave up on her dream.

That wouldn't happen. I wouldn't let it. I would see her art in a gallery. I would get all dressed up and walk in beside her, proud to have her on my arm.

As I eased the bedroom door shut behind me, I hoped tonight wasn't a rare night where Nat would jolt awake. It had been a long time since she last woke from a nightmare about her brother getting hit by the train that killed him. It had been even longer since I wasn't there to comfort her from the one nightmare haunting her.

After being crushed by her rejection, I wouldn't put it past her unconscious mind. We were similar in that way. We grew determined when set back from our goals. Though, when failure turned its ugly head, we sometimes fell into the memories we tried to keep buried.

I wanted to be here if she woke up—to wrap my arms around her so she would feel safe. But I knew she needed this more than she needed me right now. I would see her wake up happy.

Grabbing my coat before heading to the kitchen, I pulled a small pack from the drawer we threw random shit in. I felt like a burglar ransacking someone else's place rather than sneaking around my own. Natalie's heavy breathing was probably the only sound in the apartment, even though it was trapped behind the door.

I didn't think twice as I left. This was for her.

Once I was out on the quiet, dark street, my mind was static—focused as I made my way down each block. Most streets were empty. I could walk in the dead center of the sidewalk. I never heard the approach of a car. They just suddenly sped by, their headlights blinding me.

I didn't wave down either taxi that drove past. Not a trace of evidence was left behind. I wasn't about to leave a map that would lead straight to our apartment.

Getting across town was the easy part. Natalie had taken me on plenty of tours up and down the street dedicated to art. The challenge was searching for one gallery among dozens of art exhibitions and studios, walking up and down buildings with large colorful murals and strange sculptures. Even the streetlights were constructed of various materials and bent into different shapes.

It was in front of the streetlight made of lightbulbs where I found Natalie's gallery.

My frustration mounted at the sight of it. A few subtle lights were on inside, the window front covered with one of those long sliding gates. At this hour, only the homeless and a few drunks were active. Still, I couldn't do shit in the open.

I went around back, searching for cameras along every nook and cranny. The back door was simple. A dent in the door's edge created a small peephole from the frame to show that this was the employees' entrance. I could imagine the drunk, the high-and-mighty, stuffy artists stumbling from this door to climb into the limo they'd hired for the night. They wouldn't be able to deny themselves one last glass of champagne before returning to their stale lives. Galleries sucked off those people. The flashy artists who believed they were creative gods among idiots.

And Natalie would never be that. Even if—even *when* she made it big.

I couldn't even picture it. I shook those images away, spitting as a precaution.

Stepping back, I found out it took two kicks before the door dented in enough for me to yank open. Metal pieces from the doorknob clanked when they hit the concrete, echoing through the alleyway and off the walls of my brain as I rushed to head inside. My heart was soaring as I eased the door shut behind me, but I heard no one approach.

Dismissing the tension pulsing from my neck to my jaw, I went straight to the reception desk, not wasting a second before I punched the stapler clean into the wall behind it. The sound echoed off the silent walls until it faded. Cards, pamphlets, and a vase of flowers followed. The artificial candles went flying, their fake flames snapping off when they hit the floor. Fake candles. These walls had probably never seen an actual flame.

What bullshit with all the paper, wood, canvases, and flammable sculptures.

I didn't stop until the desk was empty except for a stack of business cards for the gallery.

Any of Natalie's paintings would've turned this place into something extraordinary. There were plenty of blank walls. They could've chosen any of her pieces, and it would've brought one of their walls to life. It would've sold within a blink. Unlike the splattered, smeared, abstract nonsense pieces everywhere. Natalie's art was fucking beautiful. Any of her pieces would've been the best-looking painting in the stale place.

But they had a fucking stick up their luxurious asses.

My chest heaving, I took in what I'd destroyed, my mind clear of static. This place would be unrecognizable. The fancy details would be nothing but scattered waste.

Between the silence, the white walls and the spotlights, everything about the open room was ominous.

I was ready to light this shit on fire.

I would give this place something to be stuck up about.

I dug the small pack—the one I'd snatched from the junk drawer—out of my pocket. Striking a match, I watched the orange glow for a moment. Everything else around me blurred except the flame. It had been a long time since I'd struck a match with a purpose other than to light a cigarette or a candle.

I remembered a chair swallowed up by flames.

The hair on the back of my neck rose.

Shaking off the impulse to throw the match, I grazed the flame along the closest painting instead. As I watched the canvas become engulfed, a warmth spread through me, too. Each flicker of the blaze tugged a smile to my mouth. I could almost feel the heat in my veins—like the fire ate away at my body as it did each canvas.

A rush of flare and fumes consumed the room, skipping from one decorated wall to another. I didn't bother with the sculptures, knowing it wouldn't take much for them to melt when the rest of the building incinerated.

While the flames climbed high at the door and front windows, I kept my exit clear. Bloodshot eyes stared from in the reflection, my sneer flashing back at me.

Everything was a fucking mess. Soot covered the floor, and drywall was caving in everywhere.

I did my best to stay out of the chaos, jumping back from anything that looked like it was about to topple over and shaking my coat off. I would need a shower.

Nerves raw and adrenaline high, I saved the best for last, throwing a match at the reception desk like I was trying to throw a fastball. Thanks to the cards, papers, and flowers scattered all around it, fire caught the chairs before engulfing the space altogether. I laughed as I watched it splinter under the heat. Sweat was breaking out across my skin, soaking through my shirt as the room warmed. I cackled when I used my fist to wipe away the sweat. Should've left my goddamned coat behind.

My eyes flickered, my mind struggling against the growing static to stay in the moment. I wanted to be conscious for this. I didn't want to black out. I wanted to watch the blackness eat at the white walls until the paint and drywall crumbled to soot.

My eyes were wide open.

Even as glass exploded and alarms went off, my eyes were wide open. When the sprinklers went off, raining down on my destruction, I inhaled until my lungs couldn't expand any further. The sigh following was gratifying and came from deep within my chest. Nothing was perfect, but I hadn't felt like this since I lit up my old man's chair. Fuck it. I wasn't sure I even felt like this when I tossed that goddamned lighter. That had been for me. This was for Natalie. Her paintings belonged here just as much as these fuckers. And, until she made it, no one deserved to have their art hung here.

I would not let them tear her down. I wouldn't let anyone hinder Nat's dream.

They had no one to blame but themselves.

If she couldn't sell paintings here, no one could.

Watching paint drip from the canvases and be devoured by the fire was almost as satisfying as ripping it from the wall myself.

One of her paintings would be hung up with one of those little white cards. She would get into one of the most prestigious galleries in the city. I would make sure of it. I wouldn't let them win. I wouldn't let her give up on her dream.

Pulling out match after match, I scratched them against the box before throwing them into the destruction. I pulled out every match, lighting each one to make the flames grow. The fire alarm still rattling inside my head, I watched the blaze scale the wall, spread from canvas to wall to ceiling and *everything*. Everything was incinerating.

After emptying the pack, I made it out the back exit within the same moment the fire truck came blaring down the street. I couldn't shake the impulse to yell about what I'd done. But I'd lost my chance when I walked out of the alarms.

I ran down the other end of the alley, away from the blaring alarm and the sirens. The adrenaline pulsing through me brought up memories of the night Natalie and I escaped from my old man's house. I just wished I was hopping in the car beside Natalie instead of walking home in the cold.

chapter seventeen

NOTHING BUT FIRE CONSUMED MY thoughts. I was distant from everything about my day, catching myself clenching my fists whenever I thought I felt heat on my skin, in my veins, melting the walls around me.

The rest of the night had been a whirlwind of dreams I never woke up from. I couldn't remember any of them. All I'd been able to think about was getting something in my system before I projected all over our bed.

Natalie was already in the bathroom when I woke up, light on and making a ruckus as she got ready for the day. We didn't get to talk before we rushed our separate ways, Natalie to work while I made for class.

It was only at the end of Dr. Ortman's lecture that I forced myself to return to everything around me, and it was because he called my name over the flames scaling my mind.

"You have a job interview an hour from now," he told me. "Take the portfolio you've put together for this class. And, Scott, don't mess this up."

From there, I focused on prepping for my interview.

The gallery had no one to blame but themselves.

The fire had happened. Thinking about it was pointless. I could go home to Natalie with good news.

The second I walked into the apartment, I knew Natalie wasn't home yet. And if I was lucky, I would make it out before she came in. I ransacked the closet until I found the only pair of slacks I owned. After throwing them on along with a light-blue button-down, I realized I hadn't splurged on dress shoes when I'd bought the rest of it.

"Fuck." I grabbed the nicest pair of tennis shoes I owned. I would have to stop at a store on the way. Heading for the door, I glanced at the blinking clock on the microwave. I nearly sent my shoe through the wall. "Fuck! I don't have time."

I was going to look like an idiot. I couldn't stand up in fucking tennis shoes and shake my potential boss's hand. Locking my jaw, I forced myself to turn before I did something stupid and go to the bedroom for my portfolio.

As I climbed into Nat's car, all I could think about was that I didn't want to be laughed at for wearing fucking tennis shoes with fucking slacks. The second my first paycheck was in my hand, I would buy dress shoes. I didn't care how long it took. I wasn't doing this again. I wouldn't have anyone laughing at me.

As I walked into the office, I couldn't shake the feeling of being looked up and down.

"Hello," I started when I reached the reception desk.

A petite woman with a messy bun looked up from the books scattered across her round desk. Strands of loose hair framed her face, touching her parted pink lips. She sat up straight before I could take her in any further. "Hello, how can I help you?"

I held her hazel gaze, thinking back to why I was here. "My name's Scott Nelson. I was told by my professor that I have an interview."

No matter how hard she bit her pink bottom lip, I refused to look. "Oh, yes. Why don't you take a seat, and I'll let Mr. Benson know you're here."

"Okay, thanks."

Keeping my eyes down, I wasn't sitting there for over thirty seconds before a man in a dark-blue suit walked up and extended a hand out to me. "Hi there, Scott. Gary Benson." Getting to my feet, I met to shake his hand. "Dr. Ortman told me about your application and passed on a good word, so I thought we could have a one-on-one."

"Yes, I appreciate it. I sent over my application as soon as I could."

"And you brought your portfolio. You're all set. Let's take a walk to my office."

I patted the portfolio bag. Then, as I followed him down the hall to his office, the color drained from my face when I remembered my shoes. I needed to sit as soon as possible.

Everyone I walked by—I was convinced their eyes were on me. Maybe it was because of my tennis shoes, but when I sat in the chair across from Gary Benson's desk, I felt eyes on the back of my head. It made my skin crawl. From my shoulder to my toes, my body grew tight and cold. Like a statue. I felt watched, like I was on display.

The sensation churned my stomach. It felt like they knew. They could see what I'd done.

I almost smiled. The thought was beyond ridiculous. Not to mention impossible.

I shook my head to myself. *Get a grip, Scott. Quit the paranoia. No one had a clue that I'd set fire to an art gallery last night.*

Gary Benson took his chair, opening my application before him. "So, Scott. How do you feel you'd fit in here at Pulse Marketing?"

I'd make myself fit in.

"Scott?" Natalie called from her spot on the purple rug the second I opened the door, looking up from her textbook with a mouthful of chips.

"Yes?" I asked with a smile as I shut the door and strode toward her. I pulled her to me, firmly pressing my lips to hers as my hand crept into the bag for a chip.

"The art gallery . . . it practically burned down last night," she blurted when I pulled away. "It's all anyone in the art department is talking about."

The smile slipped from my face. Swallowing suddenly became impossible. The edges of the chips raked down my throat. I made myself sound surprised. "What?"

"Yeah. Almost all the paintings are gone now. Burnt to nothing. And it just happened. Just happened." She shook her head in disbelief. "Probably a good thing I didn't get in there, right?"

I did this. I did it for you.

"It's fate."

"You're right." She threw her arms up with a shrug. "My paintings weren't meant to be there. They would've been destroyed."

Her words—her mindset—was exactly what I'd hoped for. Her paintings didn't need to be in that damned gallery. She deserved a gallery that wanted her from the moment they saw her stunning name on an application. Any of them would be lucky to have a painting from Natalie. The next better want a whole collection from her.

"Some things just aren't meant to happen. The rejection happened for a reason."

"Yeah. It was a sign—that it all happened last night."

As I nodded, something desperate turned over in my stomach, telling me to change the topic. "I start a new job tomorrow. Well, I guess not really a *job* job but an internship."

She pulled back to look at me, a glint in her eyes. "What? Really? When did that happen? Is that why you're dressed so nice?" The initial surprise seemed to wear off before I could answer because her questions were followed by "Oh, Scott, I'm so proud of you. That's such great news. This could lead you to some great opportunities."

"I had an interview today. I didn't want to tell you after yesterday."

She nodded, biting at her pinky nail, while she reached for a chip with her free hand. She wanted to act like her feelings didn't matter, but I could see the wheels in her mind working against her. I could see the tension winding through her body. It was her cycle. She only acted like her feelings didn't matter because that was how her family treated her.

"That's sweet of you, but you could've told me, and I still would've been happy for you."

When she finally spoke, it only confirmed everything I already knew she was thinking.

God, I could kill her family for treating her like shit—for making her feel like her thoughts and feelings and ideas didn't matter. Everything about her mattered, and I didn't want to hear otherwise.

"Last night wasn't the right time. It didn't matter that you would've been happy for me. What mattered was that you needed me. You being okay was all I cared about. I wasn't even thinking about the internship then."

"Because you were thinking about me?"

"Yes. You—that's all I think about. You're what matters most to me. Not some job that probably won't last. You."

Natalie shook her head. "Always know exactly what to say."

"To get your blood boiling?" I asked, my fingers catching the neck of her blouse to pull it down just enough to show off her cleavage.

A slow smile spread across her lips. "Oh, yeah? Right now?"

"Oh, right now." I pushed myself on top of her, hands grabbing at every part of her I could—her hips, her breasts, her thighs—until not a stitch of clothing covered her.

Her hands were just as greedy, winding in my hair and stripping my clothes before I moved to remove hers.

She had no idea. She was beneath me, begging me to fuck her, and she had no clue I was the reason the gallery had crumbled to ash.

The thought—just feeling her against me—

"God," I groaned into her breasts. "Fuck, Nat."

"You better," she said with an airy laugh against my neck.

I'd never been harder in my life.

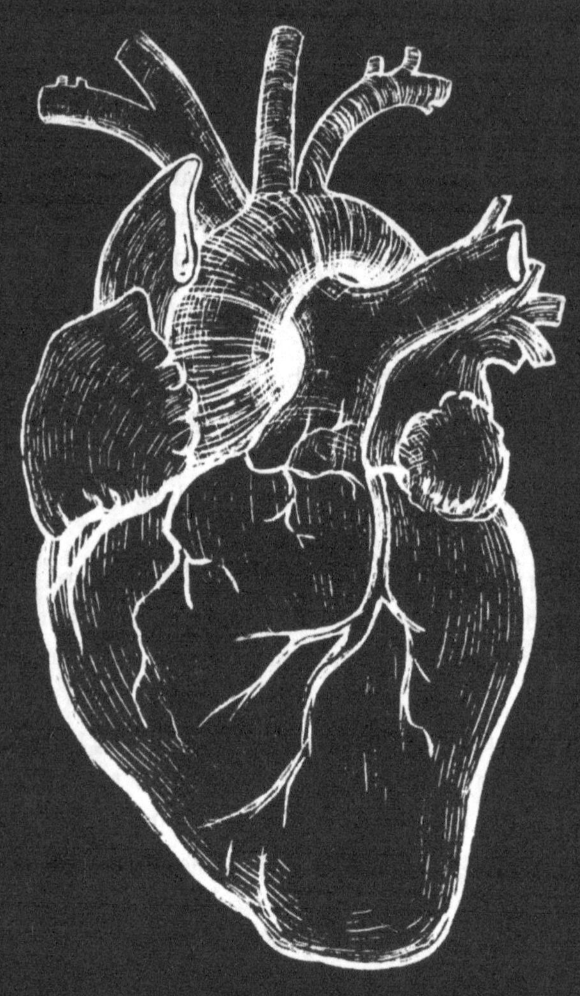

chapter eighteen

2008 (Senior Year)

THE COFFEE GRINDER WAS LIKE nails scraping a chalkboard. The sound made my head throb. I leaned back in the creaky chair and put my hands over my eyes to block out the light. Zach, my coworker at Pulse, could not have been making a bigger commotion, using his kitchen like a break room. It was after midnight, and my brain was struggling to keep up with all the paperwork.

"Hopefully, we won't get a noise complaint," Zach shouted over the grinding, only to stop the machine a second later.

"Shouting about it really isn't going to help our case, now is it?" Britney, Zach's girlfriend, chuckled, but we all knew she was serious.

Britney was too much of a coward to mean the shit she said, but she was annoyingly straitlaced.

"I think you guys are in pretty desperate need of some caffeine," Natalie said to help ease the tension. "I mean, look at Scott. His brain is about to start oozing out of his ears."

"This paperwork is just kicking our ass," Zach said. "Gary wants us to come up with a few slogans for this car company that's coming in on Tuesday, but Gary wants these on his desk by tomorrow morning."

That right there—Zach was my ticket to a job offering from Pulse Marketing.

When I got home from watching him interact with those around the office, I told Natalie she could quit her job as a hostess.

He'd attached himself to me no more than a week into my internship. Since he was the coffee-runner intern, he tried to be buddy-buddy with everyone in the office. He acted like he wasn't at the bottom of the food chain, never complained. He was too nice not to get offered a job. People liked having someone around to kiss their ass.

"That's kinda insane. Aren't you doing his work for him?" Britney said, her lips pinched as she watched Zach. "Now, on top of still having to finish your paper tonight so you can turn it in on time, you're trying to come up with a list of slogans for an unpaid job."

"They're about to graduate," Natalie piped in. "This is their test before they get a job offer."

I looked over my shoulder at her, unable to stop the smile that crossed my face at the sight of her flopping, messy bun. She beamed back at me from the couch. For once, her hair was free of paint. But she had a fleck of blue on her neck, just below her right ear. She had to know she was the glue holding this group together.

"Sorry you girls are stuck here watching"—Zach looked up at the TV but seemed to realize he had no idea what was playing on screen—"whatever you're watching."

"Don't worry about us," Britney said in the same moment Natalie responded with "Just take the time you need to get your work done."

"Natalie," Zach said as he poured our coffees, "I heard you are finally getting stuff into galleries."

I rubbed the space between my brows. While forcing myself to keep up with pointless conversations was probably the most painful part of gallery showings, my chest swelled with pride. Seeing Natalie in her element—doing the very thing she'd loved and dreamed of back in high school—was a sight that nearly brought me to my knees.

"She's sold almost every piece over the last couple of months. She's been painting more for galleries than she has been for her classes."

I spoke before I even realized what I was doing.

"I actually have a showing next week," Natalie jumped in, "at Fourteenth-Street Uplifting Art, if you and Britney would like to come. It's downtown, on the art street."

"Oh, damn, that's great. Huge. I bet you've been super excited to show your stuff off. I'm sure Brit and I could swing by, right, Brit?" She quietly responded with a "We'll see," which Zach ignored. "You're a semester behind Scott and I, right?"

"Yeah. She's taking a lighter load for the next few months because of the gallery, so she'll be done by the end of next semester."

Even with taking a back seat when it came to classes, Natalie was putting herself out there.

"Scott," Natalie said with a bewildered laugh, her words still curt, "I can answer for myself. Thank you."

Zach sat next to me, setting down two cups of freshly brewed coffee as he grimaced in discomfort.

"I'm sorry, love," I said as I rubbed my eyes again. "I'm not trying to speak for you. It just slipped out. You know I can't help myself when it comes to you."

She deflated. "It's okay. Just get your work done so you can go home and sleep it off."

Nodding, I opened my eyes to sit up straight and lean over the table of scattered papers Zach and I had accumulated. Natalie and I couldn't get home soon enough. I would kiss my way up her neck, wind my hands in her hair to keep her close, squeeze her breast before shifting my hand down to cup her—

"So, I heard something pretty interesting," Zach butted in, leaning closer so Natalie and Britney couldn't hear. "Turns out, when we graduate and become official employees, we get an intern."

I didn't bother looking at him. "You mean we'll have a minion?"

"Yup! How great would it be if we had a hot intern working for us?"

What a fucking douche.

The whole fucking reason I wanted this job was so I could give Natalie everything she deserved.

"I have a girlfriend," I pointed out. "*You* have a girlfriend."

Cheaters were impossible to understand. Men who cheated on the women they supposedly loved weren't real men. They needed a fuck to make up for the dick they lacked. And for what? To show off to other men. Being unfaithful, screwing as many women as they could—it was nothing to brag about. Society was idiotic for cheering on little peckers like Zach.

"I know, I know," he went on, "but that doesn't mean we can't enjoy the scenery."

"You don't think every guy in our office would have eyes on her if you had a hot assistant?"

"Exactly. She'd be a black sheep amongst a herd of men. Everyone would be jealous." He stared off into the distance for a moment. "God, I hope she's blonde. I was into blondes before Britney."

"Isn't she blonde? I've been around your girlfriend all night."

"Yeah, but she isn't *blonde* blonde."

I stared at him blankly, noting to ask Natalie what the fuck that meant later. "Right."

"Okay, so, uh, do we want to compare slogans and put the best ones on Gary's desk in the morning?" Zach asked, shifting through our pages of scribbled notes.

Our wadded-up papers were tossed at the other end of the table. We compared notes, Zach gulping down his coffee and cracking jokes, while I tried to hurry things along, listening enough to laugh at anything that was supposed to be funny.

When we finally finished, I leaned back in my seat and released a pent-up sigh.

"All done?" Britney asked in a grumble. "I can sleep? Please?"

Zach laughed, getting up to hug her from behind her spot on the couch. "Yes, sweetheart, you can go change into your jammies and go to sleep."

"Thank God! I've been nearly unconscious for the last half hour." She turned to Natalie. "No offense. I didn't mean it that way. I just have such a hard time staying awake. I'm an early bird, so I hate staying up this late."

"I get it," Natalie said as she stood to make her way toward me.

Damn, she was the most gorgeous, most perfect thing I had ever seen. I wrapped my arms around her waist when she reached me, wishing we were home alone.

"Ready to get going?" Natalie asked me as she combed her fingers through my hair. Trying to help soothe my headache, she caressed my forehead.

Before I could answer, Britney hopped up from the couch. "It was so nice to have you guys over. I'm always looking to meet the people Zach works with. Especially since it looks like you both are going to be there for good."

I released Natalie to stand. As we got up to grab our things, I kept a firm arm around Nat's waist as Zach and Britney walked us to the door.

She was mine. If nothing else, I could always be proud of that.

"It was nice to finally meet you, Zach. Scott talks about you all the time since you've been working together, so it was nice to connect the dots," Natalie said when we reached the door. "It was nice to meet you, too, Britney."

"Yup, totally" was Britney's response.

Once we were in the car, Natalie leaned over to rub the sore spots on my head as I drove us home.

She was perfect. She complemented me—took care of me in every way I never knew I craved. She was my breath of fresh air.

Once we were back in our apartment, Natalie leaned up against the door. The sound that left her body was a combination between a sigh and a groan. "I was really hoping I could make some touches to this new painting before bed tonight."

I brushed her hair behind her ear. "Then, sit down and work on it."

"Will you sit with me?" She stuck her lip out, just in case I thought about saying no.

"Of course I will. But first"—I pulled her in close—"I've been waiting to do this all damned day."

Pulling her by the nape of her neck, I sealed my lips to hers. I waited for her body to meld into mine before I slid my tongue along her bottom lip. I felt the nip of her teeth on my lip in response, and she released a soft moan before pulling back with a smile, winding around me with a knowing glint in her eye. She wasn't going to give in to me. Her mind was focused on art.

She disappeared into our bedroom to change into comfier clothes she wouldn't mind spilling paint on. By the time I had gone to the kitchen for a glass of water, she walked out in sweatpants and a big T-shirt that hung off her shoulder.

Natalie perched at her easel, the paintbrush she picked up an extension of herself. It gave her the ability to express her heart and soul. I carefully wrapped my arms around her as she got to work.

As I watched her, held her, I felt confident.

I knew what I had, and I would never let her go. She would always be mine. Because everything I had done, I had done for her—for us.

And that made me powerful.

I would never be the guy that let her down. I was the guy who made sure she achieved her dreams. I was the guy who would always make sure we were okay. I would give Natalie everything she wanted. No matter what it took.

I was better than men like Zach.

Burying my face in her hair, I took in the dandelions of her perfume.

I would always be there for her.

"Babe?" Natalie suddenly said, her brush still working across the canvas. "Can I ask you a question?"

I nuzzled the side of her neck, breathing "Of course" against her skin.

"I think—" I felt her hesitate. "I think that it's about time we upgraded from this dingy apartment. Our lease is up in, like, three weeks, anyway. We have to give the office an answer about renewing."

"That's not a question."

She sighed. "I'm serious."

"Oh, you do? With what income?"

"I'm selling my art now, and you're starting your official job at Pulse. I don't see why we couldn't get a house sometime soon. Wouldn't that be nice? We could start real, professional lives, adopt a pet—"

"You don't think we've already started our lives?" I asked, going stiff behind her.

"No. No, we've started our lives, but we could move, keep going, and improving when we can. We don't have to stay here forever." She spun on her stool to face me, holding her paintbrush out so it would drip on the floor instead of on us. "We came from nothing, Scott. We ran from our awful small-town lives with a mason jar full of cash. That's it. And look how far we've come already. You're about to graduate college! That wasn't something you thought you'd be able to do when we met. Things are starting to fall into our lap. Life is starting to give us a break, and we should take it."

This was coming so fast. We'd talked about all these things before, when they were distant, but she was right—everything was happening so fast now.

"But what if—"

"Uh-uh-uh. Don't pull back like you did. Don't be scared of what you might not be able to have. We both know I'll be able to convince you, anyway. It might take me a while, but I always win." Winking, she poked my nose before turning to face her work in progress.

For a moment, I considered her golden waves. Then, without thinking, I said, "My mom would never let me have a pet. I asked for a lizard every birthday I can remember until she left. I never bothered trying that with my dad. I was worried he would chuck it into a wall."

"We can have all the pets you want. I'd be okay with a lizard, so long as you don't chuck it at me." She raised a finger at me. "Don't even think about putting it on me while I'm asleep, either, Scott."

I rested my forehead against her back. "You really want all that, though?"

"We're on our way to getting everything we wanted. I think it would be good for us to move out of here, start fresh again. Besides, if we did, we could . . . start thinking about having a family?"

My head sprung up from her back. "Oh, yeah?"

I knew her cheeks were getting brighter by the second. That or they had erupted the moment the words left her mouth. Nat didn't blush about many things, but when she did, it was because she was more than embarrassed. She could talk about her work confidently, shoulders back with a straight face. She flushed when people asked about her background or when she tripped over her words and had to readjust herself. Her face would only become red when she was angry, especially if we were arguing.

"I just don't want us to change," I admitted. "What if we do all this and then something happens to us?"

Her brush paused, and she turned to face me again. "I'm talking about starting a family, and you're over here worried something's going to happen between us?"

I took her free hand in mine. "I want you to have everything you want. Everything. But what if we can't do it? What if we make a mistake and—"

She shook her head, a hint of a smile still on her face. "Stop being such a chicken. You are not a mistake in my life. You saved me just as much as I saved you. What's stopping us? What's stopping us from doing this now like we did when we graduated high school? I want a future with you—that's not going to change. It's time. You're graduating. A new chapter is starting. One where we can have anything we want."

It was my turn to shake my head. "You go on such tangents when you get like this. There's no stopping you."

"Exactly!" She laughed. "So, why don't you save yourself the earache and give in already so this can be over and done with?"

"Fine. Fine, but I have one request."

She rolled her eyes. "Always a contingency with you. What is it?"

Knowing I was about to surprise her, I smirked. She would never predict what I was about to ask her to do. It would probably be the last thing she'd ever think of, since she thought I had surpassed my punk phase. But if we were going to take another leap, I wanted something to remember these years. Something I'd wanted from the moment she finished drawing on my arm. Something that would remind me of happy memories with Natalie and so I would never forget

where we'd come from. I just needed her to redesign it.

"Get a tattoo with me."

chapter nineteen

The music was background noise compared to the chatter surrounding us. Natalie was across the room, Olivia glued to her side, while Anthony was right behind her. The three were talking to Zach and other people, while Britney wandered around, staring at every painting with the same bored, unimpressed expression. I'd be damned if I let her prissy attitude ruin this for Nat.

Every night she was able to do a showing, she'd become excited. She stressed over her clothes and little touches regarding her makeup. She strived to impress anyone she could, and though she wanted her art to do most of the work, she prepared for questions. Tonight, she was wearing a sleek black dress that stopped right over her knees, accessorized by several necklaces starting at her chest and ended at her collarbone. Just like she used to wear when we first met.

She was sexy enough to catch the attention of someone across the room. I snatched up a glass of champagne from one of the caterer's trays before stalking toward her. Goddamn, and I thought I wanted to fuck the shit out of her every night. If I thought she would, I would be in her ear, quietly begging her to follow me into a nearby closet. Natalie always wanted it dirty when we got home, begging me to fuck her as hard as I could. With every gallery we went to, I knew she was wet beneath her dress. Her nipples hardened if I so much as looked at her. Art got her going.

But she was focused and enjoying every minute of attention, so I would have to wait to take my fun later.

I came up beside Natalie and slid my arm behind her to wrap it around her waist, keeping her close. She smiled up at me when I handed her the sparkling champagne, but she went right back to listening to Olivia.

Olivia and Anthony had ended things toward the end of last year, but at least one of them had shown up for each of Natalie's viewings, kept in touch, and went to parties together. I couldn't fathom why. I hadn't seen Anthony since Olivia brought him to Natalie's opening night. And I had a feeling she'd only brought him because Nat asked her to bring someone I knew so I wouldn't be wandering around alone.

I hadn't cared. I was so proud of her that night. Every time I saw one of her pieces hanging in a gallery, I was proud.

"I heard you guys snagged a realtor," Zach said with an elbow nudge in Natalie's direction.

Before anyone else could say anything, Anthony jumped in. "Oh, you guys are moving? Do you guys need help moving? I'm down to help."

"Closing is next week. We could use the extra hand. I'll even feed you."

Conveniently, that was when Britney made her reappearance.

"I forgot all about your move. Hopefully, you guys will have enough help to get it all done."

Zach looked down at her with a frustrated expression she ignored.

"So," Nat cut in, breaking the beat of awkward silence, "I'm taking Scott somewhere after this. An early graduation present."

"Oh, really?" I asked, hearing about this for the first time.

Nat didn't meet my eyes.

"Ooooh, so mysterious," Olivia said. "Just kidding. I already know what you're doing."

"Well, shit. Then, tell me." Anthony moved closer so she could whisper in his ear.

"Don't let him hear you!" Natalie whined, panicked that the surprise would be spoiled.

Smiling, I leaned in to hear, but that only earned me a playful shove from Nat.

"You guys are disgustingly cute," Olivia told us before she leaned into Anthony to whisper to him.

"You act like we're not having a good time," he said with a wink. Turning back to Natalie, Anthony reached into his chest pocket, revealing a carton of cigarettes. My mouth went dry at the sight of the red-and-white box. "Is there a cool VIP section where all the painters smoke, or am I going to have to stand outside?"

"Outside," Olivia and Natalie said in unison.

That was when the dog made his appearance, trotting over to nuzzle his head beneath Natalie's hand. Retrievers were smarter than I thought. Had good taste, too. That, or he'd pinpointed the sucker in our group. He always waddled to Nat for love first. She crouched to give the gallery's mascot her full attention, running her hands down the length of his body.

"Your black dress is going to be *covered.*"

We all looked up from the smiling retriever. Caden was making his way toward us, his eyes locked on Loki, as if the dog was getting away with something he shouldn't be.

Caden and his wife Ava owned and ran the gallery. It was only for local artists, but Ava dressed like she was ready to star in a reality TV show, while Caden acted like a cool but aloof salesman. He wasn't successful. He liked to wear slacks with whatever shirt he thought matched but still showed off his geometric sleeve. But the cherry on top was that he always wore black leather high-tops. It aggravated the hell out of me.

"Like, I mean, covered in a bajillion of his little golden locks," Caden went on.

Nat gave Loki one last pat on the head before getting to her feet. I helped her, holding her hand.

"You act like I care." Nat gestured to her dress, which now looked like a Loki overcoat.

"Ava's gonna get a kick out of you. You look like one of her grandmother's shitty throw pillows," he told her.

"What am I going to get a kick out of?" Ava appeared, standing a little shorter than Caden in her heels. "Hey, buddy," she cooed to the dog as she crouched, "you haven't been getting into the champagne again, have you? No, I hope not. I don't want to wake up to a groaning boy tonight. No, I don't."

She was in a black leather skirt to match her husband's high-tops, thin black heels, and a red lacy top that looked like lingerie. Loki gave her zero cover from wandering eyes; everyone could see straight down her skanky top.

Pathetic. I didn't know how Natalie could like them. She practically gloated about them and how she clicked with the gallery owners the second she showed them her portfolio. They had added one of her canvases that next weekend and were as thrilled as Nat when it sold. Ava and Caden were obsessed with her art and treated her right, all the while putting up a façade of professionalism.

Still, they begged for attention wherever they thought they might get it.

"I was just telling Natalie that she looks like one of your grandmother's throw pillows after petting Loki," Caden told Ava.

She nodded with a short "Ah" before getting to her feet. "She might look like an old lady's throw pillow, but she sure does make some damned good art. We have so much buzz about some of her things. Her dripping flower paintings always stir up so much awe. I have people ask about those just about every week."

"We actually want Natalie to paint during one of our busy nights," Ava continued. "I think painting a few of those dripping flowers will make people lose their minds. Especially if you do it right in front of them. We actually want a few of our local artists to come in and work on their most-talked-about pieces in person. It'd be such an experience for everyone." I could swear on the shitty chair that would be my father's deathbed that the smile Ava directed at Natalie was on the seductive side. "It'd be a magical night for everyone."

Ava touched the bare skin of Natalie's arm, her eyes sliding to me for the briefest of moments. I hated how

Ava caressed Nat with her long, freshly manicured nails. I bristled, careful not to tighten my fist and squeeze Nat's hand.

It was like they wanted to coo her into bed with them, lure her into having a threesome. I couldn't be the only one thinking about fucking the shit out of her.

I tried to shake the thought away, knowing Nat would hate it if she knew what I really thought of Ava and Caden after how nice they were to her. Too nice.

Shaking my head, I chalked my thoughts up to paranoia. My stomach churned. The gallery was the definition of suffocating. It only got worse the longer we stayed. This was why I put all my focus on Natalie. Sticking close, I watched her, unaware of what she had planned for later.

I couldn't look at any other art in the room. I tried not to look at anything else but her.

This was because Natalie's paintings were the only ones I didn't see burning.

chapter twenty

Natalie wouldn't tell me where we were going. She dragged me to the car after we left the gallery and told me to get in. From that point on, she ignored every question. Until I annoyed her enough that she refused to talk to me at all. Eventually, when I gave up on questions, the radio was the only sound between us.

Nat pulled up to the curb in front of a shop with a *TATTOO* sign flashing green before swirling in yellow. With the sun only beginning to set, people lined the sidewalks, strolling past as they ate ice cream or sipped stupidly expensive drinks that didn't even contain alcohol.

I stared at the flashing sign, something falling to the pit of my stomach.

The giant black circle sealed to the front windows was less sketchy. Different designs covered the circle, resting behind the name of the shop, *INK METAMORPHOSES*.

"Don't be judgy." My head snapped up to face her. "Yes, you. I see you. According to my artsy sources, it's the best shop in the city," Nat said as she opened her car door.

"Really?" I asked when I jumped out of the car to meet her at the sidewalk.

"To new beginnings," Nat said, leaning in close to kiss me, "and our next step."

She grabbed my hand to pull me inside, where we were met with a girl who had to be out of high school, flipping through a dark fantasy novel as she chewed and popped her blue bubblegum.

She lowered the rock music blaring through the speakers when we walked in. "Hey," she drawled, "what can I do for you both?"

She discarded her book to lean over the counter, nearly popping out of the V-neck she had clearly made herself. The shirt was off-white with a dragon on the front that matched her black ripped jeans. They were tight. Her legs were slender. I could bet the denim hugged her ass, too.

Slut.

Natalie would never wear something so revealing. She never dressed to show off unless it was for a night at an art gallery, but even that wasn't to show off her body for attention.

"My boyfriend and I are looking to get these." Natalie pulled a piece of paper out of her pocket, careful not to show it to me as she unfolded it to hand it over to the girl. "He'll probably want it on his upper arm, and I'm getting mine on my leg."

The girl's expression didn't change as she took in whatever was drawn on the paper. "This is at least going to be a few hours. I don't think I can take both—"

"I scheduled us to get them done at the same time, so we should have an appointment with different artists right now. I sent the designs, too. I emailed them when I made the appointment."

"Great, so you're going to be here till closing." She clicked stuff on her screen on the computer next to her. "Didn't trust one of our artists to design one for you?"

Blood pulsed through the veins in my arms, bulging when I clenched my hands.

"She's an artist," I said before Nat had the chance to respond. "She wasn't trying to insult the artists. She just knows what she wants."

The girl went back to typing on that computer. "I think Jeff is across the street, grabbing a sandwich or whatever. I'll text him about your appointment." The girl looked up at Natalie. "Liam will take your boyfriend. Liam!"

A guy with double sleeves walked out from the back a few seconds later. "Oh, hey. I'm all set for you back here. You're not getting color, right?"

I looked at Nat for confirmation.

"No," she answered for me. "Just classic black."

"Nice." He gave a firm nod. "All right, then. Let's get back here and get started."

I looked at Natalie again before following him back. "I don't get to see what you're getting?"

"Nope," Nat chirped up. "Yours isn't a surprise, but mine will be." She gave me a quick peck on the lips. "And you can't convince me otherwise, so don't even try."

"Fine, fine," I called over my shoulder as I followed Liam, hesitant to leave Nat alone with such a bitch.

He was already set up and waiting for me.

"You want it to cover your whole forearm, right? Or do you want it to start at your shoulder? Your girlfriend wasn't super sure what you'd want when we talked on the phone."

"Forearm sounds good to me."

He gave another nod. "Right on."

He shuffled the parchment papers while I took off my button-down shirt, glad I had put a white tank on underneath. He had me come around to stand in front of his chair before I took my seat.

"Can I see it before you start?" I asked as he adjusted the paper against my upper arm.

"She didn't tell you what you were getting?"

"I know what it is. It's just been a long time since I've seen it."

My heart pounded at the thought of seeing the design again. I could practically smell the gravel, feel the wall beneath me, as Natalie's pen dragged across my arm.

He nodded as if he understood. He spent a few minutes quietly adjusting the paper on my arm before he sat back in his chair. "Take a look and tell me if that's where you want it." He pointed to the mirror behind him, then wiped his hands and threw towels.

It had been over four years since I last saw this design—the first piece of art Natalie had shared with me—on my arm.

It was almost permanent.

A piece of Natalie's passion would be inked into my skin.

My forearm was red and tender. When Liam put the clear bandages over it, my skin swollen to the touch. I flexed my hand, closing my eyes as the burn shot up my arm.

Everything from the branches to the trunk's roots winding through the heart was the same. Even the speckles of dirt were how I remembered it. Sturdy, grounded, with the heart at the center.

That was how Nat saw me. Even then.

"Your girlfriend's got some sick taste," he told me as he smoothed out the bandages.

"She's amazing. This—she drew this when she was seventeen."

"I'd kill for her to sketch out some stuff for our shop. She'd make walk-in folders look rad."

"It wouldn't hurt to ask. Her art has been getting into galleries, so she's been doing work outside of her classes."

"You got it, then. I'll definitely talk to her before you guys leave—give her my card."

When we were all finished, I went around to the front, and it was dark outside. The girl had her legs propped up on the desk, book open in front of her, one boot tapping the side of the computer. My teeth clamped together, and I had to turn away.

Luckily, that was when Nat walked out.

The smile on her face was vibrant with excitement. She was careful to keep her thigh covered with the hem of her dress, holding it in place as she walked closer.

"How do you feel? Do you like it?" Natalie's grin fell. "You're not going to regret it, are you? Oh god, I didn't—"

"Nat, relax." I laughed. "I don't regret it. I feel—like I'm seventeen again but also like I'm—I don't know."

"New?"

"Do I get to see yours or what?"

She beamed as she lifted the hem of her dress, then laughed at my confused expression. "Gotcha! It's on the back of my arm, not my leg." She turned to show me where an anatomical heart matching my own was now inked into her skin. Hers wasn't part of a tree, though, with no branches in sight. Instead, roses, lilies, and sunflowers sprouted from the top of the aorta. "What do you think? I sorta made them match but not too much because that tattoo has always been yours."

"I love that it sort of matches," I told her, completely in awe of her and her abilities.

I loved her. We were bound to each other. This was her way of showing me that. We were permanent. Nothing could take her from me.

On our way out to the car, Nat was all smiles. She practically skipped off the curb as she went around to the driver's side. When she climbed in, she pulled down the sun visor to flip open the mirror, leaning back as she lifted her arm so she could see the heart upside down. "Holy cow, I'm so glad I did this! Best idea I've had in a while, if I do say so myself. I love flying by the seat of my pants!"

I couldn't help but smile with her. Seeing her happy never got old. I never wanted her to lose this side of her. "You're always brilliant, and you know it. Even when you wing it like this."

"Best graduation present ever?" she asked when she turned to face me, her smile more hopeful than certain. "I figured we had to do something pretty dramatic, since we literally ran away after last graduation. Not to mention that you pretty much handed me this idea on a silver platter."

I took her hand in mine. "Leaving with you was the best thing I ever did. I will never do anything as amazing. You changed my life."

She laughed. "And I've changed your life again by surprising you with a tattoo."

With our entwined hands resting on my leg, I knew I would never let her go.

"You didn't force me to do anything. You never have. You are a million things, Nat, but no matter how spontaneous you are, you've never held me hostage."

chapter twenty-one

NATALIE WASN'T HER NORMAL, BUBBLY self. She was still in bed, buried under the covers as she watched me get ready for work, rather than perched at her easel. Jaw clenched as I got dressed, I knew her mind was working overtime. Something was eating away at her. She was just struggling to get up the courage to bring up whatever was on her mind.

We'd both been stressed between work and packing up to move. Some of our things still stirred up bad memories.

Maybe she was just pissed I was leaving her to go to work today while she had to go to class, work on a painting so her next piece would be ready for the gallery two weekends from now, and pack.

I waited as long as I could. Even putting on my shoes and my tie before confronting her.

"All right," I said as I walked out from the bathroom, straightening my tie. "What's going through that pretty head of yours?"

I knew I had waited too long to ask her, and she was probably thinking the worst of me.

"I feel like I'm forcing you."

My hands froze for a heartbeat. "Forcing me to do what?"

"Move. Leave this place for suburban life. Sort of start our lives over again. I feel like . . . when we left our town . . ." She sighed. "I feel like I'm forcing you to move on from all of it."

My hands fell from my tie. "Nat, where is this coming from? You were convinced about this being the right thing to do. You finally get me to agree with you, and you, what, want to change your mind?"

"No. No, I'm not trying to change your mind." She paused, picking at the covers. "I want you to be happy. I don't want to feel like I've forced you into this."

I shrugged. "You wear the pants around here. I don't see why that's such a bad thing."

She looked shocked by what I said. "Okay. Wasn't expecting that response."

"I have to go to work, Natalie. What do you want to hear?"

She cringed back into the covers. She quickly recovered, though, sitting up before I had finished re-looping my tie to fix what I had fucked up. "I want you to not be an asshole."

I tightened and straightened the tie one last time, pulling harder than was probably necessary. "Then, I guess you'll just have to wait to talk about this until I get home."

"What the fuck, Scott?" she snapped, jerking the covers off her but getting up. "Don't talk to me like that. *Ever.* You should know better. I was just trying to talk to you, but you can go off to your job if that's what is fucking important to you!"

"I—"

"*Get out!* I don't even want to see you right now. *Out!* I was just trying to talk to you!"

I couldn't think of anything to say to her. Not a damned word. But she didn't stop yelling as I left. Even in the hallway after I closed the door behind me, I could hear her, my heart burning.

The morning barely passed before my eyes. I processed nothing, too consumed by what'd happened before I left. I never stopped seeing red. Natalie's words screamed in my ears. I was a jackass, but I would not let her leave me. She could be done with me, but I wasn't even close to done with her. I would not let her slip through my fingers. Not after everything.

By the time I fell into my chair at work, I was practically drenched through my shirt. It'd been a few days, so my arm wasn't sore, even though we'd taken the bandage off in the shower the night before. My hand was shaking when I reached up to grip my hair, though.

"Rough morning?"

I opened my eyes to find Zach staring at me from my office door. He must have stopped on the way to his own.

"Want the rest of my smoothie? It's pineapple-orange." I stared at him. "What? I like to be known as the weirdo that brings smoothies to work every morning instead of coffee. Coffee is just too predictable. Especially in this business."

"Right. Well, I ran into Gary on my way in, and he wants us—"

"To show the newbies the ropes since we've graduated to our new, fancy jobs. I know, I know. Gotta love that we're showing interns how to function in the office when we literally just stopped being interns."

"Ready to get started, then, smart-ass?"

"That's the best comeback you've got, champ? I gotta say, I'm disappointed in you."

"I have a migraine," I lied, "so I'm not up ready to step up to the plate yet."

"You know what would help?" I rolled my eyes before he could even finish, seething on the inside. I was not in the fucking mood. Not this morning. "A smoothie."

"All right, let's go fuck with some interns."

"Ah, I love that I'm getting paid to fuck with interns now."

"Um," a hesitant yet peppy voice jumped in. A tall blonde stood frozen right behind Zach, whose eyes nearly bulged out of his head. "Sorry. This is, um, Scott Nelson's office, right?"

"Yeah," Zach said, voice suddenly gruff. "Yeah, it is."

"Perfect! Excuse me." She slipped through the door, careful not to brush up against Zach as she did. Still, she briefly met his stare before walking up to my desk.

Her eyes locked on mine, a slow smile forming on her lips. Comfortable and confident, she was slim, in heels, and wearing a pink skirt with bows going down the side. A pressed pink blazer barely covered the white shirt she wore beneath, let alone her black bra.

All the pink reflected Natalie's younger self.

I quickly tore my eyes from hers, my focus going straight to Zach. His eyes were glued to the girl's ass.

My blood boiled.

Did he not know how fucking lucky he was? His girlfriend probably hadn't screamed at him this morning. They probably hadn't fought at all, yet Zach was ogling the intern stepping into my office. He was risking his relationship—of losing Britney—and this probably hadn't even crossed his mind. Because he was too busy taking in some random girl's curves.

"Hi, I'm Hannah." She stuck her hand out, leaning over my desk. If it wasn't for the blazer, I could have seen every part of her. "Mr. Benson sent me in here. I think I'm your new assistant, but he was pretty brief with his . . . instructions? I figured I'd head straight here to get those from you directly."

In his quickness to slam his gavel of demands, she meant. It was obvious she was confident in how she looked, but she was also confident in how she spoke. She would do anything for a fucking job. I could see it in her eyes. She fully intended to climb the ladder; it didn't matter what it took.

"Yes. I heard we were supposed to get assistants, but I didn't know you were starting today."

"And I didn't know I would be working for you." She looked me up and down with a smile. "So, it's a surprise for us both."

My teeth clamped together when her eyes returned to my own. She had guts to look me up and down like that and then look me right in the eye.

Zach mouthed, *Whoa,* from behind her.

I couldn't wrap my head around people like him. It was disgusting. Zach was the closest person I had to a friend, but he made me want to warn Britney to run. But if I was in Zach's shoes, I would destroy the person who made Natalie run from me, even if they didn't respect my girlfriend or my relationship.

The sun had set, and it was raining when I finally started packing up to leave work. Still seeing red, I was reluctant to go home. I wasn't ready to go back to her, only to snap. She would not go easy on me. Tonight would go one of two ways. Natalie would either be on top of me the second I walked through the door, or she would barely acknowledge my existence.

My focus only snapped into place when Hannah passed my office on her way out. She waved, her fingers curling in a way that almost called me to her.

Zach had left a half an hour ago but not without closing my office door to voice his thoughts about my new assistant first. The other interns were male, so Zach hadn't been given one he could admire. It was all he could talk about.

It made me grind my teeth.

He had left, and I couldn't be happier. I had enough on my mind now that I was getting ready to go home. I had no idea how I would fix this with Natalie yet. But, no matter what, I wouldn't let her leave. We were in this together. We had been since we jumped into her Volkswagen Bug. She couldn't throw all that away. I wouldn't let her.

Nothing was ever wrong between us. We were just tense. Staying home to talk things out with her hadn't been an option, though. She should've known that when she tried to talk to me this morning. And she'd likely stressed herself out thinking about how we'd left things all day.

What she might've been thinking was all I could think about on the walk down to my car. I didn't even register it was raining. It wasn't until I climbed behind the wheel of the very car I had been thinking about that a raindrop fell from my brow and landed on my hand to weaken my static mind. Then the sound of rain pelting the hood of the car buffered the static.

Dark and raining. Great. I sighed, pushing the windshield wipers to the highest setting.

I zoned out again, staring off into the rain, until my eyes caught flashing yellow lights. A car was pulled off the side of the road, the hood propped up, while rapid, never-ending drops pelted every inch of the vehicle.

But that wasn't what snagged my attention.

I quickly pulled off to back up. I jumped from the car and into the rain the second I shoved the gear into park.

"Everything all right?" I asked as I came up behind her.

Hannah turned in surprise. "Oh! I don't know. I've had this car for forever, and the battery just gives out sometimes."

"Can I take a look?"

She brushed her soaked hair behind one ear, shifting to the side to give me room underneath the open hood while still hunched over. "Please."

She thought she was fucking gorgeous.

And it had been a while since Natalie had thrown herself at me in that way, always blaming her disinterest on being stressed.

Leaning over the engine bay, I saw that her soaked hair was plastered to her skin. Raindrops glided down her neck to disappear between her breasts. Her blazer gone, only her white shirt was left.

Zach would kill for such an opportunity. He would drool.

"I think it needs to be jumped," I told her, forcing myself to maintain my composure. "I'll bring my car closer."

She nodded, shivering.

If Zach were here, he would stare with a fixation on cheating.

As I got into the driver's side of my car, I knew Britney deserved better. So did Natalie, which was what kept me from drooling. I had a loving girlfriend waiting for me at home. This intern, Hannah, was nothing compared to her. I wasn't about to risk losing Natalie because of being tempted by some tramp who wore short skirts around the office, like she was ready to pimp herself out.

She wasn't Natalie. She never would be. She could dress as revealing as she wanted; she would never be as beautiful as my Natalie.

Once I parked my car nose-to-nose in front of hers, I jumped out. She stood but quickly ducked when the rain assaulted her.

I leaned into the open hood of her car to secure the red-and-black clamps into place. My arm brushed along her side, grazing her breast. I shivered, hating the way my heart pounded.

She wasn't Natalie. She was doing this on purpose.

I fixed Natalie's face in front of my eyes.

"Do you know what you're doing?" Hannah asked, her lips right at my ear. "Maybe we should just wait for the tow—"

Details of Natalie's face crumbled.

"He'll charge you a fortune."

Still leaning forward into the car, I stayed under the hood to block some of the rain. Her hand grazed down the side of my hip, moving dangerously close to the front of my pants. She had to *stop. Now. Right fucking now.* "So, what n—"

I had reached around to cover her mouth with my hand.

She sucked in a breath to scream just before my palm firmly covered her lips. With her voice muffled, her screams weren't nearly loud enough to alert anyone nearby, the pelting rain another silencer.

I wasn't Zach. I knew the value of what I had waiting for me at home, and I would never give Natalie a reason to walk out on me.

Hand gripped in her hair, I yanked her head back with a heavy breath, pulling in the smell of her perfume. Slut. A goddamned slut. She only dressed the way she did for attention. She only smelled the way she did to seduce those around her.

I held on tighter, fighting the biting temptation to wrestle her to the ground. Clenching my teeth, I took in a deep breath to steady the impulses screaming through my mind.

She wasn't my Natalie. No matter how blonde she was, no matter how much fucking pink she wore—she wasn't Natalie.

The bitch furiously struggled against me, clawing at my arms with her long, nude-painted fingernails, trying to inhale around my hand to scream. Tightening my hold around her torso and mouth, I dragged her toward my car. While my heart thundered, I was careful to walk down the side so we weren't visible to any passing drivers.

Once I wrestled the back door open, she was smart enough to brace her legs against the frame to keep me from shoving her inside. My control was slipping. She was fighting, giving everything she had to make this more difficult for me. Seeing red, I smashed her face into the side of the car.

Blood gushed, dripping down her chin and neck. She groaned, mumbling something that was lost in the river of blood flooding her words. My heart jolted, my grip loosening ever so slightly. Static overwhelmed my mind, growing louder and louder, as I slammed her head into the side again and again until she shut the hell up.

She was trying to be somebody she wasn't.

She was trying to make me into something I wasn't.

Only when her legs gave out from under her did I watch her collapse, her head hitting the asphalt in a loud thud against the rain.

Everything only came rushing back when she fell still.

My breath escaped me at the sight of her lying limp in front of me.

Her eyes were closed, but the fear in them had taken my breath away. Her skirt had ridden up in our struggle, exposing her thighs and the edge of her panty-line. If that was even what you could call her underwear. It might as well have not been there at all.

Forming fists, I had to get her out of sight. Without wasting a second, I hauled her up and laid her across the back seat before jumping into the driver's side. I angled the rearview mirror to glimpse her sprawled.

Hand on the key in the ignition, I took the moment to take in a long, deep breath.

I could see now. I hadn't given Natalie what she needed this morning. I hadn't been the boyfriend I always strived to be for her. As her person, I had failed her.

I was ready to walk through the door and be wrapped up in her scent as I held her. I would go home to her, hold her in my arms, and tell her how sorry I was. For all of it. I would beg for her forgiveness and for her not to leave me.

I wasn't a cheater.

chapter twenty-two

Putting distance from Hannah's car, I drove a few miles down.

She was still sprawled in the back. Not breathing. Probably a blessing in disguise; she didn't have to smell herself. My hands tightened on the wheel. Fuck. *Fuck!*

A corpse. I had a body in the back of my car.

Slamming my palm against the wheel, I yelled out, then shook it, feeling like I could rip it from its hold.

The bitch who had started today. Today of all fucking days. I shook my head, shutting out everything outside of the car. Everyone at Pulse would think she'd quit without saying anything. Gary didn't stand for shit like that and wouldn't call around to figure out why she hadn't come back after her first day. If anyone did, it would be his assistant, but even she wouldn't think much of it.

She'd just started. No one knew her. People would probably only be able to identify her by her revealing clothes.

No one at the office would think twice about her. If anyone mentioned her, it would be a quick question and then she would be forgotten. Zach was the exception.

My teeth clenched. He needed to get his fucking priorities straight. Fast. I had done us both a favor.

I pulled off onto a blocked-off dirt road with nothing more than a chain wrapped around a few bricks.

I wasn't a cheater. I never thought I would be a cheater, but the girl in my back seat had come close to making me one. She deserved what she got. If it wasn't for her, this wouldn't have happened. If she thought acting like a seductress would help move her up in the office, I must have shocked her when it only got her a bloody nose and a cracked skull.

After releasing a long breath, I threw open my door.

I would have to make this quick.

When I opened the door to pull her out, I stumbled back. Her face was draped over the side of the back seat, blood still dripping from her caved-in nose. Somehow, her blood was only on the small foot mat on the floor in front of her.

I cautiously turned her head toward the ceiling and pulled her out. Peeling the small mat from the floor, I was careful not to spill the blood. After dropping it on her body, I watched the blood trickle down her clothes. I kicked the car door shut before I grasped her arms to pull her into the woods.

Her body rustled against the leaves.

Her body left drag marks in the dirt. I ground my teeth, knowing I would have to fix the leaves when I got back to the turnoff. Carrying her would mean finding a way to strip and hide my clothes from Natalie when I got home.

I couldn't walk inside covered in blood.

I shivered at the thought.

I dragged her until I couldn't any further, until my arms tired out. I was deep in the woods.

Finding my way back to Nat's car would be hard enough. Nothing was around. The intern wouldn't be found for a long time, but hopefully never once I hid her. Under the trees, the rain wasn't as loud. The brush was thick, with several large branches scattered along the ground. I moved closer to fallen trees, tugging her under their trunks.

At some point, as I'd dragged her, the hem of her shirt had ridden up, revealing her slim stomach and pierced belly button. Just that little bit of skin showed off her plethora of curves. It told me everything I needed to know. She was a whore. She didn't belong in marketing.

With a caved-in nose and a split forehead, I wondered if Zach would still think she was worth it.

I stared down at her one last time. Her head was tilted toward the leaf-covered ground, revealing the worst side of her profile. Before I made her disappear, I reached for her face. Dirt made her skin rough. But more than that, she felt familiar. More than a wife or even family. She was much closer.

Using anything nearby, I covered her body with branches and brush.

It didn't take much before she was invisible, blending in as if she were just another leaf in the woods. When I stood, my head swam, and my insides felt like they were about to shudder apart. I rolled my shoulders to shake the feeling. Backing away, I saw that not an inch of skin peeked through, and not a hair was out of place. No one would notice her. Not even her pink skirt was visible. Grime hid every bit of her slender figure.

Memories of Natalie's pink-and-blue streaks flashed to the surface.

I backed away further, gripping my hair at the roots, ready to pull out every strand.

Covering her up like this had been too easy. I had no idea where the fuck I was or if this was private property. It could only be a matter of time before someone found the whore.

When I finally turned away, I ripped out a few strands.

Looking back every few steps, I couldn't help feeling someone was watching me. I was positive she was dead, but something was making me feel like I was wrong. My heart was pounding, echoing in my ears, the only sound aside from the sloshing leaves under my feet.

I followed the trail from the body back to the car, swiping my leg out in front of me to fix the leaves as I went.

Climbing into the driver's seat, I didn't let myself think.

Pulling onto the road, I cracked the back windows to let in cool air as I drove home. The rain was loud again, pummeling every inch of my car. Rain sounded surprisingly similar to crackling flames when it came thwacking steel.

Adrenaline polluting my veins, it stole all feeling from me even as I white-knuckled the steering wheel.

I buried every thought. I had to. For Natalie. Before I would get home and she ask questions.

I didn't turn on the radio. My gut felt eerily empty. I couldn't take my hands off the wheel. Listening to the cars passing me and the patter of rain, I just drove.

My thoughts had been zeroed in on Natalie until I pulled up to our complex. Cutting the engine, I leaned back into the seat, feeling drained. She was upstairs, waiting for me to walk in the door, either to ignore or confront me. Regardless, I had no idea how I would react. What would she want from me? I would do whatever she asked. I just hated when she pitched a fit and ignored me. Pinching the bridge of my nose with trembling fingers, I willed my mind to go blank again.

Only then did I make my way inside.

The second I opened the door, Natalie tossed her paintbrush into the nearest cup. I braced for her to yell. It hadn't occurred to me that she might tell me to get out of the apartment.

Until now.

She might've been waiting for me to come home just so she could make me turn and walk right back down all those stairs again. Though, I wasn't reluctant to the thought of sleeping in the back seat of her car.

Hopefully, she would not about what had happened to her car mat.

Her eyes were sharp, harsh, as she watched me shut the door and loosen my tie. So, I was getting the Natalie who would voice every thought and would refuse to back down from them.

My hand froze at my collarbone, the tie feeling like a noose.

Candles were placed all around the living room, their flames flickering. My stomach cringed deep into my body, making me sick. Making me feel like it would crawl out of my throat.

"What—"

"I can't handle you dismissing me. I can't stand it, and I won't let you." Hot tears of frustration rolled down her cheeks. I could see her desperation, see how she wrestled with herself to get her thoughts out in the open so she could have me back. "I was trying to talk to you this morning. Figure out how you felt about all of this—moving and everything else we have going on right now before I told you."

"Before you told me what?" I asked, quickly taking in everything she'd laid out.

Natalie slid off her stool to walk toward me, but she sat on the purple rug and crossed her legs, nervously bouncing them.

For a split second, my breath caught in my lungs at the thought of her telling me she was leaving me. My heart nearly launched out of my chest to plummet to my feet.

Nothing. I was nothing without her. She was my world. She was what held me together. Without her, I would lose myself. The knowledge dropped an agonizing weight in the pit of my stomach, as it was still trying to crawl up my throat. It felt like—like I was tearing out my own organs, digging and wrenching and twisting.

But then Nat opened a bag of chips I hadn't noticed. A small jar of queso was beside it.

"I thought—" She gulped. "I thought we could have some queso."

My eyebrows pulled together. "Why did you buy such a small jar of queso? We never get the small ones."

"I just—" She closed her eyes. "I bought three jars, actually."

My stomach sank back into its normal spot. "Three? What's going on, Nat? You're worrying me."

She nodded, reaching behind her to pull a brown paper bag out from the kitchen counter. She'd placed it there so I wouldn't see it when I walked in. "I'd been planning this the last two nights, but I—I didn't have the guts."

She pulled out two large jars of queso and set them in front of me, on either side of the small jar. A folded note was taped to the top of one lid. My eyes jumped to her face, suddenly unable to feel my hands. I had lost all feeling in my entire body.

Natalie gulped again, glancing down at the folded note before her eyes jumped back to my face.

She bit her pinky as she watched me.

I could hear my heartbeat echoing through the room, throughout my body. Heart thudding against my ribs with enough force I was convinced one would crack, I unfolded the paper.

We're about to add another jar to the family.

The floor—the world—fell out from under my feet. The waves of emotions flooding me made me catch my breath. I couldn't look away from the words, written neatly in Natalie's curvy handwriting. It felt unreal. Like I was dreaming. But no matter how many times I blinked, the note was still in front of me.

"I don't know how," she said, "but we've gone from 'we need to get out of this town and never come back' to 'fall in love, settle down somewhere safe, and have the chance to start our own family.'"

My grip on the jar tightened. An indescribable rush of adrenaline flushed through my body. It was nothing like I had experienced. This was a fight-or-flight reaction, not a fatal rage.

"Say something," Natalie begged in a breathless whisper. "Please."

I couldn't blame her for holding her breath.

"I can't believe this."

I was out of time. My shock was worrying her. I finally looked up from the note to meet her eyes. When I did, Natalie's face was caved in, blood oozing from where her nose had once been, dripping down her chin to land on her patiently folded hands. Sucking in a sharp breath, I blinked again. When I opened my eyes, the Natalie I knew and loved sat in front of me again, her beautiful face glowing as she waited for my reaction.

"Are y-you serious? Really? Are you s-sure?" I did nothing but blurt questions as Natalie nodded.

I couldn't let those images creep into my mind. Not now. Not in this moment.

"I took a test on Saturday and then another one yesterday and one more to be absolutely sure this morning. I wanted to be sure before I told you. I wanted us to be okay before I told you."

I set the jar down and pulled her to me, wrapping my arms around her. She was pregnant. *Natalie was pregnant.* I couldn't wrap my mind around it. We were going to have a baby.

"This can't be real. You promise this is real?" I held her tighter, cradling her head against my chest to hold her close. "I can't tell you how happy I am. There aren't words." I paused. "I'm panicking, too, but mostly excited."

"Yes!" she mumbled against my chest. "Yes, oh, I promise."

I paused, pulling her back to read her face. "You're happy, right? You want this?"

Her eyes widened at the question. "Yes! Of course I want this! This was my idea. I just . . . didn't think it would happen so soon, so quick."

I felt so much happiness I wasn't sure how to contain it. Overwhelming joy locked everything into place. I could see us moving into a house, settling in, and starting our family. Bemused, worried, fearful—so many emotions flooded through me.

"I'm sorry about this morning. I was a complete jackass. I don't know what that was, but you didn't deserve any of it. I haven't been able to think about anything else all day."

Partially true.

"This is real?" I couldn't help but ask one more time.

She smiled, nodding. "Yes. So real. We're going to have a baby."

As images of blue skin, vomit, and a caved-in face flooded my mind, I hugged her again. "I love you," I repeated into her hair, and I felt her smile widen against my chest.

chapter twenty-three

THE FOLLOWING DAY WAS MOVING day. After a night of little sleep, staring up at the ceiling, and trembling under the covers, I was reluctant to leave the warm sheets beside Natalie. But I had taken the second half of the day off so we could throw our shit into the back of our car and the small trailer we hooked it to last night.

It was just half a day. I could make it.

I spent the drive into work reminding myself no one would worry about a girl who had just started. Not after she'd spent a single day at the office.

When I got to work, the entire office was hustling. It was always busy, with people moving in and out of offices, but there seemed to be an extra kick in everyone's step today. Except mine. I took in everyone I passed, looking for anything out of the ordinary. No matter how small, I wanted to know if there was even a hint of concern over the intern.

"Good morning, Nelson." Zach appeared from nowhere, a smoothie in hand, like every morning.

"What flavor this time?" I asked him.

"Strawberry-banana. De-lish!" He took a long draw from the straw. "You should really jump on the smoothie bandwagon."

I smirked. Some of the shit Zach said was absurd. His words never lined up with his actions. "We had coffee the other night. I've seen you drink it and like it."

"Yeah, but smoothies hit different in the morning. Instead of caffeine getting your ass in gear, it's sugar that's kicking you in the ass. Hard."

I shook my head, still heading for my office. He was distracting me from reading the room. "Whatever you say. The coffee cart down the way is still better than whatever is in that shit."

"Where's your hot assistant?" Taking another gulp of his smoothie, he glanced around, eyebrows raised.

"I just got to work. I don't have a tracker on her."

"Send her off to bring you a smoothie." He grinned. "She can get me one while she's at it."

I swallowed to keep my voice even, struggling to avoid snapping. "You have your own assistant. Send your own minion for a smoothie."

Zach sighed, stopping at his office. "You're no fun. You're supposed to share your hot intern."

Jaw locked, I headed straight for my office. I dropped into my chair and logged into my computer. The screen lit up, but my eyes glazed over a second later. I didn't move to open anything on my desktop. I didn't move the mouse at all.

The crunch of her face cracking against the side of the Volkswagen Bug reverberated in my ears.

Images of blood fixated behind my eyes. Thick crimson on the side of the car between the front and back door.

Blood on the mat. Gore oozing from the girl's fractured face.

I didn't know how much time had passed.

But my eyes caught movement from the left of my office windows. Every image fell away as my stomach dropped. Gary's assistant was heading straight for my door. My grip on my mouse tightened.

Giving me a weak smile as she opened the door, she only half stepped in. "Mr. Benson wanted me to ask you a quick question. Your intern, Hannah Clark, have you seen her today? She didn't check in with Mr. Benson this morning, and it's been a few hours now."

"No. No, she never showed up to help me. Did she call?"

She shook her head, her curls bouncing against her shoulders. "No. Not a word, so we thought we'd see if you'd heard anything."

"No, but I'll let you know if I do."

"Okay, perfect. Thanks, Scott."

"Anytime." I made sure to smile before she closed the door and trotted off.

I could have sworn my heart had thudded a million times during the minute I waited for her to leave. I hated how it pounded in my ears. Pushing my chair back from my computer, I casually stood from my desk before walking out of my office. The second I was in the bathroom, I picked the last stall and locked it behind me.

I exhaled a long breath, leaning my forehead against the cool door.

Oh fuck. Oh fuck, oh fuck, *oh fuck!*

I slammed my palm against the door, rattling its hinges. Anyone walking by the bathroom definitely heard it.

Forehead against the stall door, I grabbed the ends of my hair, wanting to yank every fucking strand from my scalp.

They won't keep asking about her, they won't keep asking about her.

My thoughts were on repeat, like some busted cassette in Natalie's Volkswagen. Teeth clamped, I kept my eyes closed and focused on my breathing.

It wasn't much, but it was a start.

Behind my eyelids, I relived every action. Relived her every expression. Her terrified, muffled screams against my hand echoed. I could feel the rain running down my arms, soaking my clothes just as much as hers. The panic subsided each time I heard her face hit the door. It made me feel warm. Her blood coated my hands, and I could feel its warmth. Fresh. As if I had done it all over again and the rain hadn't swept the red away yet.

I looked at my hands and saw nothing, but I could still feel it.

The whore hadn't gotten to me. When it came down to it, I hadn't cheated. I was still loyal to Natalie and forever would be.

Something inside me coiled with a smile.

I left work right at noon and got home a little after lunchtime with Natalie's favorite donuts in hand—chocolate glazed with a million sprinkles. I stopped at the top of the stairs to take a deep breath, refusing to close my eyes and see the images I couldn't stop from surfacing. I couldn't help but *want* them to surface. Every frame from that night triggered a different feeling, pulling on the loose threads in my mind.

I only moved when I was sure the tension had left my body.

Only, when I walked in, my heart dropped when I saw Natalie walk out of the bedroom with a box in her hands.

After instantly dropping the paper bag on the counter, I was across the room within a second.

"What are you doing?" I asked as I grabbed the box from her. "You shouldn't be lifting anything. You are forbidden from lifting anything."

"Scott." She giggled. "Don't be so serious. I've been packing since I found out. I'm okay to lift—"

Moving the box away from her, I shook my head with a "Nope." I walked away, telling her the donuts on the counter were for her.

I didn't let Natalie lift a thing. Not a single box. Not even her purple rug. I let her carry our pillows and our blankets to the car, but that was all. She constantly reminded me how ridiculous I was being, but she argued little beyond that. Mostly because she was too busy stuffing her face with donuts.

It was how I bought her partial compliance.

Anthony showed up when I was halfway done loading up the trailer, declaring his last class was too boring to sit through. Natalie laughed when he tossed his textbooks into the nearest empty box. "Take 'em. This shit's boring. I'd kill to swap places with Scott and draw cartoon super teeth all day."

Even though it was a sad excuse for a joke, Natalie's laugh made me soften.

Her happiness was all that mattered now.

We were having a baby.

It still didn't feel real.

Eighteen hours had passed since she told me, and I was just as happy as I was in that moment, but I still couldn't shake the disbelief. I couldn't believe this was my life. That Natalie was mine, and that she had tied herself to me more by carrying my child. We were moving, starting our lives. Everything would move faster now. We would have so much to figure out and have only nine months to do it. For probably the first time, we were heading toward a clear trajectory. Natalie was ecstatic about this path, no matter how windy it might be.

In her mind, we were finally starting our lives. The last four years had been a struggle of survival. We had escaped our poor, abusive history. And though we had evaded the abuse, we still had struggles crawling our way out of the pit of poverty. Now, we were completely free. We had surpassed what everyone—even our families—thought we could achieve. With Natalie's art hanging in Ava and Caden's gallery and my new job at Pulse Marketing, we were reaching success.

For a split second, I wondered she would think of me if she knew about what I had—

"Hello, Earth to Scott." Natalie waved in front of my face. "Am I allowed to carry this last box, or am I too fragile to carry a small box of paintbrushes?"

"*Ha-ha*," I mocked, taking the box from her, causing her to laugh.

Anthony ran back into the apartment, huffing and puffing after running up and down the stairs. "Okay. Woo, I could do this all day. Those stairs." He cleared his throat, failing to act unbothered by the jog. "But, uh, I loaded the last of everything we took down. Anything else?"

"No," Nat said, then flashed a smirk in my direction. "Scott has the last box."

No one else but us knew about our pregnancy. It was our little secret for now.

"So, we're done," Anthony went on. It took everything I had not to roll my eyes. "When's Olivia supposed to get her ass over here to help?"

"She's in class right now, but she'll meet us at the house to unpack."

He nodded, rocking back on his heels. "Gotcha."

"What?" Nat challenged, looking fully prepared to make fun of him. I was all for it. If we had any furniture, or even just a few boxes, I would've sat back to watch the show. "Are you *antsy* to see Olivia?"

"Shut up." Anthony rolled his eyes, trying to play it off. "You have your boyfriend and your new house—"

"Awe, you *love* Olivia. You want to get back together. You want her to be your girlfriend again, and you want to live with her."

Anthony looked at me helplessly as Natalie went on and on. "Want to control your woman?"

"Control Natalie?" I scoffed. "That's a joke, right? She'll kick us both in the balls before she'd let either of us get the chance."

He gave Natalie the side-eye. "Worth a shot."

Still, Anthony wasn't subtle. When we pulled up to our new house, Olivia was already waiting, arms crossed, with her shoulder propped against the front door. From the second we had climbed out of our cars, Anthony was staring.

The second her car door was open, Nat jumped out and ran straight into the house without grabbing a box first or even waiting on the rest of us.

I laughed as I watched her disappear through the door. Grabbing a box first, I walked in after her while Anthony talked to Olivia, his eyes glued to her ass every time she adjusted the box at her hip.

The front door opened to an open and empty living room. A long counter set the kitchen apart, but off from the fridge were three steps that led to a short hallway. Natalie was nowhere in sight. I opened doors as I walked down the corridor. Two doors led to bedrooms, another to a bathroom, and then one opened to a staircase that led to the partially finished basement. The last door led to our bedroom with an attached bath. The room directly across from the master was a small room meant to be an office. Instead, it would serve as Natalie's art room. Most of our boxes would end up in here.

The door to her new art room was open.

When I walked into the room, Natalie was staring out the big window that overlooked our side yard and the house nearest us. The second Natalie had walked into this room, she'd been sold on the house, whispering to me once the realtor was far enough away that it was perfect.

As soon as she did that, there was no going back.

Natalie had something. She had a way of expressing herself, of sharing her mind and emotions with the world. And everyone walked away with their own interpretation. They understood some small piece of her and took it with them, whether they purchased one of her works. They saw a glimpse of how Natalie viewed the world.

She did all this through paint.

And then there was me. I was new to an official position, hanging by a thread to make ends meet, like the trailer park trash parents I had come from. I was still struggling to settle things with the house and the last of our bills. This was on my end, though, while Natalie had been selling enough paintings to set up a small savings for herself.

I wrapped my arms around her, my nose grazing her neck.

"We're finally here," Natalie breathed. "Can't you picture my easel here? And all my paintings could go in that corner. And look at this—whole wall is just a massive window! Hopefully, I don't get abducted by aliens or a tornado doesn't hit while I'm painting because I'd be in big trouble."

"We have to be careful not to break this window. You could get sucked into a vortex."

"Exactly!" She quietly laughed.

Our voices were still barely above a whisper.

I nuzzled her neck one last time. "We should probably go help them with all those boxes."

"I just thought I'd give Anthony a chance to make his move."

"Ten bucks says he did nothing but stare at her ass this entire time."

Nat rolled her eyes. "You think I'm dumb enough to take that bet? Ha."

We didn't have too many boxes. A lot were full of clothes and dishes, but most contained Natalie's art supplies. We all just piled them against the wall right inside the door, saving the mattress for last to throw into the bedroom.

Olivia couldn't stop gushing about the house, demanding a tour the second we set down the last of the boxes. Though Natalie relented, I could feel how anxious she was for them to leave so we could have the house to ourselves.

"Oh my god, I am so *jealous*!" Olivia gushed. "Can we trade lives?"

The second they left and Natalie shut the door behind them, she leaned against it. Then the realization seemed to hit her because she practically squealed as she ran for the bedroom.

I caught her in the hallway, carefully wrapping my arm around her waist. "Are you excited? Happy?"

She was beaming, everything about her glowing. "Very. Very, very happy. Aren't you? I mean, look, all of this is *ours*."

"We finally have a real place."

After pulling her into the bedroom, I collapsed with her onto the mattress. Natalie's hair flew up into her face, and she laughed as she caught a mouthful of hair.

"Thanks for that," she huffed as she spewed the strands out of her mouth.

As she did, I saw the girl spewing blood from her shattered mouth from my slamming her head against the car.

I felt the warmth of her blood-matted hair and the weight of her collapse in my arms.

Not now.

I blinked hard to clear my head, pushing those thoughts out as I stared up at the ceiling.

"So much is going to happen. Can you believe it?" Nat placed a light hand over her stomach. "I don't want to tell anyone. Not until after the first trimester. There's so much we have to do."

I squeezed her free hand. "We'll be ready for it. I'll do everything I can to make sure we can have everything we need."

"This house was a good first step." She turned her head to face me. "You know, you don't have to think of it as your money. You don't have to struggle. We live together, we ran away together. I think what's mine is yours and vice versa. I want you to start thinking that way, especially if we're going to have a . . . baby."

Her hesitation made it seem as if she were scared to say it out loud. Saying it out loud would make it more real. It felt like a weight between us. One that was neither uncomfortable or unwanted, just pending with wound anticipation.

"I know. I know you want me to think that way, but I don't—I don't want to bring you down. You've fought so hard to get where you are. I don't want you to worry about me."

"You just got out of your internship and started at this big, wonderful job at Pulse. Don't sell yourself short. You're only worried because we jumped ahead to get this house, and you're worried about the difference between our disgusting apartment and this new mortgage when we still have student loans to deal with." It was her turn to squeeze my hand. "We're going to be fine. I won't let you drown. If we drown, we drown together, understand?"

I nodded, but she could see there was more on my face. Falling rain echoed in my ears at the word *drown*. Then I heard the wet crack on asphalt as I recalled Hannah's skull splitting against the side of the road.

Natalie said something else, trying to reach me, but a bead of sweat rolled down my face. She turned my chin so I would meet her eyes. Hers were bright, reminding me of where I was and how I'd gotten here—of what I'd done to stay by her side. "I'm scared—terrified, really—but I know you are not your dad or your mom. Neither am I." She kissed my cheek. "We've come so far, and we're happy. Money is not going to come between us—nothing will. We won't be our parents."

chapter twenty-four

THE FOLLOWING MORNING WAS A Monday. We awoke in our bed, the mattress still on the floor but in a brand-new place. Our house. The sheets rustled when I moved closer to Natalie and wrapped an arm around her warmth to slide her into my chest. A long sigh left her body.

"Hey," I whispered in her ear, knowing she was awake.

"Hey, you," she whispered back.

"Guess what."

She giggled a little. "What, you weirdo?"

"You're still pregnant. We're going to have a baby, and you've made me the happiest man—"

Natalie jumped up before I could finish, stopping my words in their tracks. "You're right! I have to go to the store. I need to figure out what we need 'cause we are so not prepared for this right now."

"We have nine months to do all of that." I watched her slip into jeans, eyes franticly searching for a shirt. "Don't start freaking out."

"Babe, I don't even know how pregnant I am. All I know is that the pee-covered stick said I was. I need to make an appointment. I need to find out how far along I am."

I couldn't help my laugh as I watched her scramble around the room, hunting through our boxes and duffle bags to find whatever shirt and socks she was after. "Love, you don't need to be in a rush. Don't get yourself all wound up. Take those pants off and get back into bed with me. It's not like a doctor is going to let you in right now. You won't get an appointment for a while, so just calm yourself."

"Calm myself? Calm myself? I'm pregnant. I'm panicking. I don't know what I'm supposed to be doing right now. What am I *not* supposed to be doing right now?"

"So, you admit you don't know if you should've been helping us pick up boxes yesterday?"

Nat rolled her eyes at me. "Oh, stop!"

"Now"—I reached across the bed, grabbing Nat's arm and yanking her into bed with me—"get back here."

She yelped as she fell into the blankets, laughing when she landed against me.

Nothing but silence passed between us for a few minutes, enjoying the feeling of each other first thing in the morning. Her skin was so soft. No matter where I touched, my hand glided over her. I could lie here with her all day if it meant I could keep running my hand along the length of her body, from the nape of her neck to curve over her shoulder and then side before squeezing her thigh—

"Do you . . . want to tell him?"

She didn't need to elaborate on who she meant. I knew she was talking about my father. I knew she would tell her family the news in her own time, probably before she visited them next, so it wouldn't be a shock. But I wanted nothing to do with my father again.

"No. I don't want him involved. I would never leave our kid alone with him, ever. So, it'd be pointless to tell him. He wouldn't be a grandpa."

The last word made my stomach cringe back into my body. I didn't want him anywhere near me, let alone Natalie while she was pregnant—or around our child after he or she was born.

Every time Natalie went home, she asked about him around town. To see if he was still alive. But that was the extent of our interaction. I hadn't been back since I left. I couldn't even go back with Natalie to visit her family, for fear of how I would react to them after how they treated her. Every detail of her past made me want to burn the fucking world down.

"Okay, okay. It's okay." She placed a hand on my shoulder, squeezing it in reassurance. "That's why I asked. I didn't think you'd want that."

"What's the plan for today? Unpack?" I asked, changing the subject before memories surfaced.

I didn't want to think about that today. Not on my day off.

She gave a firm nod. "Unpack."

I groaned into her neck. "At least we don't have a lot of stuff."

"Yup, so if we get up now, we might have the second half of the day to ourselves."

"I like the way you think, but I also hate it because I'm not ready to get up yet."

She laughed. "I can tell. I'm already dressed, and you're still snuggled under all the blankets."

"It's warm! Not all of us can just jump out of bed and straight into jeans."

"It's a talent. I'll give you five minutes before I drag you out." She kept laughing at me rather than with me.

Nat kept to her promise—or threat—announcing it was time to get up after counting down all three hundred seconds. Once she was sure I was up and wouldn't crawl back into bed as soon as she left the room, she ran straight to the boxes marked *ART*.

"Excited to put your art room together?"

She smiled before snatching a box to skip down the hall. She never thought she'd get a room all to herself like this. She never thought she was good enough to get into a gallery, either. But here she was. With both. She was living every dream she'd had since discovering her passion for art. I was glad I could at least make one happen for her, help push the other in the right direction.

As soon as I let those thoughts in, I felt overwhelmed by how many snippets flooded my mind.

My hands trembled when I went to pick up a box and nearly dropped it, as if the cardboard had burned me. Tightly closing my eyes, I tried to shut it all out. *Can't stop, can't stop—*

The burning sensation turned into slick blood between my fingers. And then I couldn't stop thinking about the slutty intern. Her body was still in the woods. I should probably pass by the dead-end road on my way to work tomorrow, just to see if anyone had come across her— make sure there wasn't a siren in sight.

But like that, she was all I could think about. My mind jumped back and forth between thoughts of Hannah and of Natalie. It wasn't cheating. I was beginning to worry about how Natalie was handling everything today and settling into our new place while pregnant. And I was worried about what it would mean for me if the intern was found.

I wasn't even sure if the woods belonged to anyone or rolled into anyone's property. Either way, the body was hidden deep in the woods—under enough leaf-covered branches—that no one would see her. It would be even harder to see her once she started to decay. I'd scattered the twigs and leaves to cover the trail from where I had dragged her. The only thing to worry about was the smell if anyone happened to hike near where I'd covered her up.

I couldn't shake the snippets of her that surfaced. The way her blonde hair matted when I gripped it. Her hardened nipples in the rain. The shiver that overtook her body whenever the cold rain caught her off guard. The gap between her thighs, every crevice begging to be caressed.

I couldn't do this.

I couldn't keep thinking about this.

Gripping edges of the box, I could feel the panic forming into something else.

It was making my head dizzy, reliving that hour over and over. I wanted to feel her weight in my arms again. I didn't know what I was trying to see. It was like how I would relive the overdose in the bathroom all those months ago. Everything about how I was feeling reminded me of that night.

Puke around blue lips.

A caved-in face pulled back from a car door smeared with blood.

Zach could go back into pressuring his girlfriend to get him off now. I had saved myself and others from the intern's charms. I would not lose Natalie. No matter how mad I was at her. I would never do anything to make her leave. I knew what I had. I would do anything to keep her.

And now I was going to be a dad, and I would not become my father. I wouldn't let Nat walk out on me as my dad let mom walk out on us. Fuck him for not being man enough to do what he needed to make her stay.

My mind kept spiraling. I shuddered, unable to shake the surfacing images. For the first time in a long time, I wished my mind would fall into static so I could shake the twisting in my gut.

Puke around blue lips.

The guy had overdosed right in front of me, and I had done nothing but watched. I wasn't responsible. I was just there when it happened. It wasn't like I had given him whatever he'd overloaded himself on. He'd been paranoid, tripping on whatever drug had been swarming in his system.

I wasn't responsible then. I hadn't known him. He was just some guy—someone I had never seen, and he happened to shove his way into the bathroom I'd been standing in, right before his body gave up.

With another shudder, the hair rose on my arms, spreading to the nape of my neck.

A caved-in face pulled back from a car door smeared with blood.

But, this time, I was responsible. My hands were dirty, coated in my intern's blood. I had kept her from screaming by covering her mouth. I had taken care of her when she struggled, without an ounce of hesitation.

It all had happened so quickly I hadn't thought about any of my actions. My hands had acted on their own. I hadn't cared enough to stop them.

Something had swelled inside me when I heard the shattering of her face—her skull fracturing.

And even though my hands trembled, sweat sliding down my forehead, I didn't want to stop thinking about her. Part of me was still shaken, but mostly—

Fuck! I almost dropped the box to pinch the bridge of my nose. I didn't even want to let the thought cross my mind.

But I wanted—I wanted to feel that way again.

"Scott? Could you bring me the box labeled 'acrylics' and maybe bring the purple rug? I think I want to put it under my easel. I don't think it's going to work in this living room." She chuckled when I didn't answer right away. "That's my way of hinting that I want to invest in a couch."

Forcing my feet to move toward the kitchen, I set the box on the counter before letting myself lean against the fridge, the steel door cooling my arm.

Fuck, I couldn't let her see me like this.

"Yeah, I'll be right there," I replied when I could find my normal voice.

Fuck, I wanted to feel that way again. My mouth watered at the thought, and I had to swallow it back. The adrenaline was intoxicating. Just the thought of the way she'd struggled and fought against me sent something barreling through me.

Even covered in twigs and dirt, the intern had resembled Natalie. And everything had come out like it was meant for her. Getting rid of Hannah protected Natalie—protected *us*.

Inhaling a deep breath, I repeated that to myself until my clenched hands stopped shaking.

Before Nat could call for me again, I forced those quick snippets back, ignoring the twisted urge still settled in my gut. I replaced them with thoughts of Natalie and everything that was to come. I had every reason to be happy right now.

Pushing off the fridge, I wiped the sweat from my hands before finding her box among the rest of her supplies and shoved the rolled-up rug underneath my arm. When I walked in, she was standing on a small step stool, hanging a clock. "There was a nail already here, so I thought—"

I stiffened, nearly dropping everything right then and there. "I wouldn't let you carry any heavy boxes yesterday, and you thought this was a good idea? You're pregnant. Get off that damned stool."

She looked back at me, rolling her eyes. Ignoring me, she made sure the clock was straight. "Clocks. I think that's going to be my thing. You know, like how old ladies will have owl figurines or roosters all over their house? I want to do that but with clocks."

I laughed, shaking my head. She always made every worry evaporate, just by opening her mouth. "Not a chance. I'm limiting you on that."

She ignored me again, moving on to something else already. "We have less stuff than I thought. I don't think we'll come close to filling up all this space."

Evidently, she wasn't in the mood to hear my shit today.

"We'll fill in the space over time. We might even be able to get a couch before the end of the year."

"You think so? We haven't started getting anything for the nursery and that'll be a lot, so I wouldn't put your foot in your mouth like that. We could always get an okayish sofa in the meantime. Something used."

"No way," I said. "You never know where those couches have been and who's been doing what on them. I'm putting my foot down on a used sofa. If we get one, it's going to be brand new."

"Oh, putting your foot down, huh?" she challenged with raised eyebrows. "What, don't want to sit in the same place someone's bare ass might have been?"

"Yeah, someone else's bare ass, among other things."

She laughed. "God, what am I going to do with you?"

Never fucking leave me.

chapter twenty-five

I KNEW SOMETHING WAS OFF before I stepped foot into work. Fresh thoughts of how Natalie and I had christened rooms in our new home dissolved. The phantom touch of her faded instantly. Despite this, I knew how I would want her at the end of the day.

With Natalie forced to the back of my mind, the office came into focus.

Papers were being shuffled, voices were colliding, shredders were being cut off, and everyone was eyeing the two cops trudging around. Setting my teeth, I watched them from the other end of the room as I headed for my office.

They were here about Hannah.

There wasn't a doubt in my mind.

And they would be in my office within minutes.

Even with my door shut, the hustle of the office leaked through. I busied myself with moving around the slogans of papers on my desk, being sure to stare out my windows at the cops, like all the other office idiots.

The cops would find a dead-end here. Hannah had spent one day at Pulse Marketing. From our office, she looked like a college kid who stopped showing up. Hannah wasn't the first intern to decide a job as a coffee servant wasn't for them. At most, Gary Benson called to make sure everything was all right and was sent straight to voicemail. There wasn't much to tell the authorities.

Eventually, the officers backed out of Benson's office.

Clenching my knees below the desk, I rolled the tension from my shoulders. As they drew closer, I glanced up a few times but was careful not to look up too much. My pulse rushed into my ears, echoing loud enough to cancel out everything else.

Watching them step up to my door, Mr. Benson right behind them, I inhaled through my nose, steeling myself with the long exhale. They nodded as they stepped in. My head felt heavy when I returned the tilt.

Benson was behind them, saying, "The authorities have a few questions to run by you."

"Of course," I said, gesturing to the chair at the front of my desk.

The other cop grabbed the chair against the wall below the window. Benson propped himself against the glass, crossing his arms over his chest.

"I'm Officer Habel. This is my partner, Deputy Ian." He leaned forward, firmly shaking my hand as I introduced myself. Settling back in his chair, he remained upright with a notepad flipped over in front of him. "Your boss informed us you were Hannah Clark's higher-up?"

Right to it, then. They weren't here to play games or exchange niceties.

"Yes, she was assigned as my intern."

Officer Habel didn't look up from scribbling on his notepad. "When did you last see her?"

Letting a beat of silence pass between us, I pretended to think, struggling to settle on an expression. "Her first day, which also turned out to be her last day as well. I don't remember which day, but she was here sometime last week."

"It was Thursday. Then you took off the rest of the week."

Clenching my hands beneath the desk, I focused on my breathing. "My pregnant girlfriend and I just moved into a house. I took a half day on Friday so we could move everything and get settled."

"What was her typical workday like?"

Leaning over the engine bay, she had raindrops disappearing between perky breasts. I stopped breathing.

"She'd only been here a day. She didn't have a typical workday yet. I'd just been given the position I'm in now, and she was the first intern I was assigned."

Deputy Ian glanced at his partner.

I could not decipher what the look meant.

Officer Habel continued as if it hadn't happened. "Was she acting strange the day of her disappearance? Anything out of the ordinary?"

I shook my head. "She was professional. She introduced herself and went off for her office orientation for most of the day. Nothing felt off, but I didn't know her."

Heat swarmed in my core. I couldn't blink away images of smashing her face into the side of the car, blood gushing from her. Over the ringing in my ears, I heard her body rustle against the forest floor. Fuck, she had a nice one. It was hard to deny, even with Natalie's being better.

I'd done away with temptation, ignoring the crude shit that came out of Zach's mouth.

"How did she seem right before leaving work that day?"

"She walked right by my office without a word."

Which was true. I'd been relieved Zach had left so he wouldn't run his mouth about how her hips moved when she walked or stare at her long legs when he was supposed to go home to Britney.

"Is there anything of hers here? Did she leave anything behind at the office?"

I shook my head. "No. No, nothing in here. There could be something in the break room, but I don't know. She wasn't here long."

"All right, Mr. Nelson, we're almost done here." Officer Habel finally looked up at me, staring me dead in the face. "We found Hannah Clark's car abandoned on the side of the road about two miles from this office. Did you pass it when you left work that day?"

He wasn't asking if I remembered seeing it. He wanted to know if I had passed it, whether I had left before or after her, even though I had already mentioned watching her leave.

I couldn't say I left before her. They would likely check the security footage for signs of her.

Pulse Marketing had been the last place she'd been before her disappearance. No one in her life had seen her after work. Her car had been abandoned on the side of the road without a charge to its battery. Anyone could have picked her up. Anyone could have pulled over to help her and snatched her instead.

"I remember seeing a car, but Hannah wasn't around or inside. It was just there."

Officer Habel snapped his notepad shut, face unreadable as he stood. "Thank you for your time, Mr. Nelson."

"We appreciate it," the deputy added. "If you remember anything that could be important, please give us a call."

I nodded, the tension from before nonexistent after the images flashing through my mind. "Will do. I hope you find her."

"We all do," Gary Benson added as we watched the officers step out to question others. The moment the door was shut behind them, Benson groaned. "I can't fucking believe this is happening. This company is going to be under fire if this gets out. I'm going to make everyone in this office sign an NDA to keep this from our clients." He stormed from my office, eyeing the cops the whole way to his office and throughout the duration of their visit.

In need of coffee, I stepped out of my office as soon as the coast was clear, and not a cop was in sight. Because caffeine was the last surge of agitation my body was missing right now. I had a feeling the officers would be back at some point, but they were gone for now. The break room was empty, and so was the coffee pot.

Jaw locked, I shoveled the grounds into the filter. Office coffee was always shit coffee. Still, I had no intention of tasting it. I just needed something to burn away the sensation of her skin. Hannah's sweat and panic was sweet and sour on my tongue. Scorching black coffee was the only way I could get rid of it.

"Guilty, huh?" Zach smirked from the doorway when I turned to lean against the counter. "I saw you sweating from across the room."

I gritted my teeth. "Who wouldn't sweat with two cops in their office? Shit's nerve-racking."

He shrugged, briefly glancing at his slacks. "Wasn't that bad for me."

The drip of the coffee filter passed between us.

"You weren't her boss," I pointed out. "You were just the pervert watching her from his cubicle."

I clenched my hand in time for the coffee maker to chime. I turned, gripped the handle, and poured my coffee instead of gripping his neck to throw him into the nearest wall.

Goddamn, I wished Zach would shut his fucking mouth sometimes.

Zach played a dangerous game as he moved from the doorway to lean against the counter beside me while I fixed my coffee. He shrugged, his smirk still in place. "You're a shitty liar, Scottie."

And what? One of your fucking smoothies will fix all my problems?

I unlocked my jaw. "Quit being a shit, Zachery. A girl is missing."

"Well, buddy, coffee is a one-way ticket to anxiety. Black caffeine isn't going to make her reappear. With what's going on in this office right now, none of us should be drinking that shit."

If Zach kept talking, I was going to spill every last drop of my scalding mug on him.

"C'mon, lighten up, Scottie. I'm just trying to warn you not to take any more time off to mess around with Natalie, since you're already a creep of interest." He chuckled. "You don't need the cops knocking on your door a second time."

Unease set in the pit of my stomach. It was like he knew. One gulp of coffee cleared my senses and brought everything into focus. Something wasn't right. Everything he was saying was targeted at me. He was running his mouth because he was probing me for answers. I wasn't a shitty liar. Why was he taking a sudden interest in the intern's disappearance?

Staring at him from over the rim of my mug as I took another swig, I searched his face. Zach's body was casual. His expression matched his stance, but his eyes were unreadable.

"I'll see you around the office" was all I said as I left the break room.

Knuckles white from clenching the handle on the mug, I could not shake the threat behind my back.

On the drive home, Officer Habel's questions repeated in my mind. I spoke some aloud to myself. I went over my responses, where I'd given them just enough information to direct them away from me and, hopefully, the office. Once I was done rehearsing, my goal was to keep this from Natalie. I couldn't handle any more interrogations. Especially from her.

Zach had drained my patience.

I could not stand the thought of her looking at me with distress in her blue eyes. I did not want her to look at me like that. I had to keep her from second-guessing us. No matter the cost.

My chest ached at the thought of her looking at me with blank, tearful eyes as she shrank back from me. Her pulling away—I wouldn't be able to stand it. A look like that from her would break me. I needed her. Imagining her recoiling from me . . . I threw the heat on full blast to fight the cold blowing through the car.

If I slipped up, she could walk out the door with nothing holding her back. It would be over, and I would be destroyed. As my girlfriend, she had nothing holding her here, even pregnant. But as something more—as my wife . . . Marriage meant "till death do us part" and "through sickness and in health." She would be tied to me then. No matter what happened between us. No matter what she found. We would be fine. No one would come knocking on our door with more questions, but binding her to me would make her stay.

When I parked and flung open the door, I left those thoughts in the car.

I found Natalie already in bed, hand on her stomach. Popping one eye open, she watched me strip before climbing under the covers beside her.

"You okay?" I asked her, planting a kiss on her forehead.

She nodded against my mouth and nose, a long sigh releasing whatever tension she'd been holding onto. Her body deflated against mine.

Wrapping my arms around her, I pulled her against my chest, letting her settle into me. Her eyes had fallen closed again, but the silence was suffocating. Closing my eyes was impossible when my heart was jumping up into my throat. Breathing hurt as much as the silence did.

"Can you promise me something?" I asked her.

Natalie stiffened, slowly setting aside the book in her lap. Her pinky nail found its way into her mouth, between her teeth. "What's wrong?"

"I just—" I inhaled a long breath through my nose, bowing my head in defeat before I met her worried stare. "Please don't ever give up on me."

Bemusement washed over her worried expression.

"Is that what you're worried about?" She propped herself up within a blink. "How many times do I have to remind you that you're stuck with me? We're a family now, and nothing is going to take that away. It's you and me, love. To no end."

"Promise?"

Her pinky curled around mine. "Promise."

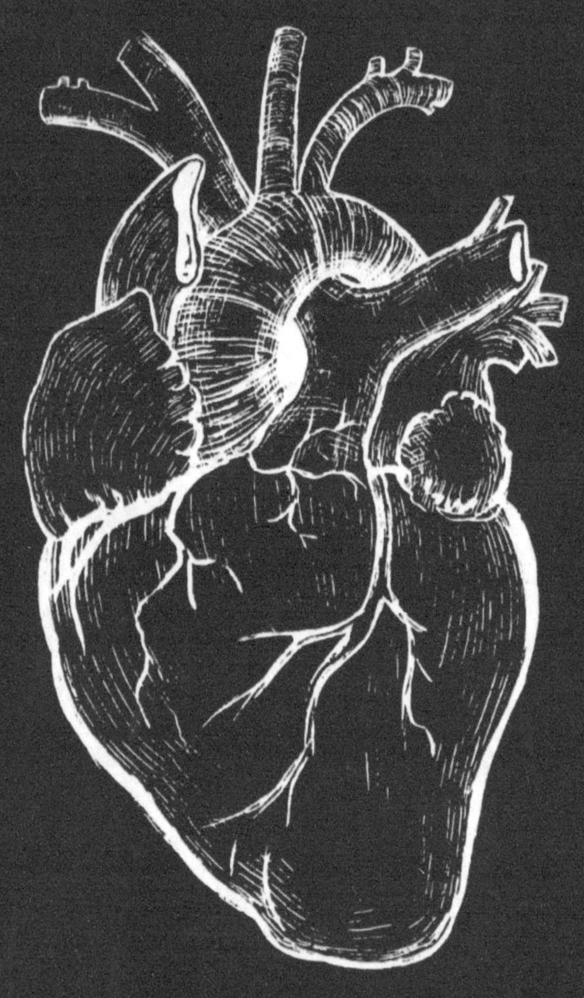

chapter twenty-six

Toward the end of 2008

I TRIED NOT TO KEEP Natalie at a distance. I did everything I could to help make things easier on her. Now that I was done with school and I'd taken up an official job at Pulse Marketing, I was gone from nine-to-five five days a week. Natalie took advantage of her alone time, spending most of the day painting for Ava and Caden if she wasn't at a doctor's appointment.

Natalie was anything but quiet, but our home had fallen into a steady pattern. Nothing was disturbed. For months, I kept everything that wasn't Natalie far away.

Though certain thoughts and impulses crossed my mind.

If she craved peanut butter-and-honey sandwiches, I wouldn't let her get up to make it herself. If she wanted something we didn't have at home, I went out to get it for her or swung by the store on my way home from work to get it.

With the baby arriving in less than two months, Nat was growing uncomfortable with every passing day. With that came panic. She worried about every little thing. When I was home, she expected me to do everything she couldn't, putting a lot on me from the moment I stepped through the front door. She barely gave me the chance to remove my shoes most nights when I came home.

A headache sprang between my brows and shuddered down into my jaw.

Everything was a lot right now.

My only chance at getting away enough to breathe was after work. I didn't—I *couldn't* go straight home most days.

Instead, the more Natalie berated me, the more I found myself parking in front of bars, watching the people who walked or stumbled out, noting every detail I could. Mostly their body language but especially how they were dressed and the color of their hair.

Before I knew it, I'd start my engine and follow them from a distance until they reached their next destination. Never getting out of my car but always watching.

Even outside of bars—random blonde women caught my attention everywhere I went.

And then I started following them, trailing them from a careful distance.

Just watching.

But with everything waiting for me at home, I didn't care about getting back late. There came a point when I had to force myself to return to Natalie. She and her barrage of questions and demands.

I could feel her growing agitation. Every time I came home late. Whenever I stepped into her art room to give her a firm kiss, her paintbrush would pause, and she would glare at the clock resting to the right of the windows. She wanted to ask. It was written all over her face. She wanted to know what was holding me up. If it was work keeping me out late or something—or even someone—else. She wanted to know.

It wasn't like her to wait so long to ask something, but it was likely because I tried to be home on time at least two days out of the week. She relaxed when I did. Watching the questions and heartbreak fade from her eyes was all I needed to know I could stay out again.

Like tonight. I went straight from my office to my car to drive home. Hand gripping the steering wheel, I struggled to keep my eyes focused on the road whenever I passed someone. Being home for Natalie was the only thing keeping me from turning down another road.

Ignoring any and every little temptation crossing my mind was the last thing I wanted to do. I followed the deepening urge to see where it would take me. I was never overcome by static—my mind was always clear. I just wanted to see how far I could go.

No one had found the intern, and no one at Pulse had asked about her since the cops stopped coming around. Her corpse had likely been ravaged by animals. I could picture her as a picked-apart skeleton underneath the underbrush. I hadn't been there since that day, but going back had crossed my mind a few times. Imagining what she might look like now sent goose bumps across my skin.

With all these thoughts whirling through my mind, I was agitated before even pulling into the driveway of our still-empty house. We'd been so consumed with saving money for the baby that we hadn't started to decorate for ourselves. Natalie's focus was on the nursery. We both wanted our child to have everything they could need. Until then, nothing else mattered.

Nat jumped up when she heard me open the door, quick to get to me despite the extra weight she was carrying. She was on me within seconds, throwing her arms around me while being careful of her belly.

"Goddammit, Natalie, can you give me a second to walk in the door?"

She jumped back as if I'd struck her.

The face I was met with was full of hurt and anger. It was beautiful. She never looked anything less. Even pregnant, she was still the most beautiful thing I'd ever seen. And though she'd talked about taking it easy until the baby arrived, I wanted her. Desperately.

"What did I do? What's your problem?"

Her questions were toeing the line between blaming herself for my reaction and asking me why I was acting like an asshole. Part of me wanted to light a match and touch it to the edge of my pants so I could watch the flames rise as I burned.

I curled my hands into fists, nails biting into my palms.

I never talked to her like that.

Opening my mouth to apologize, I reached for her.

But she quickly stepped back, holding her hands close to her chest to keep me from touching her. "Don't talk to me like that. You never talk to me like that. What is *wrong with you?*"

I'd been asking myself the same question. I never came up with an answer to it, though.

I was always just trying to do what was best for her—for us. I would do anything to keep us together. I was doing everything I could not to take my anger out on her.

"Nothing. I-I don't know what—"

Everything was hitting me at once. I was here with her, but my mind was on the body concealed in the woods, looking down at vomit covering a tile floor, feeling rising flames draw closer. I blinked, struggling to focus. The woman carrying my child was standing in front of me, begging for answers, but I was everywhere else.

"Natalie, I'm so——"

"Don't. Don't even bother." She didn't hold back the sharpness of her tone. She shook her head, and the look in her eyes made my knees weak. I never wanted her to look at me like that. Ever. "An apology isn't going to save you this time. You're going to need to come up with more than two or three words and some excuse."

My heart and stomach sank. Like some wire had snapped, my body felt like it had stopped working. I felt like a puppet with the strings cut.

"You're right. I——God! Fuck." I buried my face in my hands and then gripped my hair, fighting the urge to tear every strand from my scalp, before I looked at her again. "I didn't mean it. Please. Please don't look at me like that. I'll do anything to make that go away."

Slowly, carefully, I reached for her again to pull her into me. She allowed it but watched my every move, rigid in my arms. One hand held one of my arms, while her other was flat against her belly, almost as if she were protecting them.

Moments passed before she pulled away. "Where have you been?" Her voice was quieter, much gentler when she spoke again. She was cautious. Her eyes were wide. Not suspicious but hurt. "You've started coming home later and later lately."

She'd finally confronted me.

I didn't answer. I stood, frozen, mouth sealed shut.

"Is it me? Are you done? Is it because of this?" She gestured to her growing belly. "Because I'm pregnant? Do you not want the baby anymore?"

She was practically in tears. I could see them, but she was breathing through it, keeping her head high as she buried me in the questions that'd probably been on her mind these last several weeks.

I'd dug my grave with her. I would lose her if I didn't get my shit together.

My heart ached, my knees on the verge of collapse. I struggled for words. The *right* words. The ones that would hold her here, with me. Forever.

"I'm giving you the chance to stay and fix things for us and our child, Scott." She let out a long breath as if to compose herself. "Or you can walk out now. Doing this now will give me a chance to figure out how to get my footing without you."

She would walk out if I couldn't give her something to hold on to. Because she would never let me talk to her like this again. This was my one chance.

I saw Nat's heart start to crack right in front of me; all of it was visible in her eyes.

"No. Please." My voice was as desperate as hers, fixated on the pain ripping into me at the thought of her walking away from me forever. "I don't know what it is. I don't. I think I might be panicking about the baby. We bought this house. It's all happening so fast, and I work all day now and then I come home, and you ask me to do all this stuff." My hand twitched at my side, wanting to reach out to her again, desperate for her to see my need for her. "I'm overwhelmed. I don't know how to handle everything, so I just drive around after work and think." I reached for her again, needing to touch her. She didn't want me to wrap my arms around her—I could see that—so I cupped her shoulders. "I don't know what I'm doing—what's going on right now. I should *not* have taken it out on you like that. Of course I want you, this, us, our baby, all of it. You know I would never lash out at you like that normally. Tell me how I can do better, and I'll do it."

She took a moment to respond. "I never thought you would lash out at me like that, but with how you've been acting lately . . . I don't know what to think."

I gave in and reached down for her hand. Her fingers were cold against my palm. "I'll do anything to keep you in my life. Just tell me how I can be better for us."

Breathing felt impossible as my eyes darted across her face, searching for any indication she might need me as I needed her.

With a slow nod, she released a long breath as she looked over my shoulder. "Why don't we sleep on this and we can talk about it tomorrow, on your day off? We can work on the nursery together. I just think we both need a minute."

Silence thudded between us. The thought of losing her had a grip on my chest, lungs, and throat. There was one question I couldn't shake from my mind. I had to know. I needed comfort just as much as she did.

"Do you regret any of this?" I asked her, feeling the force of my arms shoving a fragile woman into the side of my car, images of blood erupting behind my eyes.

Natalie's eyebrows pulled together. "Regret what?"

"Leaving with me."

Understanding crossed her eyes, her brows pulling together tighter. "No. No. Why would you ask that?"

"Just please . . ." Hanging my head, I fell to my knees in front of her, gently planting a kiss on her stomach as I wrapped my arms around her. My chest wouldn't release the tension gripping my lungs. "I'll do anything. Just don't leave me."

I couldn't imagine a life without her. The thought was unbearable after all we'd been through. From the moment she sat beside me on the graffitied wall at the train tracks, I knew she would always belong to me.

Her fingers combed through my hair. "We're going to be okay."

I was excited to be a dad, to have a chance to be the dad I'd wanted growing up, but I couldn't shake the dread in the pit of my stomach whenever I tried to imagine the future. Living in the moment—giving into every thought that crossed my mind—was the only way I was making it through, day by day. How could I explain that to her?

I wouldn't take any of it out on Natalie again.

But I couldn't stop. Not now. Not if I was going to keep us together. I never wanted to take anything out on Natalie again. If I was going to keep that promise, I had to get my emotions out another way.

I would have to find a way to come home earlier, too.

I had to find a way to make her want to stay.

chapter twenty-seven

WHEN I WOKE THE NEXT morning, the bed was empty. My hand realized this before my mind. It drifted to her side of the bed, only to find it empty. The sheets weren't even warm. Heart sinking through the mattress beneath me, I abruptly sat up. With the room blurry from sleep, I blinked as I reached out in search of Natalie. It wasn't like her not to be here. She was usually glued to our bed on weekend mornings.

"Natalie?"

I was met with silence.

I didn't bother searching the floor for a shirt or socks. I padded down the hallway in boxers and bare feet, following the trail of faint music. I expected to find her in her art room, but the door to the room next to it was wide open. I paused in the doorway, taking in the mess of open boxes and packing peanuts around Natalie. She was sitting on the floor, putting furniture together. A little radio was propped in the corner, playing a tinkling lullaby, a stack of CDs beside it.

The nursery smelled like lavender and oranges. I wasn't sure how she managed it.

Taking in a deep breath, I watched her until she noticed me. Inside was warm, sunlight glowing across her face, casting shadows beneath her lashes. Her hair was lighter in the morning light. She hadn't bothered to pull it back with a scrunchie, so it was loose and disheveled from sleep. Her locks were so long it stopped midway down her back. I could imagine the purple-and-pink streaks that used to pop out of her blonde head. The teenager in me missed them.

"What are you doing?" I asked, rushing to get the words out to halt my imagination. My heart was pounding. My blood ran south. I cleared my throat to remove some of the gruffness. "You weren't there when I woke up."

"I wanted to get started," Natalie told me, untangling the mobile hanging from her finger. Her focus was on it rather than on me. My chest tightened. She couldn't look at me. "You didn't forget that Anthony and Olivia are coming over tonight, did you?"

"Do I need to grab anything at the store?"

"I started a list—it's on the counter in the kitchen— but I haven't finished it yet."

"Wine? Queso? Beer? Fancy napkins?"

She finally looked up at me, and somehow, I had earned a smile. "Everything but the queso. We still have a jar left from when I told you about our little bean." Her hand instinctively went to her stomach.

I stepped further into our child's nursery. I kneeled behind her, wrapping my arms around her so she had to stop what she was doing. My face buried in her hair, I reveled in her scent. My beautiful Natalie.

"You shouldn't be putting furniture together on your own." I spoke into the nape of her neck, her hair shifting with my breath.

"I wanted to surprise you when you got up—show you that I'm a big girl that can put baby furniture together." She didn't give me the chance to answer. "I can carry things and put things together. I don't want you to do everything for me. You don't have to protect me all the time and help me so much."

"I have to do that now more than ever." I kissed the top of her head, shutting my eyes when I felt how soft her hair was.

It was something I would've said before, words I meant, but they sounded flat to my own ears.

"Why don't we take a shower?" she asked, her voice suggestive. "I'm not over how much bigger it is than the one at our apartment."

"I don't think you'll ever stop talking about that."

"Forty years from now, when I'm on oxygen, and we can't fit our old butts in there together anymore, I'll still ramble about how much bigger the shower is."

I kissed her head again before I got up. "Leave the rambling to me."

"Is that a yes to the shower?"

I hated the way she looked up at me. The smile on her face was like a punch in the gut.

The feeling made my body go rigid.

We'd gone this long without her wanting anything to do with me. Now the tables had turned. I wanted to disappear into myself, move away from her, and the feeling sent a shot of adrenaline through me.

"I think I should get started on some things, since Olivia and Anthony are going to be here later."

An excuse to get away—that was all they were.

The corners of her lips dropped with the slightest twitch, but she kept it in place to hide her disappointment. I buried my face into her neck. I didn't want to see it, but I hoped she would assume it was because of how she looked pregnant than anything else.

"Okay, love. I guess I'll wash myself." She set aside what she'd been working on and barely let me help her up before she made for the shower.

My chest felt cleaved open as I watched her.

And I knew I shouldn't let her walk out the door, but I didn't stop her.

I wanted to bury the feeling of wanting to let her go— of wanting nothing to do with her. I'd never felt anything like it. Not with her.

"What can I do to make it up to you? How can I be better for you?"

Nat paused, hand on the doorframe, as she considered my words. "I just want you to be here. I don't want you to miss out on any more than you have to while you're at work."

I nodded. "Done. I'll be here more. No more late nights at work unless I absolutely have to."

Part of me—the part that still loved her—meant it.

She touched her growing belly, scrunching her nose with a sigh. "I miss our wine and queso nights."

"Why don't we have a queso-and-grape-juice night when I get home tomorrow?"

Her genuine smile returned. "Really?"

"I'll head straight to the store from work and be here no later than five-thirty. Think you can handle sitting on the floor with that hippy rug of yours?"

"We really should figure out what to do about that rug. Purple does not belong in an adult house like this." I waited for her to answer my question, eyes on the protective hand still on her stomach. She finally shrugged. "I hope you're okay with helping me down and then up when my legs start cramping."

"I think I can handle that."

Smile still in place, she said, "If you change your mind, I'll be in the shower."

I didn't know what to say, but she didn't wait for a response before she disappeared down the hallway.

The thought of climbing in behind her, running my hands down the length of her smooth sides, was tempting, but a stronger need was taking hold. She wasn't enough for me right now.

My mind was hazed over when I walked into the kitchen.

Natalie was bearing down on me. It was too much pressure. I couldn't handle it. I didn't know how to act the way she wanted. I didn't know how to be who she wanted anymore. That part of me was buried so deep it felt impossible to reach. I didn't remember walking out of the nursery, pulling out the pans, or cracking the eggs, but my attention snapped back to reality when I heard the hiss.

As I stared down into the sizzling eggs, every muscle in my body seized.

She was too much but also not what I craved or needed.

My vision clouded, warped, as I clenched my hands. Overcome by the thought of taking this pan to Natalie's face, I imagined her skull would sound similar to how Hannah's had cracked against the wet concrete. I dropped the pan back to the stove, clanking metal echoing in my ears—in reality and memory. The sharp emotion took my breath away. Temptation shook everything inside me, knocking the air from my lungs. The anger—the allure— was nothing I had experienced. I'd never imagined myself hurting Natalie like that before.

I stepped back from the stove, my eyes still locked on the pan but seeing none of it. I kept my hands clenched to keep them at my sides.

My heart felt like it was ready to beat out of my chest, and bile rose in my throat.

I wanted to fall to my knees.

If I turned around, I'd wind up in the bathroom with Natalie cornered. Fuck, I loved her so much. I had to get my shit together. Head in my hands, I pulled at my hair. *I had to.*

I had to keep her.

Hurting her . . . the thought was unbearable . . . I loved her . . .

I didn't bother grabbing a jacket before I forced my legs to take me out the back door. The morning air hit me, clearing my head enough to propel toward the car. We would have to get another soon. I wouldn't let Nat be home alone with the baby without a way for her to get around. Anything could happen with an infant.

I slammed the car door shut, resting my head against the steering wheel. We were about to have a baby. A baby. And here I was, running. Natalie would be pissed whenever she got out to find me gone, but that was better than if I stayed. This way, at least she was still breathing. My hands clenched the steering wheel. I couldn't say the same for the next soul that crossed paths with me. Knowing I was disappointing her and that she would blame herself set my eyes burning.

I didn't let it stop me from turning the key.

Every road I turned onto was the same. Most of it was a blur. The white-and-yellow lines, the cars, the trees, my mind—none of it was clear. None of it brought things into focus. I was driving from memory. Until I pulled into the parking lot of the bar.

After cutting the engine, I clutched the wheel.

The ones who walked out of the bar at this hour usually played out to be the most exciting.

Thoughts of Natalie at home, alone, kept trying to poke through my mind, forcing me to tighten my grip. Replacing the steering wheel with flesh was easy to imagine.

But the clock on the dash kept changing over, and the bar's parking lot was still a ghost town. The six cars in the lot me told me people were inside. They'd probably been there all night; they had to come out sometime.

I hated the silence, but keeping the car off and quiet was more important than shoving one of Natalie's clunky tapes into the old stereo. Leaning back in my seat, I trusted the tint of the windows would hide me well enough for a drunk bitch not to notice me.

My thinning patience paid off.

Exit banging open, a guy with crusty, shoulder-length hair sauntered out with an arm slung around a slender woman. A blonde woman with dark streaks drooping the front of her face, bending forward and cackling at God only knows what.

They practically looked like siblings. Yet he was all over her. My teeth clamped when he grabbed her ass. The dress was barely long enough to cover up the intimate parts of her. Cackling harder, she shoved away from him and toward what I assumed was her rusted white car. She was parked mere cars from me. Her hair barely covered the drastic plunge at the front of her skintight dress. It wouldn't take more than a small breeze or a breath against her chest to expose her breasts.

"Same time tomorrow, sweet cheeks?" he shouted to her from across the parking lot.

The pair was beyond anything I'd imagined would come walking out of the bar.

She'd be grateful to get away from that piece of shit. I would be doing her a favor.

I was doing *us* a favor.

While I had left Natalie without saying anything, it was for us. For her. Leaving was the only way to stop myself from wrenching open the bathroom door. Instead, this stumbling woman was who I had set my eyes on. It—I wouldn't touch Natalie. The unsuspecting woman fumbled with her keys, and I started the Volkswagen.

Like the classy woman she was, she turned into a liquor store. She'd likely only left the bar because her stellar morals wouldn't let her stay from midnight to noon— or the bartender had kicked her and her friend out. She walked into the store with purpose, and I pulled in right beside her car. Inhaling deep breaths with my hands tight on the wheel, my mind was racing with possibility. I could catch her by surprise, cover her mouth, and shove her into the back of the Volkswagen. Or I could force her in with the promise not to hurt her if she followed my every word.

She'd sober up real quick.

Her eyes would beg me not to hurt her as I drove us somewhere remote.

Watching the wind whip plastic bags into telephone poles and tree branches, I determined it was lucky that I hadn't grabbed a jacket. I didn't bother covering up my tattoo, either. No one would have the chance to identify me. Throwing the car door open, I knew I could make the weather work in my favor.

"Oh!" I said when the bitch came out of the liquor store as I was walking up. "I-I'm sorry." I held my sides to bear down from the cold. "Do—do you know where Gavin Street i-i-is? Can you point me toward it?"

She faced me, clenching the brown paper bag. Close up, I could see how smeared her eye makeup was from the night. Her dress was crooked, barely covering her cleavage. "Uh." Her gaze darted up and down the street as she slowly stepped toward our cars. "I'm not too sure, actually."

She took in the way I was holding myself against the cold. But she kept taking hesitant steps away from me.

"Do you need help? A ride home?"

Her questions were half-assed in forced kindness.

Selfish bitch. I was doing the world a favor.

If I were a homeless person, she wouldn't have given a shit. She was too sloshed to care about anyone. Not even herself, according to the state of her makeup.

"Could I just get warm in your car for a minute?" I asked, waiting a beat before pressing further. "Only a minute."

"No." She shook her head. "No." She was seemingly more confident in her answer. "I don't like the way you're acting. Sorry. I hope you find that street—"

She went to move past me, but I sidestepped in front of her. I couldn't risk her reporting me to someone.

Her eyes widened, her mouth gaping.

I wasn't sure what I would do next, but she knew to fear for her life.

Static consumed my mind. I couldn't keep track of time or action. I felt her hair against my fingers and then fisted the strands. I didn't hear her reaction. Disappointment tugged at the loss of hearing her gasp. But then my glance caught hers. Even smeared with makeup, her eyes were dead set in fear. It wasn't hard to see that.

chapter twenty-eight

TRAPPING HER BETWEEN OUR CARS, I got her on the ground. She didn't give me the chance to enjoy the look of her wide eyes before turning over to claw away from me, long nails chipping against the asphalt. Her screams were muffled under my palm, each shout for help suppressed.

"Shut up," I seethed in her ear, all my weight pinning her to the ground.

A sob choked against my hand, but she didn't stop squirming to flee.

Jaw clenched, I heaved her up from the ground, knocking her head into the Volkswagen's side-view mirror with enough force to make her go slack against me. I could still feel her breath—warm and shallow—on my palm. Knees buckling, I dragged her to heave her into the back seat of the car. As I maneuvered to lay her down inside, the side of her breast brushed my hand. Inhaling a deep breath, I forced myself to slam the door, barely missing the tip of her trashy heels.

Climbing into the front, I had no idea where I was taking her.

I got behind the wheel and drove.

Panic wasn't present. My hold on the steering wheel was loose. I knew I would figure out how to dispose of her. I just wouldn't stop until I found a place.

The slut was silent behind me. Not even a groan came from the back.

She was giving me the same treatment Natalie would give me back home.

Two towns over, I drove past a river I didn't remember noticing before. Natalie and I had come out this way whenever we craved Italian, becoming regulars at Lucky Papa's Pizzeria. The food was worth the drive, but I'd never noticed the body of water beside the road.

A glance in the rearview mirror told me the road behind me was empty.

I had time. There was no reason for me to pull onto the first dirt turn off ahead.

I waited until I came across a forgotten turn overgrown with branches and fat bushes, then turned down it when I felt like the Volkswagen's dingy red paint couldn't be seen from the road.

I needed a less identifiable car.

I threw the Volkswagen in park, my hands reluctant to release their grip on the steering wheel.

I'd lost track of time, but we were miles away from the liquor store, and it'd been at least a couple of hours since I left Natalie.

I couldn't waste any more time.

Walking around the front of the car, I looked down at the water rushing against stones. I'd expected the current to be harsher. We were still a ways off the road, and the river would disguise any of my stirring. The mud squelched as I trekked to the back seat to haul her out by her ankles. I didn't bother stopping to catch the top half of her. She groaned when her head hit the drenched dirt and moss, her lashes fluttering in faint consciousness.

Her eyes snapped open when I started dragging her away from the car. They weren't blue. They weren't Natalie's eyes. The brown depths of the whore held confession and fear. My hands tensed around her wrists, firmly leaving bruises, my biceps tight as I pulled her limp body through the marsh.

She inhaled a long breath to scream, and I let her. For a moment.

"No!" she called out. "Please. NO!"

Her screams were just audible enough above the static echoing through my mind.

Then my hands took everything out on her.

On top of her, I waded leaves into her mouth until she couldn't scream. Until bits trickled down the corners of her lips with saliva. Until she was choking on mud and greenery.

But that was too easy. I had to grab at her thrashing body. I had to listen to her struggle for air around the crushed leaves.

Her eyes were wider than any woman's I had seen. She was disgusting.

I shoved another clump into her mouth, and she screamed around them, her eyes watering and spilling over in a stream of tears. She had no perseverance. No survival instinct. Her attempts to push me away and reach for the debris were pathetic.

The mud would dry up in her mouth before she got away.

"Disgusting bitch," I ground out, reaching out for her throat.

Somehow, her eyes grew even wider when I tightened my hands. I felt like I could break her neck—burst her windpipe. Then, just to tease her, I would release her throat to watch her gasp and suck the leaves deeper into her esophagus. I made sure the foliage was so deep that even coughing couldn't save her. And then I would grab her neck all over again. Until she lost consciousness.

Once her eyes fell shut and her head slackened, I couldn't hold back. I clamped down on her throat. Her skin felt paper-thin and wrinkled. I could feel how her pulse struggled beneath my grip. I waited, my wrists trembling from the force of my grasp.

I lost all sense of time. I held on until my hands gave up, the static ringing in my ears fading. For a second, everything was calm, and my mind was clear.

A long breath left my body, the tension fading with the exhale. I backed away, unable to take my eyes off the disoriented and terrified look in her eyes. I waited for them to empty, but it was like she was frozen in time.

Standing, I winced from the look in her eyes, nearly falling over the woman's idiotic heels. My knees were wet and caked with mud. When I looked at my hands, only a thin layer of dirt remained, thanks to the sweat and tears.

My heart sank when my phone started ringing from the car.

Dropping my hands, I looked back at the car to find that the driver's side was still open. Knowing who was on the line, I bolted for the car.

I blinked the sweat from my eyes to see Natalie's caller ID lighting up the screen.

Fuck. I had to get home. I should already be there.

I dropped my cell back into the cupholder to return to the body, and though my heart was erratic, my hands were stable as I bent down to drag her to the back seat.

Leaving her here wasn't an option. I had no time to hide her. Getting rid of her the way I wanted wasn't an option, either.

My cell went off again.

No struggle jolted from her—no sound. My breath huffed in the cold air as I walked to the Volkswagen. The chill made me think of blue lips. The bitch's lips would eventually turn blue, but right now, I was watching the leaves crumble out of her mouth. Even limp with death, I found heaving her up into the back of the car was easier than it was at the liquor store.

The back door screeched with rust when I opened it, and I noted to oil it for Nat before she took the car tomorrow.

Before I could get in the driver's seat, my cell rang a third time.

Fuck!

A third call must have been the limit because my cell didn't ring again.

With it secure in the back seat, I hopped in the front, confirming Natalie had called three times when I flipped open my phone.

I shoved the car in reverse, hitting the gas. *Fuck!* An abrupt crack snapped before I made it out of the woods. My heart dropped for a second time. I slowly turned to my right to find the source of it. Rage rushed from my arms to my hands, clenching and unclenching my fists as

I imagined the soft skin of the whore's neck. Without a neck in front of me, I punched the steering wheel.

I couldn't fix everything, especially Natalie's side view mirror, before I went home. Goddammit, I didn't know how I would explain that one.

I hit the gas, lurching out onto the empty, damp road. Careful to keep to the speed limit, my mind grew hazy with static as my attention went on autopilot. The car was a different kind of quiet as I backed out of the woods. Her corpse was sprawled in the back like a bag of trash I was taking to the dump. It was over, but I wasn't done with her. A fulfilling tiredness settled through my body.

Then, just as I was about to clear the woods and pull out onto the road, it started drizzling.

The only sound on my drive was the patter of the rain as it poured. I shook my head to clear it before snatching up my phone again. My shoes were caked in mud. The knees of my slacks were stained, and the steering wheel wasn't in much better shape.

Eyes on the clock, I flipped my phone open again and scrolled through my contacts to click on one of the three numbers I had saved. I skipped past Anthony's name, assuming he was already at the house, and that was a reason Natalie let her phone ring.

"Pick up," I ground out.

The call went to voicemail, and I tossed the phone in the passenger seat.

I ignored the ache in my jaw. I'd left because of her. And now I couldn't be out of the house for more than a couple of hours without her calling me.

Within what seemed like a blink, I passed our town sign and pulled into the nearest thrift store. I took care not to park under a light. Glimpsing the cameras as I walked in, I slowed my pace as I made for the men's section. Soaked and muddy, I knew I had to change before going home. But I couldn't look like I was in a rush. I had to grab a pair of shoes, jeans, and a shirt, then get back to the car before anyone got curious about the lump in my back seat. For good measure, I grabbed an extra shirt or two as I sifted through hangers.

The guy at the counter barely looked up from his MP3 player.

My mind cleared once I pulled into the driveway in a new set of clothes. When I threw the car in park, I glanced over my shoulder to check the body before I killed the engine. The whore's back was damp from being dragged across the ground, hair a matted mess, but there would be no trace of the body when Natalie got up for her doctor's appointment in the morning.

Not even a leaf would be left.

As I walked up to the front door, I found myself standing before the stale house of my childhood. I knew it wasn't real. Though my gut still twisted as I turned the handle.

The shoulders of my shirt were already soaked through when I walked in. But at least I was clean of mud. No, this house was not stale. It was ours. This haven belonged to Natalie and me, and it was filled with love. I heard the pause of silverware before I felt the attention of the room.

My stomach dropped before I turned the corner into the dining room and saw the look on Natalie's beautiful face.

"Hey, it's Scottie!" Anthony cheered, raising the store-bought shot of bourbon he usually carried with him these days.

He looked like a hotel bellhop who had gone through a guest's mini fridge.

"Hi, everyone." I stepped into the room, glancing right over Olivia and Anthony to zero in on Nat. "I'm so sorry I'm late. Things . . . took longer than I thought they would."

"Nah, asshole, you just missed Anthony ripping his shirt off to dance on top of your shitty, pop-up table," Olivia said before taking a long gulp of her beer. "Those bourbons go straight to his head."

"In that case, I'm really glad I'm late." I took my spot next to Nat and reached for her hand under the table. My teeth clamped together when her hand curled back from mine.

Olivia shook her head after a moment. "I still can't believe you got your girlfriend pregnant."

"Shit, yeah, neither can I!" Anthony chimed in. "Did you get lazy when it came to wrapping things up, Scottie?"

"You're going to have a baby! When will you find out the gender?"

"We've decided to be surprised," answered Nat.

"Who woulda fucking thought?" Anthony said.

"Not us, that's for sure." I smiled at Nat, inching closer to her, knowing full well she was going to verbally rip me to pieces the second they left.

"With Scott graduating and my art career taking off," said Natalie, "we were ready to start our lives."

"Please tell me you'll have us over the second you have the little tater tot!" Olivia squealed.

"Olivia"—Anthony shook his head—"we all know that the second you find out Natalie's giving birth, you'll set up a campsite on their porch so you can ambush them when they get home."

Natalie's laugh stood out like wind chimes among the rest of us.

The second Nat closed the door behind Olivia and Anthony, my stomach dropped. All I could think about was the damp body lying in the trunk of my girlfriend's car. Her body was nagging from the back of my head. I'd have to wait until Natalie was asleep before I did anything with it. We needed two cars.

The second we were alone in the kitchen, she seethed in a whisper. "You just embarrassed me in front of our friends."

"I'm sorry." *For leaving the house without telling you. For leaving to clean and prep for Anthony and Olivia.* She knew what I was apologizing for. "I'm going to make this right . . ."

"No." Natalie shook her head. "No, Scott. You can't keep doing this. Where have you been? I did *everything* before they got here. I cooked, cleaned, and where were you? What were you doing?"

I shoved my hands through my hair and then threw them up in defeat. "I got overwhelmed. I started thinking about everything we have to do before the baby gets here, and I—I panicked, Nat. I can't explain it. It was like I lost track of time—"

"You can't keep doing this."

"I know." I nodded, my heart pounding in my ears. I could barely hear my own words. "I know. I just—I drove around for a while and then ended up at the hardware store. I bought more paint to start on the nursery in the morning." I crossed the room, taking her face in my hands. "I love you. More than anything in this life and whatever comes after it. I'm working on things—for you. I am. I'm killing to make it happen. Please, Nat, please don't even think—" I choked on my words. "Please don't think about leaving."

Her lips parted, but she was struck with silence.

I placed a gentle hand on her stomach, over our growing child. "I will do everything I can to keep us going. I'm sorry I wasn't here for you today, but I will make it up to you. I swear—on everything, I swear."

Her eyes fell closed, shutting out my only way of telling what she was feeling. Moving to rest over mine, I felt a long sigh pass through her body. "I'm not going anywhere, Scott. I just don't know what's going on with you—or us. We're not on the same page, and it's making me feel like you don't want to be here or that you want to leave."

"No. No, Nat." I pulled her into my arms. "Never. You'd leave me before I ever left you. We're going to be okay. I'm going to be better."

We held each other in silence. I could feel her distance—the way she barely held me back. She was scared. More importantly, she was unhappy, and that gutted me. I had to make things right. She was carrying my child. I had to be here. I had to put time away for her and work to make us strong again.

I couldn't keep failing her.

"I think I need time," Nat said after several minutes. "I'm not really okay after everything today."

"I'm so sorry, Nat. I know those are just words, but I'm going to make it up to you."

We had come so far. From watching my house go up in flames through the back window of the Volkswagen to now.

Her face was hidden with her hair, but I could tell I hated the look in her eyes.

"I'm going to paint the nursery first thing tomorrow, I promise."

"Don't make promises you can't or don't intend to keep, Scott."

Static rang in my ears again, but the underlying threat beneath her words tightened my chest and stopped the ringing just as quickly as it'd started. I had to force myself to swallow.

"I am, Nat. I'm getting the paint all ready before I come to bed tonight."

Nodding, she pulled away from me. "I'm tired, so I'm gonna head to bed."

I watched her walk away, heart sinking painfully slow when she didn't look back before leaving the room. It hadn't been long enough since the last time I'd seen her hide in her hair.

Down in the basement, I took in the bare bones. Empty posts where walls should be, unused carpet rolled up in the corner, a few barrels, bungee cords, duct tape, and then the paint cans lined up in front of me. My hands curled into fists, but there was nothing to punch through. The basement hadn't been finished—there was nothing to break. It looked like something out of a horror movie.

I grabbed the paint cans Nat had bought for the nursery and took my time carrying them upstairs. Oxford Gray. We hadn't even talked about gender-neutral paint colors. I hadn't sat with her to go over ideas. I had lied about picking up more canisters, like I knew what she'd planned for our child's room. I really hadn't been here for her. My girlfriend was pregnant, and I was failing her in every way. After I'd always promised her that I'd work to give her everything she deserved.

I wasn't even coming close.

Natalie and I wrapped ourselves around each other whenever we first climbed into bed. This time, however, she did not whisper about her day to me. I wrapped my arms around her, hoping she could feel how sorry I was— how guilty I felt for not being there for her.

But after the silence had dragged on long enough, she rolled over to have her own space. Falling asleep with our backs touching was how we always ended our nights, but it felt different when she pulled away. Her sigh was deep when she rolled over, her hair splayed across the pillow behind her. Remembering how long and gorgeous it was in high school, I wanted to twirl it between my fingers. The ends had become brittle in her pregnancy.

Staying completely still, I waited until Natalie's breathing became heavy with sleep before I eased from the bed.

chapter twenty-nine

OPENING THE FRONT DOOR, I was met with the damp night air as I made my way for the Volkswagen. I was barefoot, still in the pajama bottoms Nat had bought me for Christmas and shirtless when I opened the door to the back seats. Nothing felt real. Not even the wet driveway under my bare feet. Not even when I reached in for the whore I'd taken from the liquor store. She looked even worse off than when I'd last left her.

Soon enough, I wouldn't have to look at her.

Natalie would be my focus from now on.

I would put energy back into us. Because she was right: I couldn't keep doing this. I couldn't keep disappointing her. I couldn't keep pushing her aside when she was pregnant with my baby. I had to be there for her, and our growing family.

All of this was for us.

Even if it was just to hold myself back from h—

I shook my head to banish the thought.

I had to be the dad my father never was. I would not let down my child. I would not ruin Natalie and I. All of it was too good not to go back to. I wouldn't give up on us and everything we'd built. Nat and I had come too far for me to fail.

Instead, I grabbed the bitch's corpse and dragged her to the front door.

The hinges of the front door made more noise than the stairs to the basement.

I didn't stop until we were alone in the basement.

Staring down at her sprawled body on the concrete floor, her tits pointing to the ceiling, I untied the string of my pajama bottoms to drop them to the floor. Then, I kicked them to the staircase for safe keeping. I couldn't have clothes getting in my way or risk Natalie finding stains on my outfit.

I bent down and stripped the whore of her skintight dress that left nothing to the imagination. Her heels went next, then her bra, and panties followed. I kept her clothes far from my own. I'd have to decide what to do with them later.

I turned to take in the whore's body again. It was be the last time I would see her whole.

I reached for the sharp tools I'd stuffed into the rolled-up carpet. Then, after spreading out a tarp, I moved her and got to work.

My breath hot, I gripped the handles of the sharp tools as my chest twisted.

I separated skin, muscle, and tendon from skeleton, flaying the whore at my feet. Sweat dampened my forehead, rolled down my arms, collected in my hands, and moistened the parts of her I touched. Her screams did not exist but bore down on me in different ways, echoing through my mind. All of it felt real; it was just distant, my mind absent from action. I clung to the warm blood pouring from her. In no time, I was covered in her gore.

The basement was dense with the smell of decomposition.

My nostrils flared. My mouth watered. My hands moved over skin and blood slowly, taking in the way it flowed and parted at the touch. Her blood tasted metallic when it splattered onto my bottom lip. So much as piercing skin with a fingernail ruptured a person's exterior. Her blood felt slick—like oil—along my skin.

I tracked time by how much skin still clung to bone, my eyes unblinking from the tendons.

The consistency reminded me of ground beef but denser.

From head to toe, I discarded every bit of her to the other side of the tarp. I'd have to find a way to dissolve and hide the evidence. Acid wasn't just sold at a local convenience store. Last thing I wanted was for Natalie to open our freezer to find skin and internal organs. I never wanted our child to come across this and play with it, either.

I had to remove every bit of her that clung on.

Once she was stripped, her skeleton would be first to go.

When I'd finished removing every organ, intestine, strand of hair, and all of her skin, leaving nothing left but her bare bones, I took out a clean tarp to put beneath her. Staring at the pile I'd stripped, I rubbed my fingers together, smearing the blood. But it wasn't enough. Not an ounce of hesitation or second thought crossed my mind before I plunged my hands into the mound. Further coating my hands in the woman.

My breath left my lungs.

I moved my hands throughout the mush, touching blood, bits of organs, flesh, and everything between.

My toes practically curled against the concrete floor.

By the time I pulled back, she was all over me. I was up to my elbows in crimson.

I stood there until it dried and then I crept up the stairs, not bothering to pick up my pajamas when I would head right back down. The basement tools were for cutting; I needed something to lend a hand in the grinding process. And I couldn't just toss a bloody pile of skin into the freezer. Quietly opening the door, I slowly made my way to the kitchen. So help me if Natalie woke up. I was naked, covered in blood, and scrambling to wash my hands off in the sink. Knowing Nat, I know her mind would never turn to what was happening in the basement.

I wiped everything down once my hands and arms were bare again. Then, one by one, I eased drawers open and shut to keep quiet. In the second to last drawer, I found what I was looking for.

By some miracle, Natalie's recent need to learn how to cook—so we didn't have to rely on ramen for survival— had led her to buy a meat tenderizer. I grabbed a handful of freezer bags. Mallet in hand, I snuck into the nursery to bring the paint cans downstairs. I set them aside back in the basement and shoved every slab of her into the freezer bags.

My hands were steady. Even as I slid the seal closed. Even as I moved the crushed organs inside the thin layer of plastic. Even as I set them on the packs of chicken Natalie had set at the bottom.

I lost count of bags that ended up in the packed freezer, and not a single one was left.

Once the freezer and tarp were wiped clean of stray skin and blood, I knew I would have to keep Natalie from the basement for a few days.

I returned to the tarp as I wiped the sweat from my forehead with the back of my arm.

Standing over her, struggling to catch my breath, I took in everything I'd done. The only thing left to do was crush what was left.

To turn bone into dust.

Clutching the meat tenderizer, I folded the tarp over the skeletal remains and crouched in front of it to get back to work.

The splintering and cracking sensations reverberating off the walls were distinguishable. Each impression made by the mallet sent a fulfilling shudder down my spine.

Splitting a skull.

A tremor rattled up my arms at the connection of wood against bone.

A skull cracking against asphalt in the rain.

The thud against the side door echoed that of the asphalt.

My heart hammered dully against my ribs.

I let out a gasp, my arms spasming against the force.

A warmth gnarled in the pit of my stomach as I brought the mallet above my head again. And again. And again.

I couldn't stop.

I didn't know how much time had passed before I stood again. I was still sweaty, out of breath, from using my strength to bring the meat tenderizer down.

But, finally, there was nothing left of her.

Pulling back the tarp, I stared at the scattered grounds left of her. We'd come so far since I'd first took in her body on the basement floor. She was less than nothing now. I'd made her into nothing.

Pouring the dust into the paint, I stirred until bone melded with Oxford Gray.

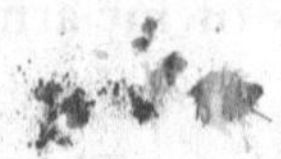

I ran a paintbrush beneath the length of the window frame. The two opposite walls were already painted and drying. The blinds were open with the window cracked to let the sunshine move the process along.

Back in my pajama bottoms, I hadn't looked in the mirror long enough to check if I had dark circles and hoped Nat couldn't tell I'd been up all night. Or wouldn't smell anything after I'd covered the basement in air freshener and lit candles. I'd scrubbed the blood out of the shower, taking Nat's loofah to my fingernails.

Nothing of the filthy bitch was left on me.

I just had to wait for Natalie to wake up to be touched by something beautiful.

I couldn't wait to have her hands on my unstained body.

With closed eyes, I tried to focus on inhaling the strong sting of paint.

Family. My family was what I needed to focus on now. I felt like her as I painted alone in our baby's future room. Except I wasn't creating art as Natalie would. The nursery walls were my canvas for bone dust and Oxford Gray paint.

Nothing had changed about the paint, which was a relief. I couldn't mess this up for Nat. The nursery was her obsession until the baby came.

Fuck, I wanted to keep her close.

Even with part of the whore still in the basement, I felt an ease in knowing she was in small pieces and unable to threaten us.

When I opened my eyes again, I dumped the brush into the paint.

I had to be better—for us.

But acid had to come first.

"Wow, it's actually starting to come along in here."

My head snapped up to find Nat leaning against the doorframe, a small smile on her face.

Her voice was filled with awe at how her dream nursery was coming together.

I forced a smile. "I told you I'd start on it this morning. I'm going to keep better with the promises I make to you."

Clarity flickered to life when Natalie stepped into the room.

I'd never felt more levelheaded.

She opened her mouth to say something but then her face scrunched as she glanced down the hall.

With my chest tightening, my hand twitched toward the brush.

"Do you smell that?"

"It smelled worse when I woke up," I said, the lie rolling off my tongue. "I cleaned it all up, but I found a dead raccoon in the basement."

Her mouth dropped.

"And I'm tossing all that chicken. I'm not risking anything."

"Forget the chicken. I'm not going anywhere near that basement."

I didn't answer. I could see she was gathering her focus to what she was about to say before.

She paused just inside the doorway, taking in the Oxford Gray walls, until her eyes landed on me, and lingered.

"I'm drowning, Scott," Nat said, wringing the hem of her shirt. "I can't do it all, and I need you here to help me."

Nothing was the same as it used to be.

The look in her eyes—the way they pleaded with me to put effort back into us so we could be saved. At one point, it would have crushed me to see such a look.

But I was numb to it.

Nothing I felt about her was the same or ever would be the same again.

Even as I extended a hand out to her and pulled her into my arms, I knew I still loved her. Natalie was still mine. Part of me still wanted to try. None of that had gone away. But the disconnect was keeping us apart. I didn't know how to fix it—fix us. I wanted to, but I couldn't bring myself to try most of the time.

With Natalie standing stiff before me, expecting me to change, I realized what she wanted was out of reach.

"I can't believe I've made you feel that way," I said. "All of that ends here. You're not doing this alone. You have me. The two of you are everything to me. I haven't lost sight of that. I've just been . . . overwhelmed to make everything perfect."

Holding her was exhausting. Telling her I loved her took too much effort. Even though it was true, saying it drained me. I wanted space. I wanted distance. I was tired of wrapping my arms around her at night, of listening to her complain about not getting enough sleep and asking for more money for things we should already have in our home. Keeping her separate from my lies was exhausting.

Yet, I could see the hope in her eyes. She wanted this, me, us, to work its way out. She wanted me. She wanted things to return to normal and for us to continue our lives with our child. Seeing me paint our baby's room was giving her reassurance.

We were failing.

She was failing. She couldn't keep up with her responsibilities, and she expected me to pick up where she was incapable. She was trying but not hard enough. And she was trying to pin everything on me. I could see it.

I still had to be there for our baby.

And I would not let her love somebody else. I couldn't watch her look at someone else with those big trusting eyes. No one but me would have her. She loved me and would only ever love me.

Even with the distance, I had to make her open to me.

With her sitting across my lap, one hand on her belly between us and the other resting on my shoulder, I knew what I had to do. If I was going to keep her—if we were going to survive, I had to bend to what she wanted.

The thought made my mouth dry.

I took one of her hands in mine and placed the other over our growing child, confidence seeping through my veins. I had to make her stay. I had to show her I would be the father I'd always wanted. We would be the parents neither of us had. I'd never been more sure of anything in my life. Not since Natalie asked me to run away with her all those years ago.

Not since smashing the intern's head against the car.

I inhaled a deep breath, held it in, and blew it out. "Marry me, Natalie. Marry me, and I will work to give you everything you want every day."

She pulled back, her own hand replacing mine when it fell away with her distance.

I hoped she would see the seriousness.

"Marry me, Nat."

chapter thirty

HEART SINKING WITH EVERY SECOND of silence passing between us, I couldn't read her thoughts through her eyes. Part of Natalie's fear came from the disconnect—the distance—in my stare. I couldn't read her stare now, and it was gnarling my insides, causing something to fester inside me.

"Are you—" Natalie laughed, hand still on her belly. "Scott, are you serious?"

I wanted to reach for her again, to be close to our baby.

With my eyes locked on the hand she had over her stomach, I said, "We're having a baby together. We bought this house. I love you and I know I've been failing you. I want us to come together again and work at this. This is too good to give up on, Nat. I want to prove to you that I'm not going anywhere and that we can make it through anything. We're survivors." I let out a laugh. "Always have been."

"But I'm pregnant."

"And? You're beautiful."

"I just never imagined I'd get married looking like this," she said as she sat in front of me. "Everyone tries to lose ten pounds to fit into a size smaller. I never thought I'd have to force my way into a wedding dress."

Fuck, I adored her.

My heart dropped as I rubbed my hands together, as if I could still feel slick blood.

I still loved her, but the compulsion to redirect hostility onto look-alikes was stronger. My gut knotted at the thought of choosing . . . because I knew which of the two I would choose.

"We can wait until after. The point is, we're worth fighting for. I don't want you to give up on us—"

All traces of a smile disappeared.

"So, what? You're only asking me to marry you so I don't leave?"

"No, no! Of course not. You know me better than that, Nat." I took her hands in mine and hoped she didn't notice how I couldn't meet her eyes. "I'm asking you to marry because I love you and want to show you that. Marriage means choosing each other every day that we wake up together. I still want to give you everything you deserve. I want to show you I'm the person who won't ever give up on us. *That* is why I'm asking you to marry me, Nat."

If I was going to put my focus back on her, Natalie would have to try harder and keep up with her own responsibilities. I wasn't the only one to blame for how things were.

Tears welling in her eyes, Nat sniffled. "I just want us to be okay. Yes, yes, of course I want to marry you. Today, tomorrow, pregnant, not pregnant, holding a screaming baby as I say 'I do'—my answer is yes."

I sucked in a sharp breath. "Yes?"

"Yes!" She threw her arms around me but then struggled to sit up when her stomach pressed into mine. My heart snapped back into my chest, pounding between us. We laughed as I eased her to sit back on her legs.

"Are we actually doing this? Did you really just ask me to marry you?"

"Nat, take a breath." I laughed. "I'm sorry I don't have a ring or even a cheesy way to put a ring on your finger, like a bottle cap rim or a Ring Pop."

Her face scrunched up. "Oh, yeah, you really suck. I shouldn't marry you."

We were going to be fine. Natalie was still mine and now mine forever. I would do whatever it took to keep her. No matter what happened or how difficult things became, I would always do what was best for us.

"Don't hate me." She tensed at my words. "Now that I've done that, I can tell you that I busted off your side view mirror last night."

She laughed. "How in the hell? Did you just propose to get out of trouble for breaking my car?" She buried her face in my chest. I kissed the top of her head, whispering, "You're so perfect for me. I love you."

"I love you more."

I shook my head, her hair tickling my chin.

"Don't shake your head. We both know it's true."

"Let's get out today. I got my paycheck yesterday. Let's get out of the house and go get things for the nursery."

Natalie pulled back, beaming. "Are you serious?"

"We need to finish things up now that the walls are gonna be done. It won't be long before it's here."

"It?" Nat laughed. "Are you going to start calling our baby a tater tot like Olivia?"

I shrugged. "Might as well until we find out what we're having."

"We'll find out when he or she is born." She pecked me on the lips before getting to her feet but not without struggling. "I'm going to go get ready so we can go." She practically squealed on her way out of the nursery.

"Don't use up all the hot water! I'm covered in paint." *Paint with bone dust.* "A cold shower is the last thing I want."

She giggled from our bedroom. "No promises!"

Watching Natalie run from one end of the store to the other, touching everything she thought our baby would love, made my heart leap to my throat. I didn't let myself blink. She was glowing in a way I'd never seen before.

Turning my back from the counter, I concentrated on the joy unfolding.

Even though we were physically distant, I'd never felt closer to her. It'd been such a long time since I'd felt a jolt—a pull—toward her. A real one. One that did not need me to drag up happy memories.

She wanted to marry me. She wanted our baby to be happy.

But I knew I couldn't revert. I had tried. While it had lasted a few months, there was a freezer filled with flesh in our basement.

And I still had to find time to get enough acid to make a body shrivel up and disappear.

Still, Natalie and I were getting so much more than anything we'd imagined when we left our small town. I'd never pictured anyone else but her, but I'd never dreamed she'd agree to be my wife or carry my child. I didn't even think I could graduate college, yet here I was, happy, healthy, shopping in a baby store, giving my fiancé the baby steps she needed.

Crossing the store to her, I wrapped my arms around Natalie and peered over her shoulder. "Elephants?" I asked. "Is that why you wanted gray-blue paint?"

"Yup!" She turned to press her lips against my cheek. "Do you like that idea?"

"I love it." I hugged her tighter. "Just elephants, or should we do a whole zoo?"

"Any animals in particular you want to include?"

"You know I have a thing for monkeys."

She laughed, the chime ringing as magically as her smile.

Fuck. She was beautiful, and I would do anything for her without a moment's hesitation. I would do everything for the both of them, everything to keep them both.

I couldn't bring down the wall between us. Not without risking my strange compulsions lashing out at her. But I would love her and keep her and our baby safe.

"I love you," I breathed softly into Natalie's ear.

"Behave yourself," she told me, pressing back into me further, caged in my arms.

I wanted her. Right here and right now. I didn't care if the woman at the checkout counter watched.

I ran my nose along her hair. "We have yet to celebrate our engagement."

When she pulled out of my arms, I wondered how wet she was. Her biggest weakness was my voice. Throughout college, she'd drop her panties whenever I whispered in a deep tone. Those days seemed farther and farther away now that we'd left that apartment behind.

Natalie paused for several moments, her mind somewhere else, almost in a daze, then looked at me with a small, bewildered smile. "I can't believe this is actually happening."

My smile didn't feel as strained as the others. "I know. I want you to decorate the nursery any way you want."

She shook her head, glowing expression still in place. "We're doing this together, love, so grab whatever you want."

chapter thirty-one

BAREFOOT ON HER PURPLE RUG and surrounded by stacks of canvases, Natalie twirled to show off the newest addition to her cocktail dress collection. The emerald-green fabric had a slit going up her right thigh, and while the sleek material covered her breasts, her back was exposed. I wanted nothing more than to slide my hands across her back and underneath the material to cup her breasts from behind.

But I didn't need anyone else sharing that thought.

"I look disgusting!" Natalie groaned, staring down at herself as she ran her hands across the dress's hem. For once, her hand wasn't on her stomach. "I can't go out like this. I look like a beached whale."

"You look amazing."

I didn't have to force a smile because it was true, but the thought of anyone else looking at her the same way sent my teeth on edge.

"Is it the *right* dress, though?" Natalie pressed, glaring down at herself. "I need to look professional but like a bride-to-be, ya know?"

We would tell our friends about our engagement tonight.

My stomach felt hollow, but my fists were ready for anything. With champagne constantly being served at these galleries, nothing was out of the realm of possibility. If one person fucking opened their mouth about our engagement—said one wrong fucking thing . . .

I pushed off the doorframe to cross her in her art room. A bright smile emerged as I wrapped an arm around Natalie's waist to pull her into me. She placed a hand on my chest.

"You have nothing to worry about. You're always the most beautiful woman in the room. If you feel good in this dress, then it's the perfect one to wear."

I'd told her it would be a few paychecks before I could get a ring on her finger, but her concern was for our mortgage. While engagement was a practical next step for us, we both were on the same page when owning a home. Nothing was more important than having a safe place for our son. Neither of us could stomach the thought of repeating the past.

Heart leaping into my throat, I leaned into her—close enough for my nose to brush along her ear. "Now go get ready so I can show you off tonight."

Nat planted a kiss on my cheek before twirling past me. "You're too good for me."

The shower turned on a moment later. I stayed where I was until I could hear her under the water and humming to herself.

Then I was out the front door.

Yanking open the back of the Volkswagen, I grabbed the two bags of lye I'd stuffed close to the seats. Hiding things was definitely a plus to being the one who needed the car more.

Except I had to get this shit out before Natalie and I left for the gallery.

Slinging the bags over my shoulders, I snuck back into the house and headed straight for the basement.

When Natalie had sent me out for groceries and freezer bags, I took a detour for a few things on my own list.

Then, after she'd gone to bed, I grabbed the barrel drum from the car and filled it with water in the basement. Since ribbons of body parts would fill the thirty-gallon vat, I didn't have to fill it completely. Then would come a good amount of lye overtop. By the time this was finished, it would look like stew.

Even now, when I opened the freezer, the storage bags looked like they were filled with ground beef.

Then, after opening up the drum, I stabbed the first bag of lye to dump it over the water. The full freezer bags went in next. The flesh and organs inside, cold and hard, I dumped every grain of shiny white powder on top of the iced mush. To keep everything below the water, I covered the top with a sheet of dirty tarp.

I couldn't tell if the shower was still running from down here. I didn't take the time to inhale a long breath. I slammed the drum's lid back over the top.

With the drum sealed, I snatched a clean tarp from the corner of the room and unfolded it over the barrel.

Backing up, I made sure everything looked normal before turning to rush back up the stairs.

Halfway down the hall, the shower cut off. I rushed to rub my sweaty palms over my sweatpants before switching out of them to throw on slacks.

When I looked up a minute later, Natalie stepped out of the bathroom, already in her dress. She'd kept her makeup simple, natural. But anxiety flooded her eyes.

After crossing the room, I planted a kiss on her cheek before she turned her head to let me kiss her on the lips. We lingered, Natalie pushing herself closer into me with each passing moment. While her lips were soft and sweet, something gnarled in the pit of my stomach. I pulled away.

Natalie looked down at herself again and mumbled something incoherent. She grabbed her shoes from the floor and my jacket from the bed. With a sigh, she added, "No time to figure this nonsense out. I'm just a whale at this point, so let's just go."

I said nothing but rolled my eyes as Nat made for the door. I threw on my jacket as I worked to lock it, Natalie already making for the car.

We barely spoke on the way to the gallery. I couldn't tell what was off with her, but I would not ask when she had a long night ahead of her.

Hell, I had my own long night ahead of me between dealing with Anthony and Zach. At least I could tolerate Zach longer than I could Anthony.

Nat and I walked into the gallery, only for her to be pulled away by Ava and Caden a moment later. I cleared my throat, glancing around, until my eyes landed on Loki trotting toward me. I met him halfway, and we wandered in search of Natalie's displayed pieces. By the time we came to a gray scale scenery piece, I remember Nat splattering with flicks of her brush. My left cuff was wet from Loki's nose and floppy tongue. My hand found the top of his head, scratching behind his ears as people filed in around us.

"Hey, there he is," one voice called above the others.

Loki and I turned to find Zach leading Britney by the hand, while Anthony and Olivia closely followed. Loki jumped, his tail wagging with enough excitement for the both of us—because I sure as hell didn't want to be here.

"My man," Anthony added as he shook my head.

I took my time reaching for it.

"Nat sent us your way the second we walked in," Olivia told me.

Of course she did. While I'm alone to deal with them all by myself.

Forcing a smile I wouldn't be able to drop for the rest of the night, I said, "I'm sure she'll pop up any minute. She always looks forward to seeing you guys at these things."

"So, we have some news."

We all turned to find Natalie stepping into the circle we had all formed around her work.

This time, my smile was not forced. *Like clockwork.*

"More news? Don't you guys think you should quit that at this point?" Zach asked, his eyes falling to Nat's ever-growing stomach.

Nat came up beside me, hooking her arm through mine before beaming up at me. "We're engaged."

Squeals erupted from both women, who quickly hushed after remembering we were in a crowded gallery.

"Let me see—" Olivia grabbed Natalie's hand, only to realize her ring finger was empty.

"No ring?" Britney asked, her eyebrow cocked as she slid her judgmental eyes to me.

"Since we just bought the house and with the baby . . ." Nat said. "The timing for a ring just doesn't feel like the smartest decision right now."

Olivia nodded, her expression glum. Meanwhile, Britney crossed her arms. It was a miracle her breasts didn't spill out of her top.

Zach shrugged. "Put a Ring Pop on it. Don't most girls think it's romantic when a guy uses something else in place of—"

"No," Britney said. "No, they do not. You might as well buy a ring at a thrift store."

Oh, she was such an obnoxious and ungrateful bitch. I couldn't wait for when Zach kicked her to the curb. With how often he looked at other women, I was surprised it hadn't happened sooner.

"Anyway," Anthony jumped in before Zach and Britney could go for each other's throats, "has anyone been keeping up with the news lately? Because Olivia has been obsessed with watching the news since these girls have been going missing."

Adrenaline shot through my body, causing my hands to clench.

"Oh, come on," Britney said with a shake of her head. "That's a little ridiculous. It's going to blow over. People are just panicking right now. The news always tries to make people panic over this kind of stuff, especially women."

Olivia's jaw nearly hit the floor. "How can you even say that?"

"All I'm saying is that you're overreacting about this—"

"How can you say that when a girl in our own office stopped showing up?" Zach jumped in. "They *still* have no idea where she is, do they, Scott?" His eyes locked with mine.

Everyone else turned to me for my response.

Hannah was my assistant. Of course everyone was looking at me. But there was no fucking way anyone had found her body. But why the fuck was Zach looking at me like that? It was like he knew something else. Was he setting me up? Bringing this up on the spot to see how I would react?

I forced myself to unclench my teeth before speaking. "Not from what I can tell. The police questioned pretty much everyone in the office who knew her, though. Hopefully, nothing serious happened and—"

"Hopefully, she isn't one of this sicko's victims," Olivia said.

Heartbeat thrashing in my ears, I could hardly keep my breathing even.

Someone was catching on. People were reporting on it now. Had someone found a body? Had they found anything? I'd kept everything hidden from Natalie, but what if I hadn't been careful enough to hide a trail that led the authorities straight to the bodies?

"Who's to say there are victims?" Britney countered. "Maybe these girls are just running off."

Olivia scoffed. "I really can't believe you said that, Britney. I expected this from the guys because they are never going to understand the constant fear we're under. They don't understand women because they don't have to worry about the things we do. Not to mention that this sicko is going after blonde chicks, so they really don't have anything to worry about."

Britney shrugged, obviously done with the conversation.

I felt Natalie's stare over her wineglass, which had been dumped for water.

My chest tightened.

"So, there's just someone going around snatching up blondes?" Natalie asked after taking a sip of her water. "I have blonde hair, for Pete's sake."

Even though my love for her was the reason these other women were on the news rather than her, I said, "I won't let anything happen to you."

I went to hug her side but then Caden appeared over Nat's shoulder, somehow patting Loki without rubbing his fur all over his suit. "What are we talking about here?"

"About the disappearances," Olivia said with a side-eye toward Zach.

Britney bristled beside him, her grip on his arm tightening.

Ava appeared on Caden's other side, a frown quickly falling. "I just got here and, already, feel like it's time for another swing by the wine. Nothing good ever comes from watching the news."

I had to find out more.

My eyes darted from Zach to Britney to Natalie and then back to Zach. This couldn't be happening right now. But I felt like Zach's stare hadn't left me. Inhaling a shaky breath, I clenched my hands to stop the raw nerves shooting through me.

I leaned into Natalie to whisper, "I'm going to run to the bathroom. I'll bring you another water on the way back."

She beamed up at me as I moved away. I smiled back at her before slipping through the crowd, surveying the surrounding art.

People were drifting closer to Natalie's work, which would leave her and Caden and Ava distracted for a few minutes. Zach would be wise to stay where the fuck he was, too.

I had to know if the bodies had been found. There was no way to watch the news now, but that couldn't be the only way this was being reported.

Moving through the surrounding people, I kept my eyes on the red *EXIT* sign. I had to be quick. I needed to be back before Natalie questioned where I was. Least of all, I didn't need Zach questioning my whereabouts. I had no idea what made him bring up the missing girls, but I didn't appreciate the look he gave me, either.

My hands balled into fists, I shoved the door open. I barely had time to process the chill before I noticed a line of newspaper boxes out of the corner of my eye. Luckily, the street was empty, but I was out of breath before reaching the street corner. In front of a blue newspaper box, my eyes jumped to each headline until it landed on the article I was looking for.

LAW ENFORCEMENT CONTINUES SEARCHING FOR MISSING WOMEN - POTENTIAL PREDATOR AT LARGE?

My body deflated. Snapping open the yellow box, I snatched the newspaper to read the headline on the way back to the gallery. The article was just some big stupid warning to scare women. The authorities hadn't found the bodies. Authorities were aware of the missing women, but no bodies had been found. There was no point in changing anything now.

chapter thirty-two

NATALIE'S STOMACH ONLY GREW AS the last couple of months of her pregnancy passed. We were pouring everything into the approaching due date. And, because of how close she was to being due, I was home more. The nursery was full of elephant plushies, trinkets, and a crib mobile. We were on track—back to sharing a routine and the same thoughts. We fell asleep beside one another. Nat wrapped around the body pillow I'd bought to help her sleep while I wrapped myself around her. Every night, she fell asleep holding my hand.

But everything was routine.

I did everything she asked. I forced myself to act normal, and a small part of me fell into that pattern. But the other part was still wrestling to the forefront. Not a day went by where I didn't feel robotic. I was distant and slipping farther and farther away with every little thing she did or said that set me off. I never snapped at her. I held my tongue. But I could feel something building. To where my blood would scream to take it out on something.

I loved her.

Even if I felt trapped.

Everything was building, ready to explode. Those feelings needed to go somewhere.

I could never take it out on her.

Whenever anxiety and stress got the best of her, I should've been the one parting those waves trying to crush her. The one holding her above the surface so she could breathe. But I couldn't. I loved her, but I couldn't. I did not have the energy all the time.

I watched over her every day, on edge for her to deliver. The thought made me smile but also sent a sinking feeling through my chest. I didn't know what would change or how much. I couldn't wrap my mind around bringing a baby home. I didn't know what to feel. I didn't know how I felt whenever I looked at Natalie, either.

Everything was slipping out of my control. Too quickly for me to process it. It was easier to let it all happen and grasp whatever power I could have. It wasn't much, but it was the only way I could get out of bed in the mornings without heading straight to the bar.

Eyes wide open, I inhaled a long breath and then forced myself to get out of bed. Natalie had coffee ready and waiting when I walked out of our bedroom dressed and ready for work. Her smile was bright, her belly so gigantic that her pajama shirt barely covered it.

Eyes on her stomach as I made around the counter to her, I said, "You'll call me?"

"You think I want to go into labor without digging my fingernails into your arm?" She stood on her toes to kiss me.

I stood, frozen, as her lips met mine. Then, barely muttering a "Goodbye, I love you," I was out the door.

I did everything she asked. I could force myself to act normal, but it was all done with a vast distance between us. Our connection was lost. Neither of us knew how to get it back, how to lessen the disconnect. That wasn't stopping Natalie from trying to force an emotional reconnection.

She was panicking about how things had changed since telling me about the pregnancy.

I knew Natalie was hurting, and I felt that in the pit of my stomach. But there was only so much I could do.

Behind the wheel, I leaned my head back to close my eyes for the moments I had to spare before I would be late. Feeling like I could blow smoke out of my nose, I forced myself to start the car. Sticking to the ritual I kept to once every couple weeks, I drove past the dead-end road. Thoughts lingered on the debris hiding the decomposing carcass, my breath hot, my body bracing for the twisting in my chest, my tongue soon following.

I could only imagine the smell.

I could only imagine the curves of her decaying body.

Inhaling deep breath after deep breath, I forced my grip on the wheel with shaking hands.

The dead-end was overgrown with vegetation, empty of red-and-blue lights. Hannah's body was still waiting for me, hidden.

Coming to a red light, I dropped my head in my hands as sweat rolled down my forehead. Teeth clamped together, I had to fight the urge to turn and relive driving down that road.

Work. I had to go to work. I couldn't afford to take the time to revisit the slut. My eyes snapped open before my brain could conjure the image of my hands sliding up her decomposing sides until they met her chest.

I shook my head, realizing the light had turned green, when I blinked those images back.

It was getting harder to ignore the urge twisting in my gut.

With every blink, I saw red.

Blood gushed.

Blood dripped down her neck.

Blood streamed, staining my hands.

I wanted to feel that way again. My mouth watered at how she'd struggled. The elation snatched my breath away. I drove to work based on memory and memory alone, reliving every intoxicating moment I'd spent denying her for Natalie. Every small struggle—every advance she made toward me—escalated until I had no choice but to protect my devotion to Natalie.

Eliminate temptation. Eliminate the look-alikes trying to coerce me from my one true Natalie. I needed my way back to her. Could I . . . once everything else was out of the way?

I shook my head. Whether I was removing all risk of losing Natalie, I failed her. There was a chance I could lose her either way. Because I couldn't stop seeing those who were trashy copies of the woman I loved.

None of those women compared to my Natalie. And that was all I could think about most days, wearing down every bit of energy I had until I couldn't even pretend when I went home to her.

I didn't want to lose her, but my grip was slipping.

Pulling into the Pulse Marketing parking lot, I snapped back into myself, stomach dropping and static subsiding. Regret instantly lodged in the pit of my stomach when I realized I'd parked next to Zach. My surroundings came into focus to find him waving from the front of his car.

Fuck.

News about missing girls had quieted, but I still caught Zach watching me from across the office sometimes. Whenever I locked eyes with him, it sent my teeth grinding.

I closed my eyes briefly, shutting out the thoughts screaming at me, before throwing open my door to meet Zach and go on with my day.

Like every night since rededicating my time to Natalie, I left work, weighed down by a constant ringing in my ears. Exhaustion was not enough to subside the fire in my chest. It took everything I had not to drive by the dead-end road, to take a detour to visit what I'd left hidden. Through the struggle of keeping my breathing even, I had to remind myself my pregnant fiancé was waiting for me at home.

When I pulled into the driveway, I didn't give myself the chance to sit and think or even collect myself. I was out from behind the wheel the second the car was in park.

Inhaling a long breath, I balled my unsteady hand before opening the door.

When I walked in, Natalie was sitting at the kitchen counter with her pregnancy books laid out in front of her.

I slowly set my bag down, cautious to know what kind of mood I'd caught her in. "Hey, you."

"I think I've come up with a name for a girl" was Nat's response while I slipped out of my shoes.

I walked into the kitchen. "Oh, yeah? Let's hear it."

She looked up with a fake gasp. "You're expecting it to be stupid, aren't you?"

"Not at all." I kissed her on the head, then pivoted to make my way to the fridge so I could throw together a sandwich.

"Angela."

I dropped salami and provolone over the spicy mustard smeared across the bread on my plate. The final touch was rolling up a couple of slices to shove in my mouth. "Huh."

"You hate it?" Her pinky nail found its way into her mouth.

"Not at all. I just expected something more . . . artistic from you." I smirked, taking a bite out of my spicy salami sub.

Nat glared, her arm dropping from her face. She could barely sit up to the counter, her stomach keeping her practically a foot away.

"Ha. Ha. You're hilarious."

"I'm glad we're on the same page about that." I grinned through another bite. "What about a name for a boy?"

"Oh, god." Natalie put a hand to her forehead. "Could you imagine having a little emo boy running around in a diaper and a boy band T-shirt? Ugh, he'd be just like his daddy."

"You say that as if it's a bad thing." I smacked my chest over my heart. "I take offense. My heart is wounded."

"Hmm, I think you'll recover. At least until the baby's born and then the doctors will have to peel you off the floor to revive you."

She made me smile. Things between us almost felt normal. For a moment.

"So, now you think I'm going to faint in the delivery room?"

"Olivia might've bet money on it."

"Bitch," I muttered.

I walked around the counter to her and stopped behind her to wrap my arms around her. She smelled like strawberries. Just like when we were kids.

Relaxing back into me, she released a heavy sigh.

"What?"

"No matter how things are going, you still hold me like I'm yours."

I kissed the top of her head. "Because you are. Always. To no end."

She looked up at me, my favorite glimmer in her ocean-blue eyes. I should take her to see the ocean one day. Another way to celebrate escaping our old lives. Neither of our families had ever taken us to the beach. Now, we could take our own family.

"To no end?"

"It's just you and me, baby." I trailed kisses down her neck. "Always has been, always will be."

When she turned her cheek, I didn't hesitate to press my lips to hers. Her mouth opened with a sweet breath, her tongue sending electric shocks through my body. Everything screamed for more. I wanted to grab her, yank her to me so that no space was between us, and burrow my way inside her until I was covered in her.

I clenched the counter, pulling back from her to clear my head, blurting out the first thing that didn't involve her skin. "I'm going to buy us another car."

"Oh, is that why you're kissing me like this?"

I shook my head, but my lips never stopped. "No. It's just a bonus."

"Wait, really?" She pulled back to look at me. "You want another car?"

"We're going to have a baby. We need more than one car in case of an emergency. I'm not going to take the car to work every day and leave you and the baby without a way to get around. What if she starts choking? What if she hits her head or gets a fever? I don't want to leave the two of you here without a car."

A wide smile crossed Nat's face. "She?"

"Well, you said it, didn't you? Angela?"

She shrugged. "We'll see. In the meantime, you can get back to kissing me."

"What about a name for a boy?"

I needed another moment.

"Not so confident it's a girl anymore?" she asked, eyebrow cocked.

"I don't care what we have. We're going to be the family we never had."

"We already are." Before I could answer, a smirk spread across her face. "Are you going to go back to kissing me?"

Humming in her ear, I muttered "I have a better idea" before scooping her up from her chair.

"Whoa, whoa, whoa!" Nat laughed. "I am way heavier than I used to—"

"Does it look like I'm having trouble?" I carried her to the bedroom, planting my mouth against every inch of her exposed skin the second I had her on the bed.

Light giggles shook her body. My lips froze between her breasts.

A thrashing body with leaves crushed between smudged red lips.

Warmth sped through my veins.

Inhaling her fragrant skin, I had to remind myself to breathe. Breathe to hold myself back. Breathe to build a wall against those thoughts.

Natalie. I'm with Natalie. My Natalie.

This was Natalie, and she was only giggling.

My body felt like it was lit on fire—like one of those canvases—every second that I battled against the muddled static, refusing to make anyone or anything that wasn't Natalie my prime focus. I couldn't stop all night. Even once Natalie slept peacefully beside me, I had to spend every waking second reminding myself she was pregnant with my child.

chapter thirty-three

LUNCH WAS THE FURTHEST THING from my mind as everyone else left for the new Thai restaurant down the street. Papers were scattered across my desk, many of them stamped with notes of slogans and marketing plans underneath the company logo. As soon as noon rolled around, people started walking past my glass wall from the corner of my eye.

When I declined Zach's offer to carpool with him, he gave me an odd look that caused the hair on the back of my neck to rise, but he didn't get to say anything. Zach quickly left with his intern when he offered to pay for them both. The second he was gone, I blinked against the ringing in my ears, inhaling a long breath to return my focus to the work in front of me.

The ringing and muddled feeling hadn't left me all day. Burying my head in my hands, I pressed my palms into my eyes. No matter what I did or how much ibuprofen I took, I couldn't focus on anything outside the ringing in my ears. Lunch was out of the realm of possibility; I was too behind on work.

But I needed to focus.

My chair hit the wall with the force I used when I jumped out of it. I didn't bother grabbing anything but my keys off the desk. The shitty office coffee wasn't going to be enough. I needed a strong latte to knock out whatever strange procrastination this was.

The parking lot was almost empty by the time I made it out to the Volkswagen. I hooked a few turns before pulling into a nearby neighborhood to stop at the coffee cart. It sat between an apartment complex and office buildings. The guy who ran it was a genius. Zach's fucking smoothies didn't compare to a coffee from the cart. I wish he was my intern. I would've sent his intrusive ass out to get me a latte before letting him go to lunch.

Since graduating, I hardly stopped by anymore because Natalie had time to make coffee before I left for work. Jeremy's Coffee Cart never failed to give me the extra kick I needed to do homework when I got home from interning. It would be just the thing I needed to crank up my motivation. If my head didn't feel close to splitting, I probably would've played Eminem on the way back to the office for a little extra oomph.

With the ringing still loud and clear in my head, I was quick to cross the distance before someone else got in front of me. A couple was waiting to be handed their order while another guy stood, chatting on the phone away from them. Stopping behind him, I didn't need to scan the menu. A few people walked around on phones or were coming home from the grocery store, but it wasn't crowded.

Which was why I froze mid-step when I caught sight of a dog. I was next in line, the guy in front of me ordering and talking on the phone at the same time. I thought the dog was alone until a woman stepped onto the curb from the parking lot and whistled for the dog to come trotting back to her. She hooked a leash to the teal collar around the black lab's throat but barely held onto it as she headed toward the apartments.

Her hair was in a high ponytail, which swayed with her every step. She was dressed in workout clothes, a layer of sweat glistening across her chest. Her sports bra exposed just enough to reveal her bouncing breasts. Her yoga pants were cinched around her ass. The space between these two pieces of clothing showed off her toned torso.

I wanted to pull her waistband down, drag my hands—

"Next!"

My head snapped up, the ringing returning to my ears. Jeremy was at the window, the man in front of me having left already.

"Oh, sorry." I stepped up to the window, pulling out my wallet. "I spaced out. My wife makes fun of me for doing that so often." I forced a smile. "Just a latte, please."

Jeremy grinned as he took my change. "Sounds like your woman is looking after you."

"Yeah." My eyes were still tracking the woman. "Yeah, she does. Can I get two of those lattes?"

Once I had two steaming cups of coffee in my hands, my feet led me in the direction of the woman. I sipped, watching her from over the rim of the lid. I thought she would have looked back, but she never did. Her dog didn't even seem to be aware I was trailing them, either.

Watching her walk into the main entrance of the apartment complex, I focused on her thin hips. They did nothing special, had no extra sway to them. But the curve of her side was almost an invitation. I wanted to grab the warm skin there and force her close. I missed pulling Natalie close like that. I let the coffee burn my tongue, forcing the image of her coy smile to leave me.

Keeping a good distance back, I watched her lead her dog inside the apartment's main entrance. When she pressed a fob against the keypad at the door, I gripped the coffee intended for her.

I would not let her out of my sight.

Inside, a maintenance man was vacuuming the rugs outside the elevators. He looked up when I tapped on the glass door with my coffee, gesturing to the closing elevator doors. She had disappeared inside, the dial keeping track of each floor she passed.

"My girlfriend forgot I don't have my keys," I told the maintenance man through the glass.

He looked back at the elevator that had shut. When he looked back at me, he still seemed unsure, but he turned off the vacuum, which I took as a good sign.

Awkwardly fumbling with the cups in my hands, I flashed a sheepish smile and shrugged to let him know that, even if I had my keys, I wouldn't have the coordination to unlock the door or hook one of my full hands through the handle to open it.

The dial indicated the woman had stopped at the sixth floor.

The bastard needed to move.

I needed to make it to her apartment.

Finally, the prick made his way to the door and yanked it open with a grimace.

"Thank you" was all I said as I brushed past him for the elevator.

As the doors were closing shut, the vacuum turned on again.

I slouched against the back wall, keeping my head downcast for the cameras. My hands were sticking to the cup sleeves, but nothing beat out of the ordinary. My breaths were easy. The ringing in my ears was gone. Instead, unease rushed to my fingertips. My body was anything but at ease.

Two coffees. It had taken two lattes to get into the building.

The elevator doors dinged open.

The jangling of keys snagged my focus.

"Wait. You dropped this. I just—my hands, they're full—"

The woman looked up from the door, eyes shooting to me in surprise while her dog stepped back to glance around her. Her keys were paused in the door. "Ye—"

I had reached her within a few strides, forcing her inside.

I felt and heard her gasp.

The sound sent a wave of pins and needles down the back of my neck.

Both coffees fell to the floor.

I kicked the dog into the bathroom on the left, swiftly shutting the door before it could lunge. Once the door muffled the mongrel's barking, I turned to the girl.

Her eyes were wide with fear, but she didn't scream. Instead, as if meeting my eyes had released her from shock, she shoved off the wall to make for the kitchen. She didn't look back. Like an idiot. I slammed into her when she reached the knife block, wrestling her hands away from it and over her head.

Her back hit the cabinets, and I hoped it wasn't loud enough to alert anyone.

She released a gasped sob against my hand, eyes wide with terror, but she didn't stop trying to wrestle her hands free. I removed the space between us, pinning her to the cabinets. Though my knee and thigh were between her legs, I kept my face away from hers to take in her every expression—to see every question swimming in her glassy eyes. She thrashed harder at the lack of space between our bodies, panicking at her vulnerability.

Time felt so slow, but everything was happening within a matter of seconds. The frenzied pulse of my heart was the only thing grounding me.

She slammed herself back into the cabinets to make noise with what little force she had.

Ignoring the knives in front of us, I pulled her away from the wall of cabinets. The kitchen floor was the last place I wanted to be. I wanted her defenseless, not surrounded by knives, pots and pans, and whatever else she could turn into a weapon.

While she flailed, I pulled her into the bedroom—to the carpet, where she couldn't make so much noise. I didn't mind the struggle so long as it didn't draw attention.

Shoving her onto the bed, I wrapped my hands around her neck within the same second the image of her pale face and lips crossed my mind. She would look like that soon enough. With my hands bearing down on her neck, she wriggled her hands free from our bodies, throwing them between us.

The moment she had me off balance, she scrambled for the edge of the bed, gasping. Her eyes were on the bedroom doors—her only way out.

"What do you want?" she did her best to yell, her voice strained from the pressure I'd placed on her throat.

I swung around, my arms flinging to grasp her waist and throw her back onto the center of the bed. She cried out, which was cut short when my hands were on her neck again. The dog in the bathroom barked louder.

Her skin was soft and decadent, leaving me convinced she had some skincare routine. I wished I could have shared this woman's beauty routine with Natalie. My mouth watered as I thought of Natalie's skin feeling so soft beneath my palms.

My hands tightened around her before I used one to grab her hand. Slamming her wrist into the covers, I pressed my knee against her palm.

"If you don't quit that," I gritted in her ear, "your neighbors are going to think we're up to something kinky."

Her mouth opened as if she were screaming. She had no air. Meanwhile, my own breath hissed through clenched teeth.

Once I did the same with her other flailing hand, she was entirely exposed to me. I breathed her in, my nose brushing along the soft skin of her neck. Lilacs and something too refined for me to know emanated from her. Natalie never wore stuff like that, even when she had a night at the gallery. Yet, this woman had just come back from a run with her dog and had sprayed herself with perfume beforehand.

The woman's chest trembled beneath me, either from fear or her desperation for air. Then, slowly, my tongue followed the same trail.

She was salty with sweat.

She winced back into the covers.

When I looked up, Natalie's face stared back at me, her blue eyes wide with disbelief as her lips lost color. Her hands strained against my knees, body thrashing from its lack of air. I froze above her, staring down into her eyes as the awareness in them faded.

The panic had left them, and the fight was leaving her body. My grip tightened, my pants feeling more and more restricted. Knees digging into the mattress on either side of her, I didn't wait for death to take her before I unbuttoned my jeans.

Looking down into the pale face, I saw Natalie. She was beautiful. White as snow. She was mine. I had to have her. Fingertips stroking her lips, I caressed their pale rim with a scoff. I was nothing without her. Long after the woman stopped struggling, I stayed on top of her, stripping her, running my hands over her, grabbing and sliding against her.

She felt like velvet.

chapter thirty-four

THE FUCKING DOG WAS STILL going fucking nuts. The bathroom door shook every time the mutt clawed at or slammed himself against the door. Not one complaint was made, and no one knocked on the door. To everyone else in this complex, he was acting like any lonely, sad dog who missed their owner.

But she was dead in her bed.

And I had a feeling he could sense it.

Still, I took my time with her. And then I took my time lying beside her, running my hand along her thigh and over the curve of her hip until I reached her lips. Her white complexion reminded me of the guy who had overdosed. Except I wondered what her skin—cold and pale—would feel like against my tongue. But rigor mortis had finally set in, leaving her as of no use to me.

When I got up to put my clothes on, my gaze wandered to her dresser. At first, I reached for the top drawer in search of panties but then I caught sight of a carton of cigarettes. The hair on my arms rose to point at the ceiling as warmth, like smoke, flooded through me. I flicked open the carton to find it half full. Every nerve ending was on fire, even before I brought a cigarette to my mouth.

But having the cigarette in my mouth wasn't enough.

I rushed from the bedroom, scrambling around until I found a lighter beside a candle.

As I lit the tip, I stood in the living room, facing the kitchen. The candle scent was freshly cut cedar. It was unlit, resting on the coffee table. A pot of succulents sat beside it. A glass of water adjacent. Then I closed my eyes to savor the first drag I'd had in years. Smoke ran along the roof of my mouth, seething down my throat, until it filled my lungs.

I pulled from the cigarette until I couldn't.

For the first time in a long time, I watched the white paper burn. I could almost picture the train tracks. Gravel, railroads, high walls, and graffiti replacing the luxury apartment before my eyes. I felt the same hunger for smoke, inhaling my lungs with grime for the first time in years.

I shook those images away.

Pacing the room, I wandered from one drawer to the next. I wasn't looking for anything in particular this time. I'd found all I needed. The carton of cigarettes was burning a hole in my front pocket. Instead, I rummaged through each drawer, tossing things out here and there, then got bored.

Turning, I faced the bedroom and the bitch lying still. I wished her dog was in the same fucking condition. But maybe leaving the dog alive would lead it to rip her corpse to pieces. Within strides, I was in the kitchen with the knife block in front of me. Ironic how she had tried to use it on me, only for me to be the one standing here now.

I could see myself running the edge of the blade along her collarbone, down her chest, until her breasts were covered in thin bloody cuts. From there, I would only travel lower. The fresh meat would drive the mutt mad.

Before I could reach for a knife in the block, my phone rang from my back pocket.

Closing my eyes, I took another drag from the cigarette between my teeth before I flipped open the phone. Natalie's caller ID was plastered on the front screen. Answering wasn't a choice.

"Scott?" Nat groaned out the second the phone was against my ear. My heart lurched. The cigarette fell from my fingers, and I ground it into the kitchen floor until only a dead bud and black soot remained. Then, before I could say anything, she was gasping. "Ow. Ow. Ow. Okay, shit, ow."

My grip on the phone tightened, my eyes wide open. She sounded panicked.

"What? What?"

Static slamming into the walls I'd built up with full force, I lost all ability to breathe and move.

Fuck.

Fuck! Not a miscarriage. No—

"Shit." It was time? It was time. "Shit, are you serious? Are you okay? What do I need to do?"

I moved into the bedroom before Nat heard the dog barking. Running a hand down my face, I wanted to remove every bit of skin and muscle.

She let out a breathless laugh. Not an ounce of humor was behind it, though. "Help me. Call an ambulance."

Adrenaline was pounding through me, and she sounded so delicate.

"I can't remember the last time you cursed."

"I'm in pain. I have zero control over what comes out of my mouth right now."

Glancing down, I took in every curve of the paling body on the bed. Walking out of the room took everything in me. Walking out of the apartment took even more. Especially when I snuck past the bathroom.

"Censorship isn't exactly a priority, got it."

Someone would find her eventually, and it would look like a tragic break-in when they did.

Rather than taking the elevator and losing signal, I raced down the stairs. I was out the exit and in my car within minutes, keeping Natalie breathing on the other line before and after I called for an ambulance.

All I could hope for was getting to the hospital at the same time as her.

Fuck. I wanted to pull out another cigarette. The carton felt like a weight in my pocket.

"Where are you?" I asked her as I sped down the road. "What are you doing right now?"

The other line filled with the sound of Natalie breathing, straining against the pain.

"Well, I was in bed when my water broke, so those sheets are nasty now," she said once she'd composed herself. "I'm kind of slumped on the couch right now."

"The ambulance will be there soon."

I wasn't sure which of us I was trying to convince more. Even though everything out my window rushed by, I felt like I was driving as slow as a goddamned snail.

"Did you tell anyone you were leaving the office, or did you just run out like a madman?" she gasped out.

"Fuck 'em. We're having a baby. They can load me up with all the paperwork they want."

She groaned on the other line. Meanwhile, I was passing cars whenever I felt like the Volkswagen could take it. I ignored every bastard who flipped me off. No one would ruin this for me. No one would stand between me and getting to the hospital before Natalie. I would get to her in time.

"Um, so do I need to worry about my hand during labor?" I asked, looking for a way to distract her.

"I might be small, but I'm about to pop a baby out of me, so I'd be worried about every bone in your body if I were you."

Sirens blared in the background, and I knew I could race to the hospital rather than home. If the ambulance hadn't shown up when it did, I likely would have headed straight home for her.

"So, I might check myself into the hospital after this."

"Don't be a smart-ass."

Blood pumped through my veins. Tension made me almost hyperaware of every tick and jolt of my body.

Staying on the road was all I could zero in on.

"Are you okay?" I asked when Nat let out another long groan.

Natalie groaned the entire way from the couch and to the door. "Oh, yep, totally. Our child is just trying to wreck me like a wrecking ball."

"I'm scared," I whispered.

I could barely breathe. I was barely processing through the static.

"Me too." Nat groaned again. "I cannot believe this is happening right now. We were *just* talking about names the other night, and now it's happening? Oh, my god. It's happening. Not to be cheesy, but holy shit, the baby's coming."

I stepped on the gas, not giving a damn if a cop tried to pull over our Volkswagen Bug piece of shit.

Pacing closer and then away from Natalie, I had no clue where to stand, what to do with my hands, whether I should step back or be right by Natalie's side. My pockets were empty of things to fidget with, since I'd stuffed the cigarette carton in the glove box before coming in. I'd have to find another hiding spot later. For now, Natalie wouldn't find it. She was already propped up in a hospital bed, her head thrown back over a pile of pillows, her hands on either side of her belly.

"Is this happening? I can't believe this is actually happening."

Natalie was rambling. Breathing through her teeth was enough to tell me that she'd put me six feet under if I made so much as the slightest joke for the next several hours.

The nurse laughed. "Ah, the words of every first-time mother." She smoothed Nat's hair back once she was hooked up to all the machines. "You're doing great, so don't worry. The doctor will be along soon."

"Soon as in right this very second." An older man in a navy scrubs and a white coat walked up behind the nurse. He smiled at Natalie, gray scruff perking up with the grin as he took in the both of us. "Hi, folks, I'm Dr. Shetfield. How are we doing in here?"

He shook my hand and smiled at Natalie so she could stay relaxed. Or as relaxed as she could be, at least.

Her head lulled toward the doctor. "Please tell me this isn't going to take forever."

Fuck, she was a sexy, sweaty mess, and she was about to have our baby. My heart dropped into my stomach again. She was having our baby.

"Are you okay, love?" Natalie asked me through a long painful breath. "You look like you're going to be sick."

Dr. Shetfield chuckled deeply. "I've had more than a father or two pass out in the delivery room in my time."

I shook my head, trying to stifle the feeling threatening to crawl up from the pit of my stomach. "Yeah. Yeah, I'm fine. It just—hit me is all."

Nat let out a laugh. "It just hit you that I'm pregnant?"

My head was swimming.

"Now's about the time that it feels real for us fathers," Dr. Shetfield said with another chuckle. "I know it only started to feel real on the drive to the hospital."

"He freaked out about me lifting a box when we were moving, so I just thought it would've felt real a little *soonerrrr*." Her groan was the longest, most brutal she'd let out. "Shit. Oh my god, oh my god, I feel like I need to push. Right now."

My heart plummeted to my stomach. Swallowing back everything turning over in my stomach, I was at Nat's side before she finished calling out. She released her grip on the scratchy hospital sheets to turn her tight grasp on my arm.

Dr. Shetfield glanced up from checking on Natalie. "Well, it better feel real now because it looks like you're having a baby right this very second."

I removed her nails from my arm to hold her hand, letting her squeeze as hard as she needed to. The urge to pull her into me—to take her pain—washed over me. In that instant, I felt tied to her. The piece missing between us snapped into place. This was the blue-and-pink-streak-haired girl I met on the train tracks years ago, the girl I'd jumped into a rundown Volkswagen Bug with after setting fire to my dad's piece-of-shit chair, the girl who'd helped push me through college, who I burned down the world for.

And she was about to have our baby.

My heart pounded in my ears, doing flips in my chest, like I was a teenager.

Nat threw her head back in laughter when she saw the look on my face. "I think you better start telling my husband to breathe before he passes out."

The doctor laughed while I was hung up on one word that'd left her mouth.

"Husband, huh?" Hyperaware of the distance between us, I ignored the churn in my stomach and the weakness in my knees, then moved in closer to her.

Eyes meeting mine, she smiled up at me. "Oh, shut up. I'm busy giving birth here."

My life had been turned upside down. A tiny defenseless baby boy was cradled in the crook of my arm. He was so small, while his eyelashes were massive. He had a decent head of hair on him, too. I stared down at him as if he held all the answers, fidgeting around the room with him in my arms. If Natalie wasn't beaming from her pile of pillows and IVs, I would've accused my eyes of lying. I would've assumed that—as Nat liked to remind me—I had "zoned out" too far and that everything around me was made up.

He was too perfect.

"Isn't he?"

My head snapped up to meet Natalie's beaming gaze. "Did I say that out loud?"

"He is perfect, though, isn't he?" Even sweaty and exhausted, she was still beaming. "I never thought I could feel this much. My love is already so strong—stronger than anything I've ever felt."

I know what I feel is already stronger than anything I've ever felt for you. I couldn't take my eyes off our son, even to look at her. From the moment I saw him, I knew I would crawl through broken glass, cut off my right leg, drive a knife into my own stomach to protect him. I would let the world inflict whatever pain it wanted if it meant he were protected.

I would do anything for our perfect baby boy. Every bit of tension in my body thrived with this certainty. I would be the father my dad never was—the father my dad never would've come close to.

"His hair is too light to be like mine," I pointed out, "but it isn't exactly blonde, either."

Nat smiled, reaching up to ask for him. My jaw tensed when my heart cramped at the thought of letting him go. Inhaling a long breath through my nose, I slowly placed him into her waiting arms.

It wasn't like I could tell her no.

Staring down at our bundle, she lightly combed his hair to the side. I almost couldn't believe it when the nurses cleaned him up. He had much more hair than either of us expected. "He's the perfect combination. It might change, too, as he gets older."

"Hopefully, he's like his mom through and through."

She turned her smile to me. She hadn't stopped since they placed him in her arms. "You don't mean that."

"You're the love of my life. Of course I mean it," I said before kissing the top of her head.

That was the moment he yawned and cracked open his eyes. My chest felt like it was expending; my focus was on him and only him.

Nat gasped. "Hi, Desmond. Oh, gosh, look at you. Your daddy is so right. You're too perfect." She glanced up at me, tears in her eyes but still smiling.

I could feel my own hot tears forming.

"Are you sure we'll be okay to go home tomorrow?"

Reaching back above her shoulder, she placed a hand against my cheek, her voice trembling with tears. "We'll be just fine. Everything's ready. We're ready. We already have his room set up and waiting for him. He's going to be a happy and healthy baby."

"You sure?" I asked, leaning into her warm hand.

"Yes. We're a family, and we've got to start acting like it sometime. If the doctor's saying that it's time to go home, it's going to be okay."

I'd wreck the fucking world if the bogus doctor was wrong.

Desmond was ours.

chapter thirty-five

AFTER SPENDING ABOUT TWO DAYS at the hospital, our home felt eerily quiet when we opened the front door to introduce Desmond to his new home. Natalie sighed before stepping inside in first. She went around to flick the lights on. Lying awake in his carrier with an elephant blanket tucked in around him, Desmond gawked up at me.

Surprisingly enough, he was just as silent as the house. To where I worried if we'd taken him from the doctors and nurses too early.

As Natalie turned on lights and quietly fussed over how things looked, I made my way to the living room. I carefully set Desmond's carrier beside the couch before Natalie and I tiptoed around the house. Even without the blanket tucked around him, the carrier seemed to swallow Desmond. And the car seat weighed more than he did. We'd been excited to bring him home, but another night in the hospital might not have hurt. Just to be safe.

"He's so . . . small," I whispered when Natalie came up beside me. The longer I stared down at him, the more I wanted to feel him in my arms again. He would be safer cradled than in the carrier. "Where's the handbook on keeping a baby alive?"

Natalie eased back into the couch, closing her eyes, while mine were locked on Desmond. "I wish there were blueprints or some kind of instruction manual. I mean, they do for the most part with 'this is how you change a diaper,' 'this is how you should feed your baby,' and 'this is everything you should check for when they cry.' I am just as clueless as you are. Lucky us, right?"

I sat beside her on the edge of the couch. Desmond's tiny lids started to droop. When I looked at Natalie, she was sunken into the cushions and huffed with her arms crossed over her stomach. Her breathing shallow and even, her body was spent.

"You're exhausted," I murmured, touching her shoulder. "Why don't you head to bed? I'll take care of Desmond."

Natalie let out a small grumble, waving to lazily brush my hand from her shoulder. I jumped up, taking her hand to help her up. She peeked up at me as I brought her to her feet and guided her down the hall. Once in our bedroom and in a large T-shirt, Natalie wrapped herself in a burrito with the blanket. She was out again the second her head hit the pillow.

With her hair laid out behind her, she looked peaceful.

The longer I watched over her, the more the image of Natalie blurred.

For a moment, twigs and dirt were lumped through her blonde locks. Blankets faded into tree trunks and debris, leaving the blonde figure buried.

I watched her until a tightening in my chest had me rushing back to the living room. The tension eased when my eyes landed on Desmond. With his eyes closed and his mouth parted, I carefully lifted him from the carrier. Chin to chest, I held him close. An overwhelming sense of love and affection washed over me.

In the living room, we stared at each other for what seemed like forever before he gave up again and let his eyes fall shut. I couldn't move. I couldn't tear my eyes from him. The longer I stared, the more I wanted to keep him close—the more I wanted to protect him.

Desmond was my son. My entire world. And there were no boundaries—no line I wouldn't cross for him.

When I finally pulled myself out of the trance enough to make for the nursery, he was snug in my arms. It took everything I had to place him in the crib. I draped his blanket on the side of the bars, but he still had his circus-themed onesie on. Then, like his mother, he instantly fell asleep.

Placing my hands on the top rung of the crib, I inhaled a deep breath. Natalie had mentioned something about a new baby smell at the hospital, but all I was reminded of was fresh paint.

My hands tightened around the rung.

I woke up to neglect. Cooing crackled from the monitor. Two weeks of sleep deprivation hit me at once. Rolling onto my stomach to bury my face in Natalie's pillow, I stiffened when I didn't find her in the bed next to me. I had left her in the nursery. With Desmond, which was where the sounds were coming from.

Sitting up on my elbows made my head swim.

That was when Desmond's babbling erupted into wails and massive tears. Gritting my teeth, I shot out of bed. Natalie was in the nursery with him, and she wasn't doing anything to comfort him. Despite being half awake, I felt my way from the room, blinking against the pounding in my ears. He clearly needed something. And his mother wasn't doing a damned thing about it.

My shoulder caught the doorframe on the way out. Barreling into the nursery, I swallowed back the hiss threatening to slip through my teeth.

Natalie flinched awake from the rocking chair when I stormed into the room, heading straight for the crib. She blinked, taking in the strain of my muscles and veins. I stared at her groggy expression, careful to keep my distance from her to focus on Desmond.

"I think he's awake," she mumbled.

"You think?" When I reached down into the crib, Desmond's face was beet red from crying. "I got him."

The size of his tears always caught me off guard; they seemed too big for such a small body. Before he was even in my arms, I felt tethered to him. I couldn't shake the awe I felt whenever I looked at him—whenever I realized he was mine. My son.

The tension in my body uncoiled the moment I picked him up. He felt and looked so small and fragile in my hands.

"I hope that feeling never goes away," Nat said. "The one where we look at him, and we just feel so much love. It makes me seriously wonder how our parents could do all those things to us growing up."

"My theory is that he's cuter than we ever were."

My voice had lost its gruffness with her.

Natalie's smile turned into a scowl. "Not funny."

She sat at the edge of the rocking chair, holding the blanket around herself for warmth.

"We'll be better parents than ours ever were," she said. "Than they ever thought about being."

Desmond bawled, probably sick of hearing us talk instead of trying to figure out what he needed.

"We have examples of what *not* to do, but we still have no clue what we're doing."

Nat sighed. "I have a feeling it's only going to get harder before we have a routine."

Desmond sniffled before letting out another shriek. Adjusting him into the crook of my arm, I gently rocked him.

"It's been a couple of weeks now. I miss sleep."

"You're telling me. At least your boobs aren't sore twenty-four-seven."

"Maybe I could help with that. A massage probably sounds really nice right now, no?"

Desmond wailed louder.

Natalie got up, wrapping the blanket around herself to take him from my arms. Smiling, she said, "Nah, I don't think so. I'm a new mom. The luxury of massages is gone." Desmond fussed louder, his face swollen with impatience. "Probably for the next eighteen years."

Scooping him from my hold, she unwrapped his swaddle and put him on the changing table. I stepped forward to watch his arms shoot up like he was at a rock concert. We laughed. All he needed was a lighter.

"He's the cutest fucking burrito I've ever seen."

Nat smiled, responding with, "Are you ready to learn how to change him?"

My heart dropped. "He's just so small. I don't want to break him."

Nat laughed, and Desmond stared up at his mother, almost as awestruck by her as we both were by him. "He's not a butterfly wing, Scott."

"Still!"

"You're going to have to wipe his ass eventually. At least just watch me. I'm going to make you do it next time—face your irrational fear of crushing our child."

We kept poking fun at each other, pointing out every feature we thought came from one other, while Natalie changed him. Desmond lay there quietly, staring up at us with the big blue eyes that matched his mother's. He had her ocean-blue eyes, but he had my dark hair and narrow nose. The biggest surprise was that he had Natalie's gentle smile. So much of her in him sent my heart soaring. His smile shot through me the same way Natalie's did, compelling me to do anything for him.

"All right, you're almost done," I said. "How about I trade you? I can go make some breakfast while you finish up with him."

"Hmm. That might seem like a fair trade, but only if bacon is involved."

"You got it." I gave her a peck on the cheek before heading for the kitchen.

Once everything was sizzling on the stove, I thought about going to grab the paper, but I was lazy, and yesterday's was already on the counter. I brushed aside the wedding magazines scattered across the counter and found it. With eggs cooking behind me, I shifted through the pages, not giving a shit about sports or inaccurate weather reports.

My heart dropped when I caught a large black headline out of the corner of my eye.

WOMAN'S BODY FOUND BY KIDS PLAYING IN LOCAL WOODS

Everything in my body sank. Everything in the room, including myself, becoming distant. Pulling the newspaper closer, I couldn't stop staring at the black text. I couldn't even stomach the thought of reading the article. My brain was too clouded, making everything harder to digest.

How many fucking people have seen this? Did Natalie see this? It was under the sports page. Maybe she hadn't gotten to it yet. She's been too busy adjusting to mom life to do anything more than glance at the headlines. It wouldn't matter if she did. There was no way to tie it back to me. The slutty assistant had to be drastically decomposed by now. She wasn't even identified. I didn't see her name anywhere in the article.

Shutting the paper, crumbling its edges, I buried the article in the trash can. I threw every abandoned paper towel on the counter on top. Then I'd burned the first egg I'd dropped, so it went on top, too. The yolk ran over everything until the page was unreadable.

I couldn't afford to think about that—about Hannah or any other thrown-away body. It was done. I wasn't responsible for them anymore. I was responsible for my family—for being as good a dad as I could be to Desmond. That was what I had to focus on now. Natalie needed me to make her breakfast, and we would spend the rest of Sunday together before they were left alone when I had work tomorrow.

Still, the headline burned in the back of my mind for the rest of the day.

chapter thirty-six

WAKING IN AN EMPTY BED, I knew Natalie wasn't there without reaching across the sheets to search her side. Natalie was almost glued to the nursery, reluctant to leave Desmond's side. Part of it was due to her paranoia of something happening to him while away, but mostly her awe kept her there. Sometimes, I could convince her to leave the rocking chair to come to bed with me, while other times, I got sucked in to watching him sleep. Natalie and I would sit on the floor together, whispering in disbelief. Sometimes, it felt like there wasn't much of a point going to bed when he'd just wake us up crying every couple of hours.

There were also nights like these where Natalie snuck out of bed to take care of him. I didn't take the time to glance at the clock. I was out of bed and down the hall to the nursery within seconds. My chest felt tight. I had to make sure they were okay.

The door was cracked, and Nat was sitting in the middle of the floor, eyes drooping, as she ran her fingers through the carpet. Airy, tranquil music chimed from the CD player on the shelf. Desmond seemed to still be swaddled in his crib, sound asleep, thanks to the lullaby.

She looked up at me when she noticed the door opened and whispered, "What are you doing up?"

"What are you doing awake in the middle of the floor?"

She smiled, turning to look through the rungs of the crib. "I can't sleep. He doesn't sleep much, and when he does . . ." She shook her head. "He's perfect."

I sat beside her, leaning my shoulder against hers to playfully knock into her. "I know. We made that."

"Wouldn't it be perfect if he was the right combination of you and me?"

I followed her gaze to the crib. Not even eight weeks old yet, he was still so small.

"I have the perfect nickname for him," I told her without taking my eyes off him.

He was swaddled in the circus blanket I'd picked out for him weeks ago, long lashes casting shadows over his smooth, chubby cheeks.

"A nickname?" Nat whispered in excitement. "I hadn't thought of that!"

"Dezzy. I think it fits him."

Nat gasped, leaning back to rest against my chest as she beamed up at me. "That's perfect! How did you think of it?"

I shrugged. "No clue. If you had asked me if there was a way to shorten Desmond without just calling him 'D,' I would've said no way." I chuckled quietly. "It just . . . it's him."

"It is. Gosh, Scott. I just can't believe it. This—that he's ours. I can't stop staring at him."

"I know. I've been mulling over nicknames since we decided on a name. I'd always thought it would be cool to have a nickname, but there's no way to shorten 'Scott.'"

"I could start calling you 'Scout' or 'Scottie.' Oh! Or 'Scooter'!"

I scowled. "I'd never do anything you asked me anytime you used it."

She pushed away from me, turned to me, and crawled into my lap. With her knees digging into the rug, she straddling my lap. Her arms were draped over my shoulders, a massive smile on her face. I loved how often she smiled lately. "You call me 'Nat' all the time."

"I've been calling you that for years." My heart pounded in my ears, blood pumping through my entire body, as I placed my hands on her waist. "You can't tell me you hate it now. It's too late. You're my Nat."

Rolling her eyes, she said, "You just made me sound like a bug."

I shook my head, leaning forward to press myself against her. I took in her head, her smell, the feel of her chest against mine—she was so delicate and smooth in my hands.

"But you're mine."

A spark in her eyes, she rocked her hips against me. My mind spiraled, erupting in flames.

"And I'm yours."

I barely heard her reply.

"I mean, you're kinda stuck at this point," I said, nodding to the crib.

Hands dug into her hips, my chest rising and falling, my lungs were about to give out. My control was slipping with every breath. She was mine. She was perfect. And I wanted her. I wanted to feel her hips move against me, wanted to feel her skin slide against mine, wanted to grab at every part of her body—right this second. Until we were one. Or I would explode.

"That's just awful to hear," she teased before pressing her mouth to mine.

Not an inch separated our bodies.

"Fuck, Nat," I breathed in the moment our lips pulled away before returning for more.

Thousands of images exploded behind my eyelids.

A caved-in face pulled back from a car door smeared with blood.

Natalie's lips caressed mine, forceful and open, her tongue warm.

The touch of a cold body enveloped me, feeling like velvet.

Nat rubbed against me, hips rocking into mine.

Body parts scattered across blood-smeared tarp.

Nat opened herself to me, letting me push her off of me to climb on top of her.

Bones ground to dust. Bones plastered all around us.

Decomposition inside a barrel, where all of it would stay.

Caging Natalie below me, I stripped her of her clothes. She tore my shirt over my head but paused when she hooked her fingers into the waist of my pants. She pulled back with a gasp, placing a hand on my bare chest, over my pounding heart. I blinked, shaking my head to clear it until the images fell away and Natalie came into focus again.

"I'm not sure I'm ready to have another one of those," she said, nodding to the crib as I'd done.

"I don't—"

"I stuffed a few in the second to last drawer." She glanced above us, at the bookshelf, and the set of drawers at the bottom.

"What? You were expecting this? In here?"

She threw her head back in laughter. "What better way to use the nursery?"

"Fuck, I love you." I kissed her one last time before jumping up to search the drawers.

Back on top of her, I removed the rest of the clothing in our way, then pinned her between my arms. Her smirk sent a thrill racing down my spine.

From the moment I slid inside her, I was aware of how different she felt from the woman in the apartment. My body braced and tensed above her. I couldn't hold back the images whenever I shut my eyes. Natalie moaned, opening wider as she arched against me. I froze with a grimace, shuddering above her. My thoughts wouldn't turn off. She was warm and tight but not enough. Flashes of memories raced through my core.

I felt myself rock into her fully, but my mind was somewhere else, comparing every thrust to another time and place. Natalie only returned any force I used against her, digging her nails into my back. I stifled a flinch at her touch. It wasn't right. She was squirming beneath me, but she wasn't fighting. She shouldn't be touching me.

Needing her to be still, I grabbed her hands before they could stroke my back. A small sound escaped her when I fixed her wrists to the carpet. Withdrawing and returning, harder, seeking more of her, none of it was enough. It wasn't the same. She still writhed beneath me. She moaned and strained against my grip. She didn't fight back. She didn't cry. Life flashed in her eyes instead of distress.

Every thrust sent a jolt curling up my shins and into the base of my spine.

It wasn't what I wanted, but it would do.

Ignoring the arch of her back, the strain of her hands against my fists, and the sounds she released, I focused on the tick of the clock on the wall behind us. In time, with each rock of my hips, I imagined Natalie lying still below me, rigor mortis stiffening her body.

Urgency drove my hips harder, faster, forcing myself deeper, as I dug my thumbs into the curves of her hips. Her hips still jutted out like they did when we were kids, defined over her low-rise jeans. The arc of her pelvis was solid beneath my touch. Shutting my eyes, I focused on the feel of her bone there, pressing into her harder as I leaned into her taut skin.

She gasped under me, the sound resembling that of a last breath.

I shuddered above her. I didn't roll onto my back.

I pulled away from her, my body sagging, completely detached. The only thing I could think about now was sneaking out of the house for a smoke.

When she looked back at me, my own blank stare reflected from her glazed gaze. My face and the moonlight gleamed in her questioning eyes. She sat up and followed me as I moved away. I didn't gather my clothes. I didn't look down at her. I didn't look her in the eye at all.

Sensing my sudden distance, she leaned back with a smirk, exposing herself to me further rather than covering up.

"You coming to bed?" I asked her.

Predatory bumps rose along my skin. It felt weird to speak. She was sitting up but still in a vulnerable position on the floor.

Her intense gaze flickered across my face, trying to read me, before falling down the length of my body. She settled on my eyes longer than any other part of me, waiting for me to meet hers. But I never did.

Breaking from her further, I made for the door without waiting for her answer.

"Are you okay? Is something wrong?" she whispered in the dark.

Pain stabbed at my stomach before my heart slowly dropped to the floor. I stopped in the doorway, still unable to meet her eyes. I couldn't let myself fixate on her.

"Yeah."

"Okay, well, I'm going to stay here for tonight," she told me, her voice quiet against the darkness.

Her words didn't match the look in her eyes.

I nodded, closing the door behind me.

chapter thirty-seven

EARLY-MORNING HOURS. LUKEWARM BOTTLES. Countless diapers.

Our lives revolved around Dezzy.

Exhausted didn't even come close to describing how Nat and I felt. Staying up well into the morning to write an essay for a class didn't even come close. I felt more tired than I ever thought possible.

Yet, we were getting along more than we'd ever been.

Every morning began before my alarm went off to get me up for work. Natalie would either groan from the rocking chair or into her pillow beside me. One of us would roll out of bed to take care of Dezzy, while the other turned off the useless alarm clock before it rang. Then we would switch.

This strange routine of ours sufficed, and I always had plenty of time to get ready for work. I didn't want to go until Natalie took a shower because I knew she wouldn't leave Dezzy alone to take one, and taking one together wasn't an option anymore.

I missed seeing Nat's long sleek legs. Sweatpants, a stained T-shirt, and unshaved legs were her new-mom uniform. I always gave her time to get ready and do her hair in the morning, but it was always up in a messy bun by the time I got home.

She'd gone from being covered in paint splatter to being covered in Dezzy's spit.

Shoving a lit cigarette between my lips, I briefly wondered if she felt restless being home with the baby all the time, without the outlet of painting.

A lot of restless things were building up for both of us.

Every day—every single damned day, I had to swallow the urge to drive by the dead-end road. She wasn't there anymore. She wasn't mine anymore. She was gone. I'd hidden Hannah well but not well enough to keep pesky kids from stealing her from me. Right from under my nose.

Weeks had gone by, but not one cop had shown up to question anyone in my office. I prepared for it every morning I drove to work, but my workday always dragged the same. Pulse Marketing was the only link Hannah's body had back to me. But still, nothing exciting ever threw a wrench in my day.

Aside from Zach. I was tired of looking up from a measly task to find him staring at me from a cubicle. We talked less and less, but he still kept an eye on me.

The more time that went on, the more I thought about what could happen. Of what I might have to do if Zach kept this up. I kept my distance for now, but I couldn't shake the feeling that he knew something or that he was watching me.

That didn't stop me from thinking about what I'd done to Hannah. Replaying every second I could remember. From the feel of her soft inner thighs under my calloused hands to the pelting of cold raindrops against warm blood. Thoughts of the woman from the liquor store rose with it. Followed by the one still dead in her apartment.

With each arising memory, a shiver stalked down my spine.

I had to shove those thoughts and images into the back of my mind whenever I was at my desk or at home.

At home, pushing back those thoughts and images was easier. Everything was easier to ignore. It wasn't quiet like the office. I had an entire room to myself at work, while Desmond's cries didn't give me room to think. Just seeing him made everything easier to block out. Whenever he stared up at me with Natalie's eyes, everything all built up from the day disappeared in an instant. Everything was easier to ignore, even Natalie.

Blocking out those thoughts was nearly impossible otherwise.

Needing a change—desperate for a change of scenery whenever I drove, I finally went out and bought a truck, leaving Natalie's Volkswagen Bug behind in case there was ever an emergency at home while I was at work. I missed the Volkswagen and all the memories its back seat carried. All the secrets it held. Even the busted side view mirror I had to fix. I thought the change would help, but I had to almost force myself to look forward to coming home. Thinking about Desmond was the only way I could ignore those thoughts and head straight home from work.

I couldn't wait until he was big enough to sit in the middle of the living room when I came home, playing with building blocks, green army men, race cars, and everything else I couldn't have but would spoil him with. He would have everything Natalie and I didn't growing up. We'd make sure of it.

We lay awake, talking about it most nights. Listed all the things we wanted to do differently. Well, it was mostly me listing things I wanted to do for Dezzy for the short time he was awake when I got home. Where Dezzy's eyes were bright and happy the second I took him in my arms when I walked in, Natalie's looked hollow with exhaustion.

I was working as much as I could to start saving for toys and anything he might need. He was my motivation every workday and my priority the second I came home. All of Natalie's paintings had come to a halt the second she had Desmond.

Ava and Caden had told her to take as much time as she needed before trying to get something to the gallery. But Natalie hadn't mentioned them since we'd had Dezzy. I knew Olivia had been to the house to see the baby multiple times, but Natalie hadn't talked about their visits together, either.

I didn't know what to think about any of it. I was trying to give her space, spending every second I could with Dezzy.

Ready to see him, I dropped the cigarette to crush it beneath my shoe, taking one last moment to enjoy the smoke in my lungs. I was down the street from the house. I just couldn't let Natalie see that I was smoking again. As much as I tried to hide it, she probably knew. I couldn't get rid of the smell entirely. Still, she hadn't said anything.

But more than that, I refused to be around Desmond with a cigarette. I even kept the damned things in the truck. The thought of him being around cigarettes and smoke made me nauseous.

I hopped in the car to drive down the block, quickly chewing gum, before pulling into the driveway. Once inside, I found Natalie in the living room, smooshed into the cushions, with Desmond cradled to her chest.

"Not a bad view to come home to," I said, causing her head to snap up with a gasp.

"Oh! You scared me."

I shoved every nicotine-induced thought to the back of my mind.

"I'll be sure to walk louder when I come home from now on. Maybe slam the front door."

Natalie nodded, a smile tugging at her lips. "If I was bottle-feeding right now, you'd have warm formula heading straight for your face."

I dropped into the spot beside her. "So violent."

Reaching toward her, all I had to do was wiggle my fingers, and she knew to set Dezzy in my arms. Relief in knowing he was safe washed over me. I felt lighter as I propped his little body against my legs, cradling his head above my knees.

Cooing, he stared up at me as his tongue popped in and out of his mouth. I couldn't help but chuckle.

"What a goober. You're gonna have your mom's sense of humor, aren't you? I'm gonna be done for."

His tongue stuck back out as he jerking to the other side with an unusual, small sneeze-like sound.

Dezzy's tiny hand wrapped around one of my fingers. The touch was like a scene from a movie. Only, it felt like an explosion of emotions. A flutter rushed through my stomach, and I leaned closer to him.

"I'm going to go grab a glass of wine. Do you—"

"You're breastfeeding. Are you sure that's such a good idea?"

Natalie froze the second she stood, glancing down at me from over her shoulder. "Why are you asking me that?" An edge slipped into her voice. "I just thought I would have a small glass. I know I'm breastfeeding our child, Scott. The doctor said a small glass was fine. I'm not getting wasted."

"I'm sorry, I just—" I swallowed back any excuse I could come up with. "I don't know why I said that."

"Just forget it." She plopped back down into her spot, aggressively crossing her arms.

"I'm sorry. I—this is not how I expected the night to go."

"What were you expecting?"

"I just wanted to spend time with you and Dezzy," I lied, partially.

Staring down at him, I thought I couldn't imagine wanting to be anywhere else.

Adrenaline shot through my veins in response. Reminding me of the one thing I'd rather be doing right now.

Rocking Dezzy, I tried to ignore the ringing in my ears. His little hand tightened around my finger. I still couldn't believe it. Even when I looked at him, he didn't feel real.

"I know we've been too busy—too fucking tired—to talk about this," I said, "but do you still want . . . to get married?"

She laughed. "Nervous to ask?"

My laugh was awkward.

"Mostly didn't know how to ask."

"Well, we can't afford to do the big wedding thing. Not right now." She glanced down at Dezzy with a smile.

She wasn't complaining. Her love for Dezzy was more important than anything she wanted.

"Do you want to wait? Save up for that?" I asked, knowing I would have to push myself harder to save for her and Dezzy. "I want you to have what you want."

She deserves that much.

Nat shook her head. "No. Any money we set aside . . . I'd rather save it for him. A big, fancy wedding was never something I dreamed about. I'd rather we spend that money on life. On turning this house into a home and then having more . . ." Her eyes fell back to Dezzy, who was still clutching onto any finger he could reach.

My eyebrows shot up.

"More? You mean, we're not just gonna keep the one?"

Nat laughed. "Um, we're keeping him, but I'd like to have another. One day. Not anytime soon. I'm in no position to put myself through that again so soon."

A beat of silence fell between us, but neither of us broke eye contact.

I was frozen, the fever spreading through my body, leaving me tongue-tied.

I didn't know what I wanted anymore. Nothing was clear.

"You've been thinking about this, haven't you?" I finally asked.

Smiling, she said, "Yeah. I mean, I'm home with Dez a lot, so there isn't much else to do but think about the future. Is that not something you see for us?"

I nodded, playing with Dezzy's little fingers instead of meeting her intense, questioning gaze. "When was the last time you painted?"

I knew she could feel the sudden withdrawal. I could see it on her face—the hurt in her eyes.

But I did nothing about it. Not even reach out to her. I sat, frozen, holding our child, letting her feel the distance I put between us.

She let out a frustrated breath. "I don't understand this, Scott. I thought we were doing okay. You asked me to marry you. We just had Dezzy, and you ask me if I still want to get married just now but then pull back?"

I flinched from the force in her voice.

"Just—just stop it, Scott. Stop it. I don't know what you're doing. I feel like you're going to leave. Nothing's changed. If you want to leave, leave. Don't feel obligated to stay. If you don't want this anymore, Dezzy and I will be better off." Her voice was strong, forcing me to look up and take in the tears slipping down her cheeks. She didn't wipe them away. She let them fall. "You know what? You're right." She jumped up and left the room without looking back at me. "I'm going to go paint."

My heart didn't drop in my chest. There was no sinking feeling in my stomach as I watched her leave the room. Her long hair was the last thing that disappeared down the hallway. I leaned back into the sofa, turning my attention to Desmond. A small smile was tugged on his lips, even though his eyes were falling shut with blinks that became longer and longer.

"It's okay," I whispered to him. "It's going to be okay. You can sleep. I've got you."

A sigh relaxed through his infant body. A lightness in my chest followed the fever in my veins when Dezzy nestled into his dad's arms.

Carrying Dezzy to his nursery, I took in all the elephants. Natalie had picked out most of them during our shopping spree. His favorite throw was draped over the side of his crib, waiting to warm him. He deserved all the circus animals. Not just elephants. His favorite blanket—the one I gave him—had all the animals.

I carefully lowered him into his crib, heart pounding as I thought of him waking up. Holding my breath when he reached for the bundle of blankets, I stayed tense until he settled, then stepped back from the crib. His breathing stayed even, his eyes shutting tight—he didn't stir.

I was unable to move, dreading the thought of going to bed and facing Natalie. I'd heard her leave her studio for the bedroom about an hour ago, and while I could hope she'd fallen asleep, my gut told me she was waiting up for me.

Closing my eyes, I was suddenly overwhelmed by snippets flooding my conscience all at once, mind turning hazy with visions of touching those who'd been sprawled in my back seat. Whenever I spent time in the nursery, I couldn't ignore the way my stomach gnarled, knowing that the whore from the liquor store was all around us.

Intense desire jolted through me, rising from somewhere deep.

The impulse to duplicate the snippets rattled around in my head.

Quietly backing away from Dezzy's crib, I didn't fight the echoing static. I couldn't push back the ache of the images flashing across my mind. Even though my eyes were wide open now.

I shook my head, but I couldn't shake the warm, slick feeling between my fingers before it stiffened to a crust. With a shiver shooting down my spine, I couldn't deny my want for that feeling.

chapter thirty-eight

SWALLOWING BACK THE TEMPTATION TO leave, I forced my legs to carry me back to bed after one last glance at Dezzy. Tense, I spent the night forcing the urge to leave as far down as possible. The night passed excruciatingly slow.

Then I left for work, feeling like a zombie.

Natalie noted how zoned out I was but seemed to decide not to say anything about it. When she planted a kiss on my cheek, it didn't feel like my cheek. She and everything else around me felt distant.

Once that was through, the workday passed in a sweat. Focusing on anything for more than a few seconds was next to impossible. Even when a coworker talked to me, I didn't fully process what they were saying. Everything was muffled, distant, and hazy. And I couldn't shake it. No matter what I did, it felt like I was walking in fog— another dimension.

I was fighting a constant battle, where most of my focus was on restraining the impatience festering inside me.

The hands of the clock in my office barely seemed to move, even the seconds. Sweat beat down my forehead. My palms dampened every piece of paper I touched. I was scared to look at my reflection in the dark screen of my computer.

A knock briefly snapped my focus back to the present.

"Hey," Zach said, walking right on in before I had the chance to tell him he could. His steps slowed as he neared my desk. "You okay, buddy? You look pretty stressed. Is it the missus? The baby? Regretting the whole thing? It looks like it's taken *years* off your life."

Questions from Zach were the last thing I needed. He was already on my radar. And since I was on his, I would have to do something about it.

"Yeah. No. No, no, no." I wanted to drag my hands down my face. "Everything's fine at home. Natalie and the baby are great. We don't regret a damned thing—"

"But you are stressed."

I held back the need to snap at him, trying to keep my tone even. "I have a newborn at home, Zach. Who wouldn't be?"

"Yeah," he said, "I don't envy you in the slightest. Thanks to you guys, Britney's got baby fever, and I'm too fucking young to have a kid. So, do me a favor and tell Natalie not to encourage her at dinner tomorrow."

And too much of a crude, disrespectful prick.

When I didn't continue to fill the silence, he stepped forward to place a sheet of paper on my desk. "Alrighty, well, Benson wanted me to bring you this list of clients to focus on starting Monday."

"I'll start on this first thing next week, then. Thanks."

Zach nodded and started to leave. My annoyance leaped to the surface when he stopped at the door. "We all should try to get together soon. I'm sure Natalie could use a little break."

Nobody gave a shit about the new father. I was here, working my ass off, trying to convince Benson to let me take on a few extra roles to move up and make more money, when I would rather be home with Dezzy. Exhausted from being woken up three to four times a night with Dezzy, I considered suffering through a cup of coffee more and more every time I straightened my tie to leave, just so I wouldn't be dragging my feet all day. I fucking hated being stuck in my office all day while Nat got to be home with our son. I'd give anything to swap places with her.

Tension spreading through my body, I forced a smile. "Yeah. Yeah, we'd both like that. It'd be easier to have you guys come over—I don't think Natalie is ready to leave the baby for a night out—but I'll let you know next week."

He wanted to see how we were doing—wanted to know what I was up to. Of course he would want to come over to the house. He'd likely been hoping for the offer all along.

He gave the doorframe a little smack, giving an "Awesome" and a thumbs-up before leaving.

I sat back in my chair and raked my hands down my face. My palms came away sweaty. I wasn't sure how much longer I could fucking do this.

My gut twisted every time I looked up at the clock. Getting tighter and tighter with every hour that passed. The way my organs gnarled forced childhood memories to the surface. To the time just before Natalie planted herself in my life. Reminding me of the dread I used to feel whenever I had to go home.

For the last hour of work, it felt like the walls were closing in on me. I didn't know what I was doing. I didn't feel or process anything. Nothing made complete sense. No matter what I did or tried to distract my mind with, I couldn't grab hold of it for long. There was too much backed up in my mind.

The second my clock hit five, I was out of my chair, grabbing my things and heading for the nearest exit. I couldn't be surrounded by walls for another second. Not without hurling up the few bites of lunch I managed to get down.

When I stepped out of the building, I was met with sticky, humid air. The weather was getting warmer, and its fight against the cold made being outside gross. I quickly got into my truck and peeled out of the parking lot. I didn't know where I was going, but I knew home would not be my first stop. I needed more time.

Careful to keep to the speed limit, I circled the nearby offices to see who else was leaving their nine-to-five on time. Jerking the dial on the radio until the truck was silent, I kept the windows rolled up to watch everyone I passed while locking out the humidity.

A couple of managers. A few women in pin-straight skirts that didn't dare rest above the knee. A few guys Zach would probably get along with walked some girls out to their cars, hand on the small of their back the entire way.

None of them looked right. With their hair up, I couldn't tell if their hair was long enough. Familiarity didn't trigger me closer. Clamping down on the steering wheel, I knew the festering in my stomach and chest reached an all-time high. Screaming at me to take action.

All consciousness I had faded.

Stepping on the gas, I blindly headed down the main road that would take me to the closest town. Then I drove straight through it to the next passing the creek I'd found some weeks ago. It was an older, limited area compared to the neighborhood Natalie and I lived in. A diner and a small strip of random stores made up the whole thing. Large homes were scattered about, too, but this left the people who lived nearby to commute to the next town if they wanted fast food or needed a better selection of groceries.

I turned down the first street, but between the setting sun and the sticky air, not a single person was outside. The more streets I drove, the more the sun fell behind the trees.

All of it was a blur.

Every house looked the same. All were empty for all I could see. The car was quiet, leaving my mind to eat away at itself in the silence. I barely felt the steering wheel beneath my hands. Nothing was anything more than a shadow. It wasn't until I went down my fifth or sixth street that I finally saw someone who wasn't a young child playing basketball in their parents' driveway.

Heart leaping into my throat when she came bounding out the front door, I saw her keys jangle at her side after locking it. Her hair moved with her—long, wavy, and light like a ray of sunshine. Wisps of it whirled around her body, nearly touching her butt. Jaw locked, I curled my hand as I thought of running my fingers through the length of her strands. Shutting my eyes, I thought back to all the times I'd combed my hands through Natalie's hair whenever she rested her head in my lap. I could practically feel—

Her car door opened, causing my eyes to snap back open, only to realize I'd stopped the truck.

Carrying a small backpack that probably wouldn't carry more than a phone and a tube of lip gloss, she slung it into the passenger seat of her car so she could adjust the T-shirt she'd twist-tied in the front. Because of the knot, the shirt barely hid her young curvy frame. She couldn't have been over seventeen, but her shorts rode up her ass.

Where the fuck were this girl's parents?

Climbing into the driver's seat, she threw her hair up into a high ponytail before shutting the door to start the car. Her shirt had ridden up with the action, revealing a perfectly flat torso. Perfectly taut skin inviting—begging— to be touched.

Inhaling a deep breath, I gripped the steering wheel to hold myself in the car. Despite that, I couldn't stop myself from thinking about what it would feel like to bite that curved spot right above her bony hip. That was Natalie's sweet spot. I wondered if this girl would giggle the same. I wanted to test every sound she could make. Compare it all to my Natalie.

After backing out of the driveway, she didn't even look in my direction when she drove past. Keeping my head down, acting like I was scrolling through something on my phone, I waited a few beats before I followed her. She came to a stop before turning out of the neighborhood.

My heartbeat accelerated with the truck.

When she came to the next stop sign, I didn't hesitate, didn't think.

My body moved impulsively, my mind reckless. My truck was thrown in park in the same motion I opened the door. My actions didn't feel like my own. I wasn't overcome with panic. I simply walked up to her car window and tapped. She jumped at the sound, then froze when she looked up at me, mouth falling slightly agape. I could have sworn I heard a little gasp slip past her young, loose lips. I wanted to grab that mouth. Bring it close to my face and make her stare me down. Because her eyes— her hazel eyes—reminded me of a deer. Big and hesitant, waiting for a reason to run.

But I smiled before she had the chance to. "Sorry, I didn't think asking for directions would scare you."

She cracked open her window, frozen in her seat. I could still see a sliver of skin. She was revealing everything else, including her slim, long, lotioned legs, but she was hiding her mid-section. Horny girl . . . it made me want it even more.

She knew exactly what she was doing.

Tempting those around her.

Forcing my focus on her rather than on Natalie. She was desperately trying to draw me in. In ways Natalie had not achieved when we first met.

"I'm pretty sure I made a wrong turn," I continued when she said nothing, worried she would step on the gas. "I'm looking for the diner."

Another moment passed before she finally smiled up at me. It didn't come close to Natalie's. All of them were whores. Useless and selfish. None compared to Natalie. No matter how hard they tried.

"Not from around here, are yeh?"

My heart plummeted.

For a moment, I was thrown back to my stale prison, surrounded by beer bottles, while the kitchen was empty. My dad was in my face, beating the shit out of me.

"If yeh mother hated yeh before . . . I would hate to think what she'd say 'bout yeh now."

"No." I blinked rapidly, relying on every inhale and exhale to rebuild the walls I'd cemented to keep those shouts in the deepest parts of my mind. I clenched and flexed my hands as static rang in my ears. "No, ma'am. Just passing through."

"Okay, well, I guess yeh could just follow me there if yeh wanted."

"I'd really appreciate it," I said, reaching for the handle of her car.

It was rusty. How did this little horny girl open such a heavy, rusted, piece-of-shit door every day?

I could easily wrap my hand around her wrist and snap it without effort. She seemed delicate, like a bird. A caged bird with clipped wings. She was a creature ready to take off. She was cautious—waiting for the right moment.

Yanking open her car door, she was next.

I couldn't give her the chance to leave.

Her hazel eyes shot wide open, jaw dropping, with an inhale to scream. The palm of my hand covered her entire mouth, muffling everything and making it harder for her to breathe. She wrestled against me as I pulled her from the car, flailing to the ground. If that was everything she had, everything would be just fine.

She tried to stay on the ground, making me work for every step closer, as I dragged her to my truck. Jaw clamped, I knew I didn't have time for this shit. She was putting more effort into saving herself than the others.

Her muffled screams abruptly stopped, making me turn to look down at her at the exact moment she dug her teeth into the palm over her mouth.

"*Fuck!*"

A sting shot up my arm. Blood pooled in the palm of my hand. My other hand came down across her face. Exhaling through clenched teeth, I barely had time to take in the bite mark she'd left. It was only when her head fell back hard enough to hit the ground that I realized I hadn't used an ounce of restraint.

Her eyes rolled back for a moment, her shirt rising up enough to expose her abdomen. "This is a sick joke," she sputtered after several moments of rapid blinking. Head lulling from side to side, as if she were trying to figure out where she was, her mouth opened and closed like that of a fish.

She was still conscious, but she had no fight left in her.

"No," was all she could muster as I started dragging her across the ground again. "No. No, please. Please."

Ignoring her, I picked her up once we were beside my truck. I missed the Volkswagen, but shoving her in the back seat of my new truck would make it easier to hide any trace of this girl. Natalie and I always used the Volkswagen as our family vehicle. She'd sat in my truck twice since I bought it. Getting rid of all evidence of this horny bitch from Natalie would be easy.

This would be the first time I was dirtying up this truck.

Her head continued to move from side to side as I lifted her, eyes rolling every which way, as if she were in a trance. The sight brought a familiar feeling to the surface. She was struggling to clear her mind. Fighting for even a bit of control after the blow to her face.

She was powerless now. I hadn't meant to strike her that hard.

Watching her from the rearview mirror, I left her car behind with the door wide open and scuff marks in the gravel, driving until I reached the wooded creek area.

"Don't," she mumbled when I threw the truck in park and cut the engine.

Ignoring her, I reached into the glove box for the wad of napkins, wiping away the blood I'd smeared on the steering wheel.

When I looked back over my shoulder, the girl hadn't moved. She was still fighting to stay aware.

I climbed into the back seat, leaning over her, close enough to breathe the same air. Her eyes opened weakly. Reaching out, I could hear the frantic beat of her heart. Sweat dampened her hairline, and I couldn't help but wonder what else was damp. I grinned. Such a horny girl. So young, so naïve.

She sucked in a long breath to scream. It froze in her chest when I pulled the hair tie out to let it down. It was too beautiful to be trapped in a ponytail. I wanted it to be free. Running my fingers through her hair, I felt like I was a kid again, pinning Natalie in the back of her Volkswagen, combing my fingers through her paint-splattered hair.

"You don't even come close. You're so young, and you dress like such a whore." I placed a hand on her exposed thigh. Her legs were so long. "You want this—"

"No."

"You do. You're begging for this kind of attention." I climbed out of the back seat, bringing her to the edge of the seat by her legs.

"No, no. *No!*"

There go the waterworks.

When she flailed again, I dragged her out by her hair. She screamed when she hit the dirt. Her pain rang through the trees.

"You look like my wife when she was young." I pulled her through the woods and stopped only once we were close to the creek. Thanks to the running water, her screams would be muffled. "You should've gone with a band T-shirt instead of this see-through piece of shit." I ripped her shirt straight down the front.

"What the fuck is happening?" she yelled, throwing her arms up to protect her face. "No! You're psychotic!"

I straddled her waist, grabbing her hands when I had the chance. "Stop," I ground out.

Terror consumed her eyes when she looked up at me.

Flinching whenever I moved to touch her, feel the softness of her skin, she screamed and tried to wrestle out from under me, force me off of her. All I could do was laugh at her attempts and keep touching. So soft. So young. So naïve and innocent. So completely helpless.

I let her keep at it until I touched her with enough force to leave bruises. Grabbing at her arms, digging my fingertips into her thighs, pinning her arms above her head to lean in close.

None of it was enough—violent enough.

Reaching out from her, I searched the ground for something with weight. My hand was coated in dirt before I had a rock clenched in my hand.

When I tried to consider doing this very same thing to Zach, I knew it wouldn't feel the same. The adrenaline rush wouldn't satisfy me. His shouts would never compare to shrill screams.

Her voice strained from all the screaming, arms flying to scratch at me before I could bring down the rock. Jagged and rough in my hand, the rock would destroy her already severely plain features.

I brought the rock down on her again and again. Without aim. I just swung my arm downward and listened, felt, and saw the rock split apart flesh and muscle. My arm didn't stop until fatigue took over.

My shaky hand dropped the rock. It landed beside her unrecognizable face with a thud.

My hands slick with blood and membrane, I clenched it within my palm and fixated on her new look. Every bit of her was slick except for the brain matter. I closed my eyes at the texture, a shiver racing down my spine.

A long breath left my body, the tension fading with the exhale. Transfixed by the woman at my feet, I took in her blood-stained clothes and the bite mark I had left on her lip. Even more crimson trickled down the side of her face before ruining the deep plunge of her dress. She wasn't beautiful, but I found myself unable to look away. She was what I wanted her to be. I made her.

She'd been enough for me—in the moment.

I mutilated the temptation from her. Left her as something less than a woman.

Her blonde hair wasn't as shiny as Natalie's, her skin blotchy with freckles and acne. The little girl dressed like a streetwalker instead of a teenager, artist, or a mother. She was trash—nothing compared to the love of my life.

When I couldn't look at her anymore without seeing her face blend with my Natalie, I pulled her up by her arms. Her head rolled to the side, shoulders dragging dead leaves, twigs, moss, and straw with us as I led us closer to the river. I dragged her across the stones that lined the water, blood darkening puddles, staining the path we had come from.

She'd clung to life as long as she could, but I didn't know when the light disappeared from her eyes. They were no longer there. One punch from the rock took care of that. Covered in her own blood, it was impossible to tell if her skin had paled.

Warmth spread through my body when I pushed her into the racing river, her skull splitting open further before she was swept from the edge.

I didn't bother to watch her body vanish from sight.

The ice-cold water would turn the horny bitch's lips blue eventually. Her body would be bloated before anyone found her.

I still had to make one more stop before going home.

Then, just as I was about to clear the woods, it started to rain.

I froze, realizing what I had done. I let go of the steering wheel, jolting at the sight of the horny girl's blood smeared across it. I didn't dare look in the seat. I couldn't go home with the truck looking like this. *I* couldn't go home looking like this.

Before stopping the truck, I pulled forward until it was concealed again. Throwing the door open, I ran back to the river, careful to avoid stepping in the bloody path I made. She was nowhere in sight when I made it to the edge. Her corpse had already been swept down the river. Her body had likely thrashed against the boulders until it sank.

Crouching where I'd shoved her in, I rinsed the blood off my hands. The water fucking cold as hell, I snatched them from it the second they were scrubbed clean. I'd have to use soap under my nails when I got home.

Raindrops showered me when I lifted my shirt above my head, goose bumps spreading everywhere cold water had hit me. Blood darkened the water around the shirt as I rubbed it against stone. I wrung it out on the way back to the truck. My pants weren't as bad.

I wasn't fully aware of my actions again until I pulled into the parking lot of the Goodwill down the road from our neighborhood.

Slamming the door shut, I looked down to check for blood. Most of it had come out of my shirt, and I could use it to cover the splatters and smears on my pants.

I went around to collapse a back seat, ignoring the rain. Crumpled-up receipts, a screwdriver, a set of paintbrushes, and other junk cluttered the back. I grabbed one of my large, wadded-up sweatshirts thrown in the corner and headed inside.

A few people were browsing around inside, so I wasted little time. I grabbed the first blank T-shirt I touched and then a pair of jeans similar to another I had already owned. I didn't let myself look at anyone for too long. They didn't matter. I had to get home. Nat would be pissed enough as it was. No one else mattered except Natalie, and I had let her down again today.

The second I was back in the truck, I changed and then stuffed my dirty clothes underneath my pile of sweatshirts behind the back seats. I'd decide what to do about them later.

chapter thirty-nine

SITTING IN THE TRUCK OUTSIDE the house, I breathed in and out as I eyed the windows, preparing to go inside and face my life. As I prepared to act like I wasn't thinking about the young long-legged girl. The one who had begged for my attention from the moment she stepped out of her house with a strip of her taut stomach exposed. I'd left her with bite marks to return the favor she'd left on my hand, though, where she had drawn blood.

Shaking my head, I shut my eyes to block out the feel of her skin between my teeth.

I forced myself to leave the truck, checking my clothes the whole way to the door before I walked inside.

"Late night?" Natalie called from the kitchen when she heard the door shut behind me.

Inhale through the nose, exhale through the mouth.

I slipped off my shoes, leaving them by the door, next to Natalie's boots. "Yeah. Sorry I didn't call. Zach was up my ass."

Knowing it wasn't a complete lie, I took in the room for anything out of the ordinary as my muscles tensed. I couldn't shake the feeling that Zach was on to me. The long stares at the office, the questions about Hannah, the way he watched me whenever we were around each other outside of the office. Everything he did set me on edge.

I shook my head, quickening my pace to cross the room.

Natalie didn't come around the corner to greet me anymore. She was keeping her distance. Which I deserved. I couldn't give her what she needed. Not anymore. But I didn't know how to keep her here—force her to keep holding on for the both of us.

"What happened to your work shirt?" she asked the second I walked into the kitchen.

Dezzy was in his bouncer with Nat in front of him, who leaned back against the counter as she watched him. At first, she didn't get up.

I stood in the doorway, eyes darting from one to the other. Dezzy was smiling from ear-to-ear, drool blubbering out of his mouth.

I sighed, pulling an excuse out of my ass. "One of the printers stopped working tonight, and ink exploded all over me when Zach decided to play repairman."

"So, if I asked Zach about this, he would verify this?"

Natalie didn't look at me, wiggling Dezzy's chubby little arms.

Swallowing hard, I breathed through the sudden metallic taste of venom in my mouth, keeping my anger behind my teeth. "Nat? What are you saying?"

"Are you cheating? Just tell me. Please, tell me."

While my heart sank, my hands balled into fists at my sides.

"I am *not* a cheater."

"You're coming home late again, Scott. What am I supposed to think?"

"Anything but that! You're supposed to think about all the years we've been together and remember that I asked you to marry me and realize that I would never cheat on you."

"You haven't even bought me a ring, Scott! None of this is real anymore!" She released a sigh when she couldn't yell anymore. "I feel like you're going to leave."

I couldn't unclench my teeth to answer.

Panic flashed across her eyes when I said nothing. I was frozen. I wanted to tell her I wasn't going anywhere—because I wasn't—but I couldn't get the words out.

I couldn't make declarations the way she did.

"I want a future with you—that's not going to change."

"I'm not going anywhere, Scott."

"I feel like you're going to leave, and it's scaring me."

Tears pooled in her panic-stricken eyes. Natalie always tried to put on a brave face. After her brother died, she'd been taught to dismiss her tears. And here she was, blocking out her vulnerability for me, not letting her weak side show.

"Natalie, I'm not cheating. I would *never* do that to you. That isn't what's happening here. I just—I don't know how to tell you or anyone else what's going on right now because I don't even know. But I'm not cheating, and I'm not trying to make you think I'm going to leave."

I wanted to cross the room and bring her into me, but something kept me still, holding me in place. Nothing could convince me to move. I didn't feel a pull toward her. The disconnect was growing, and I didn't know how to shove it back.

All I knew was that I didn't want her to leave me. I would fall apart. I would be nothing without Natalie. A lump forming in my throat, I knew I couldn't bear it if she walked out.

Natalie got up from the floor, keeping her back to me as she went over to the stove to stir whatever was in the pot, then wiped her face with her sleeve.

My heart plummeted.

"Did you seriously walk away while he's in his bouncer?"

Natalie's head shot up to face me, eyes wide and blotchy. "I'm right here—"

"You have your back turned," I said, pushing away from the door to pull Dezzy from his chair. "It isn't safe. He's a newborn, Natalie. You can't turn your back on him. Not even for a second."

"Scott"—Natalie let out a low, unamused laugh, like she couldn't tell if I was serious and wasn't sure how upset she should be—"I'd never let anything happen to him. He's perfectly safe."

"Is this what you do all day when I'm not here—you leave him in his high chair while you do whatever?"

"No." Her voice had turned exasperated. "But you're here—his father—and I thought that, if I was at the stove, you would have the common sense to watch him for a second."

"What happened to being better parents?" I snapped.

Natalie dropped her spoon on the counter, stepping back from the stove to face me head on. "Is this seriously want you want to do right now, Scott? Really?"

"You started this—you accused me of cheating."

"You don't talk to me anymore, Scott. I'm worried about what's going to happen to us if you keep refusing to communicate. Whenever I try to talk to you, you shut down."

My arms tightened around Dezzy. "I told you I don't know what's going on, so how am I supposed to talk about it with you?"

She threw her arms up in defeat. "I don't know! But at least I'm trying. I'm trying, while you won't even meet me halfway here."

"I don't know how to talk to you!"

Dezzy burst into tears, his cheeks reddening with his cries.

"He probably needs to be changed," she said. "I'm not hungry, but dinner is ready. I'll leave it here."

Then she left the room without another word. Meanwhile, Dezzy was screaming into my face, ready to blow out my eardrums.

How could I have been so blind? Natalie was just like every parent. Terrible. Neglectful. Indifferent to Desmond's crying. My jaw locked as I reminded myself to breathe, so I was gentle with Dezzy.

His own mother abandoned him.

I carried him down the hall to the nursery, seeing that our bedroom door was already shut. The door to her studio was cracked open. It was like she wanted to set me on edge. Had she been painting? Did she do it during one of Dezzy's naps, or had she left him in one of his rockers as she worked?

Setting Dezzy down on his changing table, I smiled at his innocent face, some of the tension leaving my body, even though he was still crying. His cheeks were getting chubby. Pretty soon, he would have a round belly to match. I copied all the steps I'd seen in the videos Natalie and I had watched while she was pregnant. Dezzy's tears subsided as I fumbled with the different wipes and powders.

When I finished, I hoped that I'd done everything right, but if it weren't, it would have been because of Natalie. She should be the one changing him anyway. And he seemed to know it.

He stared up at me with big watery eyes. Wanting to change his tears into a smile, I blew raspberries against his little tummy. With eyes closed, he smiled widely. One of his small hands reached for me but then he shook his arms out straight, like he was trying to stop me from tickling him. The more I took him in, the more warmth I felt.

By the time I lifted him off the changing table, Dezzy was as quiet as a mouse. I walked him around the room, rocking him and watching his eyes fall closed with blinks that seemed to last minutes.

During those minutes, my heart felt full.

I couldn't bring myself to put him down, and before I knew it, half an hour had passed, and I convinced myself to lay him in his crib.

Quietly stepping out of the nursery, I wrenched at the dread settling in the pit of my stomach as I made my way down the hall. Before making for the bedroom, I peeked into the cracked door of Natalie's studio. I stepped inside until my foot touched the edge of her favorite fuzzy purple rug.

A tall canvas was propped up, a set of freshly used brushes resting in a cup of water beside it. The spread was overwhelmed by bloodred clouds against a gray background. Lightning struck the flaky brown ground she'd dabbed across the bottom. It was simplistic but powerful.

Backing away, I couldn't stop taking in the smears of the clouds—the sharp strike of the lightning.

For a moment, I wondered what she saw while painting those crimson clouds, then shut the door.

She was being careless with my son, and she was hiding her art rather than taking it to Ava and Caden.

I didn't let myself hesitate outside our bedroom door. I could already tell by the faint light coming from under the door that she was still lying awake with one lamp turned on.

My eyes immediately landed on her, who was curled into the blankets pulled up around her shoulders. She was a ball beneath the duvet. Tears clouded her eyes, yet not a single one fell. Her cheeks were dry. She hadn't been crying, but she'd been close to it this entire time. Before the static settled in, I was aware my heart hadn't dropped from seeing her like this.

"Are you okay?"

The question was forced.

She looked away from her phone to glance at me out of the corner of her eye, putting her pinky nail in her mouth.

I sighed. "You're like this because of me."

She said nothing.

I walked into the bathroom to brush my teeth. Standing at the sink, I braced my hands against the counter's edge.

Terrible mother. She doesn't deserve him. She probably hated her life, and I don't want her to hate him or me.

Images of my own mother appeared behind my dark eyelids. To where I could feel the tender purple splotches on my arm, across my chest, similar to ones my dad tried to copy years after she'd walked out.

The mistreatment had started with neglect when I was young. Before she'd start smashing my toys, throwing them out of windows, or melting them in pots like the fucking psycho bitch she was. She told me she didn't love me just as much as she showed it. Then the physical abuse cranked everything up a notch. All of it led to abuse. All of it was abuse. Those nightmares still traumatized my dreams on bad nights.

Neglect was where it started. Neglect was only Natalie's beginning, and that burned in my chest like a brand.

Before I went to close the door, I heard her release a small sob. Once it clicked shut, all of that was blocked out once.

chapter forty

MORNING PASSED WITH A BLUR. Natalie drifted through the house like a ghost, silent, dressed in rags, the bags underneath her eyes darkening with each restless night. She hadn't forced me to sleep on the couch, and she came to bed as soon as she got Dezzy to sleep. The emotional distance between us was like a taut string tied around us. I could feel her toss, and I didn't think she ever slept more than a few hours at best.

I could tell she was trying to distance Dezzy from me.

In the recent weeks, she would always pop up the second he cried, lift him into her lap the second I walked through the door, or keep him on her hip at all times. She never set him down when I was home.

Having to find a chance to hold him sent tremors down my arms, forcing me to flex my fingers. Everything in me surged with the idea of crushing a windpipe.

During the few moments Natalie met my eyes, I wanted to storm out the door.

She barely looked at me. But when she did, her eyes were pled for the chance to fix it. However, something in her glance almost confirmed she could feel my urges in the way I looked at her, like she knew the news headlines were about me.

I wondered if Zach had gotten to her—told her about his suspicions. About Hannah.

Sitting on the couch with my head in my hands, I tried to shake the feeling.

Natalie walked out of the bedroom, and my head snapped up. My hands ran down the length of my pants as the look on Natalie's face made every organ in my body drop.

"We're almost out of diapers for Dezzy, and we need to grab a few things for dinner tonight," she said. "I was going to make a trip to the store unless you wanted to come with us."

She didn't want to leave me alone with Desmond. I swallowed back my accusation, clenching the outer seam of my jeans to give my hands something to do. She was distancing me from Dezzy. An abyss divided us. She could feel the disconnect, but I could tell she had not given up on us. Even when we fell asleep beside each other, the black hole between us was impossible to ignore.

"Yeah, I could use a minute outside of the house," I lied.

I didn't want to go anywhere. But it was for Dezzy, and I had to be there for him. I had to make sure Natalie didn't fuck up.

I couldn't even trust her to get diapers alone with our son.

Natalie got Dezzy dressed and ready to go while I double-checked his diaper bag. Sure enough, only a couple of diapers were left inside it and only a few by the changing table.

She'd let them run low.

How could she justify keeping Dezzy from me when she barely parented him as it was?

Little was said as we got the truck situated. Since getting the truck, the Volkswagen had taken a back seat as our family vehicle. The truck was larger and more reliable, and we just felt safer with Dezzy in it rather than the chipped, janky car we'd run away in during our teens.

On the drive to the store, hope rolled off her in waves. Natalie kept glancing at me out of the corner of her eye from her passenger seat. Not once did she ever look back at Dezzy in his car seat. As I turned into the grocery store parking lot, my grip on the steering wheel tightened. Why was she trying so fucking hard for us suddenly? Desmond was the one who mattered—who needed his mother. I did not understand how she couldn't wrap her mind around that.

Natalie made no fucking sense.

"I was going to make my penne casserole tonight," she said, breaking the silence. "Unless you had something else in mind?"

I shook my head. "I think that's good. We both know Zach will eat anything you put in front of him."

"What about dessert?"

"I think we're fine." I threw the truck in park.

She nodded and grabbed her bag, biting her pinky nail as she got out of the car.

She was quick to get Dezzy out of his car seat, her eyes flashing to me when I opened the opposite door to grab his bag.

I slammed the car door shut, images of smashing Hannah's face into the side of the car rising to the forefront of my mind. I blinked, and it was gone, but a flash of warmth stirred in my chest, and I paused for a second before moving toward the store.

Natalie grabbed a shopping cart near the car and set Dezzy's carrier into the child seat.

He cooed, kicking his tiny socked feet around. He was in his blue outfit today with an elephant beanie, a circus ball balanced on the tip of the elephant's trunk. He smiled the biggest, goofiest smile, blowing bubbles.

I couldn't stop the laugh that escaped.

The second the automated doors opened to let us inside, I was ready to turn around and go home.

"He's cuter than we ever could've imagined, isn't he?" Natalie asked me.

I didn't answer her.

There was too much to keep up with.

People scurried around with carts full of groceries, children either following their parents or sitting among the food, old women zooming about on electric wheelchairs.

I already had a headache.

Even though we supposedly needed a few things, I followed Natalie through produce and then to the cereal aisle. Natalie stuck to pushing the cart, her gaze jumping from keeping an eye on Desmond to searching for what she was looking for and back again. I walked beside her, and while she talked to me the entire time, she barely paid me a second glance.

"Any cereal in particular you have to have?" she asked, even though we'd only come in for diapers and tonight's dinner.

And then she stepped away from the shopping cart.

I gripped the side of the cart, the grated metal digging into my palm. "What the hell do you think you're doing?"

Natalie's head snapped up at my question, her hand frozen with a box half off the shelf as her eyes widened.

"Don't just walk away from the cart like that. Someone could knock his carrier off or walk off with him . . ."

I lost track of everything I said, my ears ringing over the static.

She was a fucking terrible mother. I could see how she would spiral to be like mine. Natalie would resent our son the older he got. The change would start with stern punishments and shouting until that wasn't enough. Holding herself back was too difficult to be worth the effort. She would give up and leave bruises on Dezzy like my mother had once done to me. I wouldn't let my son repeat my childhood.

Fuck Natalie. Fuck her incompetence. Fuck her inadequacy as a mother.

I would rather die than let him go through what I did. But what if I was his only chance of being saved from that future abuse?

No child deserved that—to have their innocence beaten out of them.

The world snapped back into focus in time for me to hear someone on the aisle gasp. I didn't look at anyone else, though. My eyes were on Natalie and Natalie alone. Her eyes glazed over, tears welling in the corners.

"What is wrong with you? Why would you say that?" she snapped. "What do you think you're doing?"

My chest heaving, I went to pick up Dezzy. All I could think about was getting him away from her. She'd abandoned him when she stepped away. Anything could have happened to him, and she didn't care. She never even considered it.

But when I moved toward Dezzy, Natalie beat me to him, snatching him from his carrier. "Don't."

My mouth went dry, but my tone was seething. "Don't act like you give a fuck about our child."

Her mouth fell open before she collected herself enough to speak again. "Why are you acting like this?"

"What did you expect? Maybe you shouldn't have tried to force a connection back into place and act like you love him and I."

I watched her heart break, every thought and emotion reflection in her gleaming eyes.

My own heart aching in my chest, I stepped back with my eyes locked on Desmond. I had to find another way. I couldn't let her do this to Desmond. I wouldn't let history repeat itself.

A guy hovering on our aisle stepped up to me, shifting around like he was going to put himself between Natalie and I. "Hey, man, don't talk to your wife like that."

I swallowed a scoff. Like he could do a damned thing.

I turned my back on Natalie, silently promising Desmond I would be back. I needed a goddamned smoke first. "I'm leaving, anyway."

I didn't look back. I had better things to do than pick a fucking box of cereal.

I didn't stop until the grocery store was out of sight. Coming face-to-face with a gas station when I turned a corner, I didn't hesitate to go inside for Marlboros. The second the carton and lighter were set in front of me, I flipped open the top to pull one out. It was lit the second the cigarette was between my lips.

I leaned against the wall, just out of view of the windows.

The sting of the smoke ignited my lungs. I could almost feel the heat from when I set the gallery ablaze.

When I exhaled, my eyes landed on newspaper boxes.

Again, my entire body deflated, and my hand shook when I went to move the cigarette.

MULTIPLE BODIES FOUND WITH CRUSHED SKULLS

MORE BODIES FOUND IN LOCAL CREEK

COPS DUB CREEK SERIAL KILLER "SKULL SPLITTER"

The cops were catching on. They knew I'd become addicted to the sound—what splintered skulls and splattered brain matter looked like after the light drained.

My heart jolted into my throat.

CORONER ANNOUNCES CHUNK OF FLESH MISSING FROM SKULL SPLITTER'S LATEST VICTIM

Investigators were bodies behind from finding my latest victim. But they'd found the body belonging to the one in the dress. I'd tasted her like no other. I could still taste her salty skin in my mouth, sweaty from her fight. I'd probably let them all have that chance from now on. Let them fight until their bodies were covered in sweat, dripping between their breasts. Let them think they had a chance. Until I followed that trail of sweat.

SEARCH FOR BODIES AT LOCAL CREEK ENSUES

Sweet and salty and beautiful. Even the blood and muscle beneath.

It left me wanting more.

CURFEW TO BE SET IN PLACE AS SEARCH FOR SKULL SPLITTER CONTINUES

The headlines didn't stop.

Each fucking bolded word was worse than the worst.

I shook my head to clear my thoughts, throwing the cigarette back in my mouth to walk away.

But when I turned, I thought I saw bodies discarded on the roadside. Natalie's face reflected back at me everywhere—bashed in like roadkill, the side of her face crushed, pieces of her missing and falling out onto the concrete.

My breath caught, my hands forming a death grip on the Marlboros.

chapter forty-one

THE TAXI DRIVER DIDN'T SAY a word after I paid him and got out. My focus was on getting through the front door to look for Natalie and Dezzy. Every muscle in my body was stiff. My hand barely wanted to put the key in the hole, let alone twist to unlock it. All I could think about was making sure Desmond was taken care of. If I found his mother had walked out and left him . . . I didn't know what I would do.

The second I walked into the house, I felt defeated. My shoulders were weighed down, my chest numb. Static had caused a headache between my eyes, but the ringing had mostly stopped.

Despite having smoked, I let out a long breath when I found them in the living room.

Natalie was on the couch with Dezzy tucked into her chest, breastfeeding him.

She looked up when my legs took me no further than the kitchen. "Lucky, I had the extra set of keys in my purse, no?"

Relief quickly turned into a burning sensation within my chest.

I tried to ignore Natalie, swallowing back everything about her that was making me sick. After watching her be so thoughtless with him, finding my son soothed and tucked into her, pulling from her, my stomach churned.

I crossed the room within strides, taking Desmond from her arms. She flinched back, but I didn't say a word. She didn't deserve him. Not when she turned her back on him. Not when she was this fucking neglectful.

While she sat there, in shock, I set Dezzy in his bouncy chair.

Picking up the nearest rattle, I shook it in Dezzy's face. He grinned, shaking his arms and spitting up bubbles of saliva. He spat up like that whenever he was in the bath, too, like he was trying to mimic the hundreds of bubbles in the warm tub. I couldn't do anything but smile, blowing a raspberry in his face long enough to make him grin back. *That is my kid.*

Natalie suddenly gasped, sitting up from the couch for once. "They're putting a curfew in place."

Natalie was holding a newspaper wide open. The headline from the gas station rose from where I'd tried to bury it. *CURFEW TO BE SET IN PLACE AS SEARCH FOR SKULL SPLITTER CONTINUES*

When I went to swallow, my throat was dry. Spit scraped my esophagus.

"I might just have to be a hermit—a complete homebody," she added. "From this moment on, I might not leave the house."

I snatched the paper from her. I wanted to crumble it but thought twice about it. "Don't be so dramatic."

"Whoever this sicko is, he's killing blondes, Scott, and I fit the bill."

Her voice grew louder and more frantic the longer she talked.

"You have nothing to worry about."

"But what—"

"Goddammit, Natalie, I said that it's going to be fine!"

She flinched back, blinking rapidly as she made herself small against the cushions. The only thing she could seem to say was "You called me Natalie. You yelled at me and called me Natalie."

"I—" I shook my head to clear it. "Nat, I—"

She pushed up from the couch, and all I could do was watch as she picked Dezzy out of his bouncy chair. "You know I can't stand you when you talk to me like that. I don't think I've ever been nasty to you like that." She tucked Dezzy close to her chest to storm out of the room.

Nerves raw, my eyes darted to Dezzy.

"Be careful with him," I said, jaw clenched.

She paused long enough to glare at me. "Get it together, Scott."

I stepped to follow them. I hadn't decided my intention, but I felt a surge of something.

Natalie didn't even look over her shoulder, snapping, "Don't."

I stopped right there, listened to them disappear down the hallway with a sinking feeling in my chest.

But I let her go.

"Lets just get through dinner."

Her voice from the hallway went right through me.

Hands clenching and unclenching at my sides, I focused on my breathing to stop thinking about all the ways Natalie could hurt him.

Every one of Natalie's smiles were forced. I could see how dead her eyes were. Her pupils flared with anger, sadness, and disappointment throughout the night. Every single time she looked at me. All of it twisted my stomach into a mangled mess. Her glare reminded me of how miserable she'd look whenever she sought me out at the train tracks on those bad family days.

Every time her icy blue stare found me, it was kindling to the ire building in my veins in the same way canvases and melting paint had been to the gallery fire.

"I was just making a joke, Brit. Don't take it so seriously."

"Don't do this now, please. I just don't like it when you make jokes like that." Britney turned to me sharply, forcing my thoughts to break away from Natalie.

However, Britney seemed to change her mind about me and turned to Natalie instead.

"Ugh." She stabbed at the potato salad on her plate. "Does Scott ever do this? Completely challenge every word that comes out of your mouth?"

Natalie sipped water, her eyes meeting mine for a moment. "Sounds like it's time to change up Zach's treats so he's better behaved."

Britney cackled, nearly spewing her wine.

"Wow, Brit, I don't think it was funny enough to spit up wine," said Zach.

"Oh, shut up," she said through the hand covering her mouth. "You're just being whiny because you were called out."

Natalie snickered.

Zach seemed to think better about responding, turning to Natalie instead. "How is it being new parents?

"I've never been so exhausted yet more happy," she answered. "He's just the sweetest thing. For the first few weeks, I couldn't believe he was real. Now, I can't imagine doing anything without him."

You leave him alone. That's what fucking worries me. And then you hover like a vulture, waiting for an opportunity. Like my mother used to.

"By the way, thanks for the pressure, Scott."

I stiffened, my hands curling under the table, as I looked up at Zach.

I couldn't imagine what Natalie had been telling Olivia and Britney these past months. While Natalie could gossip and complain about how things were between us all she wanted, her friends were the least of my worries.

Zach, on the other hand, had been testing me lately. Ever since Hannah disappeared, he was always lurking around my office. Knowing he was watching my every move, like he knew I was involved. Then there was Natalie, who made me feel a twisting in my gut.

While I was facing Zach, my eyes were on Natalie.

When she looked at me, the sharpness in her eyes made me think of the bite she had the night we met.

She'd stormed away from her asshole of a boyfriend. Then she'd stormed into my life. She was pulling away from me now. And instead of panicking, I felt numb to it.

It was the thought of her walking into another man's life that made rage seethe through my body.

"The last thing I needed was Britney begging me for a baby, and it's already started," Zach said with an eye roll.

His joke wasn't convincing. I could see the truth in his face. Being stuck with Britney would be his worst nightmare.

"Oh, don't be silly. You act like I'm ready to start poking holes in condoms. We can't have a baby without getting married," she countered. Turning to Natalie with a smile, she asked, "When is the wedding? Maybe we could double up."

"We've known each other since high school," Natalie laughed, "followed each other to college, and we got engaged. Dezzy was just kind of a happy accident. Scott's had a lot of buildup to this. None of this was random."

A happy accident. My hand tightened around my fork. *An accident.*

"Hide your boxes," I jumped in with a forced chuckle.

Save yourself from having a child with someone who doesn't give a fuck about 'em.

"He speaks!" Zach said. "What've you been thinking about over there? You said more at work. Yesterday anyway. You're usually pretty quiet around the office."

Fucking bastard. Zach was such a goddamned prick.

"Yeah," Britney chimed in before taking another gulp of wine. "I could see that, since you've barely said two words all night."

I was done with them. Zach and Britney were just a distraction from Natalie.

I tried to shake off the tension twisting through my body before any of them saw the tightness in my muscles.

Zach just didn't know how to leave things the fuck alone. He was getting dangerously close to stepping into something he'd wish he hadn't.

I could do other things that didn't involve mutilating him. If she hadn't already been found, I'd fucking leave his corpse next to Hannah's. Drop him next to her before, just to rub it in his face. Watch him realize he was right and then split his skull clean open.

But he wasn't what I wanted right now. Zach was nothing. An afterthought. My focus had always been and was on Natalie. Even if it sickened me.

"And he's silent again," Zach said, earning a giggle from Natalie.

My eyes sought hers, heart plummeting with an overwhelming high. No static followed. Only clarity.

The corner of her mouth twitched in a hesitant smile.

"Zoned out," she mouthed before sipping from her glass.

Momentarily glancing down, I tightened my grasp on my silverware.

"I'm exhausted from today, and you're all ganging up on me like pricks," I said with a laugh, though my jaw was clenched so tight it ached.

The ache only worsened when Natalie's pupils flared again.

Releasing one final, long breath, I gave myself permission to admit what I really wanted.

chapter forty-two

I WAITED UNTIL I HEARD Natalie close the front door. Once Zach and Britney were gone, I gripped the railing of his crib. None of the tension in my body released. The second I was leaning over his cot and saw his blue eyes from the shadows, I was usually overcome by release.

But not this time.

Seeing him lying there, staring up at me as he waited for me to pick him up, only made my chest sear. While I inhaled a long breath, the heat spread further. I wanted nothing more than to pick him up.

But my hands ached to take hold of Natalie. Twitching, I curled my fingers into a fist when goose bumps spread down the length of my arms. The prick even surged up the back of my neck.

"Is he down?"

Natalie's voice came from behind me.

Shoving back from the crib, I forced my hand to drop to my side.

"You don't give a shit," I spat.

She flinched from the doorway. "Are you really doing this? Again?" When I watched her close her eyes and pinch the bridge of her nose, my blood boiled. "Do you have any idea how I feel right now? Do you care? You're not communicating—not talking to me. If you don't see that as an issue, I can't do anything about it, but I feel like this is something that could be a serious problem for us down the line."

She was laying everything out on the table, her body shaking with the effort to hold herself together. She crossed her arms over her chest, propping herself against the doorway. A hand gripped the edge of the door from under her arm.

"You disappear for hours on end. I don't know how you are, what you're feeling, or what you're doing. Because you don't talk to me. You come home, but you aren't really here. No matter what I do, how much effort I put into us and trying to make you happy, you aren't really here. You aren't *trying*, Scott. I feel like I'm doing everything I can, while you just sit there. You let me give it and give nothing back. I can't even tell if you see me half the time." Her breath caught in her chest. But she gulped down whatever feeling was building to the surface. "You want sex, and if I can't give that to you because of my period or me not being in the mood, then I'm just cast aside like I bring nothing to you. Do you know how that makes me feel? I feel like I'm living with a roommate, not my husband. I'm living with a roommate who just happens to share a bed with me. That's it, Scott. That's it."

Heat seared through my veins, obliterating every goose bump on my body, as I inhaled again. For whatever reason, I could hear my father shouting obscenities at me.

"That's enough!"

My voice bounced off the walls. I didn't think. My body was moving. Crossing the distance between us, I snatched her from the doorframe to send her into the hallway. With eyes widening, a gasp deflated her chest. I thought it sounded like my name. I didn't care over the roaring in my ears. Against the wall, she was numb with fear.

"You just don't know when to shut the fuck up anymore."

Veins blazing, I snatched Natalie by her hair. She reached up to where I'd snatched a clump from her scalp, screaming. Dragging her down the hall, I heard the breath leave her body. Mine scorched across my skin—boiled in my blood.

Snapping back into herself, she clawed at my hand to free herself. "Scott. No, Scott. Please. What are you doing?"

My vision blackened. I pulled at her hair harder. I felt strands break. With her second scream, Desmond stirred before he was fully awake and crying at the top of his lungs. "Look what you've done now," I spat. "You're a shit mom."

She collapsed, still struggling against my grip. She only got louder as her panic grew.

I shook her, blonde strands breaking in my hand. "Shut up, Natalie. You'll wake the baby."

Reaching the stairs of the basement, I hurled her onto the steps.

She screamed, crying out at the pain as her hands flailed around my grip. "Scott!"

"I am so sick of this, Natalie. I can't keep it up. We have everything we'd always talked about when we were kids, and it isn't enough for you." I let her go to dig my hands into my own hair. Still lying on the stairs, she was pale and frozen. I stood in the way of her only exit. "I'm not the problem. It's you. You're acting like my mother. You bitch like her, you neglect Desmond like her, and I won't let you hurt him—"

Gripping the step in front of her, she balked up at me. "I would never! You have to know that."

My mind was crystal clear. Muffled. I knew what I had to do. I was keeping my mind out of it, letting my impulses take over.

"I don't fucking believe you! I've seen you leave him alone."

I won't let Dezzy go through what I did. I'm not going to let you hurt my son.

So fast—too fast—she started down the stairs, practically crawling backward.

"You're the one breaking your promise, Natalie." My voice echoed down the staircase. "I won't let him have the same childhood we did."

I was on her within seconds, dragging her down the rest of the steps.

She wrestled and kicked the whole way down, her cold hands prying at mine to get me to let her go. When I finally did, it was to drop her in the far corner of the basement.

"Scott?" A tear escaped, rolling down her cheek as she choked out my name. "You've never touched me. Don't start now."

I swallowed the bile rising in my throat.

I brushed along the length of her hair, releasing the broken strands in my grip. She did not melt against my touch. Forcefully grabbing the back of her head, I made her lean against my leg. I kept my eyes open, taking in the empty basement to keep my thoughts focused away from Natalie. Paint cans were stacked against the wall. The barrel drum was shoved into the corner. Natalie's toolbox was beside it.

Tonight would be a repeat of the alcoholic blonde I brought home. Without the paint. Or anyone waiting for me upstairs.

I went to move away from her, undoing my fist from her hair. She was the mother of my child. I could not let her suffer. I could not take my time with her. Not until she was dead. Then and only then would I let myself loose.

"Don't start now." She gripped the leg of my pants, staring up at me. I refused to acknowledge the look in her widened eyes. "What are you doing? Scott?"

I moved back from her.

Fuck Natalie.

I went to snap the lid from the steel drum, only to watch the lid fall off when it hit the cement floor.

She fucking brought this on herself. Fuck this. I fucking love her. Fuck no—but Desmond. Fuck Natalie. The mere thought made me hard.

Then I saw it. My right hand balled into a fist. I could see it. The realization was written all over her face—fear, disbelief, denial, confusion, more denial. Her eyes were wide, her arms coming up to wrap around her shoulders.

"You—you're him? The guy they've been talking about in the news? All these months?"

I swallowed, focusing on her face and the strain on my wrist.

"Skull Splitter."

The name was barely audible, but the room was quiet. Hearing Natalie say the name the newspapers used made my mouth water.

"Don't—"

Dropping to the floor in front of her, I didn't let her flinch back. With a death grip on her face, I snapped. "Stop it, Natalie."

"Please." She choked out a sob. "Please. Don't do this to Dezzy. Don't do this to me. To us—" Her breath hitched in her chest. "I love you, Scott. I love Desmond. Don't take me from him. He needs me."

"You should have thought about that before. He'll be better off without you."

She swung at me.

Without a thought, I shot my hand up, catching her wrist.

I was not fazed by her pleas. I was not fazed by her screams. All of it was stopped—cut off with my hands. Her wrist snapped in my grip. I moved up her body, forcing her against the ground.

Cradling her arm but still wrestling against me, she screamed, "*Why?*"

With her wrist limp against her stomach, she only had one arm to fight with. Her screams fell on deaf ears.

"Why? All I wanted was for us to be a family. I just wanted us to be okay."

My hands found her neck, forcing silence to envelop the room.

"It comes down to because I want to."

She fought, she spoke, but all of it melded together in a blur. Eyes closed, I tightened my grip further around her.

Dezzy would never experience the difficult childhoods we had. He wouldn't have abusive or neglectful parents. He wouldn't live in a trashy home full of empty beer bottles or be surrounded by family who ignored him. He wouldn't fall apart at train tracks, smoke, and wonder if he should lie on the tracks to put an end to the miserable life he had. He would have it better than Natalie and I ever did.

Because I wouldn't let her hurt him, neglect him.

Hands shaking around her throat and every muscle strained with force, I did not take in the terror in her eyes until they were empty of life.

That was when I knew Dizzy was safe. His mother would never have the chance to hurt him.

My child was safe.

Leaning over her, hand grazing her breast to lay it over her unmoving heart, I found my heart frozen in place.

I flinched when I felt something roll down my left cheek. When I looked at it after wiping it away, I was surprised to find it wasn't blood.

"No," I said as I pulled my hands away. Her neck already splotched with dark bruises. "*No*. NO!"

My vision clouded. My image of Natalie was corrupted. I shook her shoulders, but her eyes were catatonic, glassy, open. I shook harder, striking her against the concrete floor. But she did not move.

Blood pooled between her lips.

Releasing her shoulders, I reached for her again. Caressing her hair, her cheeks—but she remained frozen. Looking away from her for a split second, I looked at the barrel but had no intention of touching it.

She deserved better than that.

I lay down over her, motionless, as I stared at her lips. My chest seized at the fluttering in my stomach. Inching closer, ever closer, I kissed her long and slow. Salt and copper trickled from her mouth and into mine. The taste sent warmth seeping through me, my hand trembling as I stroked her cheek one last time.

chapter forty-three

A TREMOR THRUMMED THROUGH ME, causing my mouth to salivate. The meat pulled, red and tender, delicately from the sharp knife in my hand. I couldn't deny the delirious thrill as the seconds ticked by on the clock hanging from the wall while I cut and anticipated the taste.

At the dinner table with his eyes half open, Dezzy sat in his carrier, facing me, so I could keep an eye on him. He cooed as I filleted.

With the lights dimmed and the house eerily silent, the suspense raced along my spine in waves. The divine smell of cooked meat, wine, and bleach was heavenly and caused my fingers to grip the utensils harder.

I couldn't help but flinch when the metal scraped the plate. The rake against the ceramic echoed, ricocheting through the empty rooms. I took in a long breath against the stillness before proceeding to carve bite-sized pieces— dainty cubes of medium-rare nourishment. With nothing else present to disturb the flavors, the plate was clean of distractions.

The slab of meat parted perfectly from my knife to reveal the bloodred vibrancy inside.

The first bite was marvelous—rich and divine; it practically melted in my mouth. The taste of beef or veal but softer, a tad sweeter. The succulent muscle fell apart between my teeth, dissolving against my tongue.

Closing my eyes, I allowed the sensation to overwhelm me. The taste, the thrill of chewing and ingesting something so unspeakable and vastly unacceptable, the recollection of how I had obtained the slabs of flesh. The elation of it all rushed through me. It was something I simply could not deny. Extraction had always snarled within me, endlessly threatening to be unleashed, and I could not quiet it.

It was something I could not control, nor could I bring myself to truly want to restrain myself.

Although the first bite was something I savored, I devoured the second as if I were famished. Bite after bite after bite went down with wolfish laxity.

Until the plate was clean of everything except scarlet remnants of fluid.

I sat back, carefully angling my fork across the plate, followed by the knife, hesitant to disrupt the stillness plaguing my surroundings. The silence was foreign to my ears after so many hours of screaming, yelling, and seemingly endless sobs—and then again, after numerous hours of sawing through flesh and bone.

The power of knowing she could never leave . . . was the most satisfying feeling I had ever experienced.

With the basement bleached, blood scrubbed from the walls, bones discarded in a trash bag, and meat preserved in the freezer, the house was finally hushed. I hadn't felt this smug since taking Natalie. Though, I could not remember the last time I had felt so full.

Younger women had luscious skin, their meat sweeter, skin softer. Natalie was no exception. Her skin tasted sweeter than everything between her legs. Biting into her flesh satisfied me more than she ever had.

Though every victim after this would be unmatched, they would resemble her. I could see it. How I would "accidentally" bump into them at the coffee shop they frequented during their lunch hour or wind up in the same elevator to go to the same floor in any building they wandered into. I would shed my sinister exterior, presenting only my charm until I had them alone.

Until I determined they were someone I wanted to be part of me forever.

Murmuring came from the cradle I'd placed beside the table, and I looked up long enough to see Desmond restlessly fist his shirt.

With Natalie . . . the urge had been building—the impulse to lure another victim into my grasp, only to subdue and consume them. She had deserved every second for how she treated Dezzy. For every minute of heaven and hell she put me through. Every second between us—it had all come to this. Removing the flesh from her skeleton had been euphoric, powerful. An act few could carry out without hesitation. A person's conscience often interfered with pursuing such acts.

I reached for the glass of wine resting above my empty plate, swirling its contents before taking a long gulp of the merlot, confirming my assumptions. Her flesh had tasted sweeter than the finest of wines.

And now, I would never be alone.
She would always be with me.

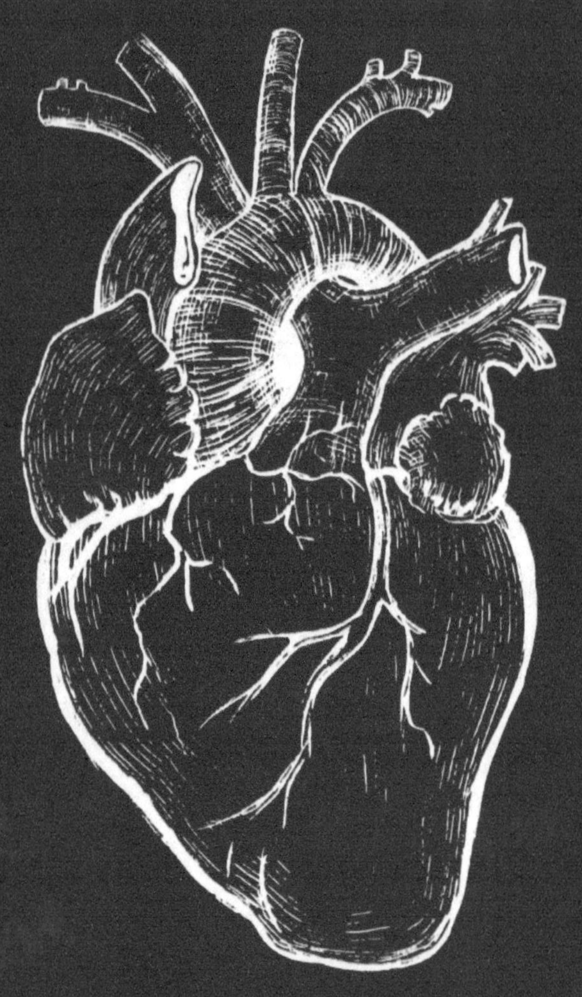

acknowledgments

I would like to acknowledge and give my warmest thanks to my team for helping me make this book happen. Not only did my amazing editor, Samantha of Miss Eloquent Edits, make this book read pretty between all the gruesome descriptions, but she even made the interior of this book look pretty eerie, too. Along with that, my book cover designer, Bianca of Moonpress, did an extraordinary job of bringing my vision to life.

To my family, for encouraging me to follow my dreams of being a published author from the moment I wrote my first book at fourteen and then continued to back me when I majored in Creative Writing when I started college. My mom especially deserves this after enduring years of me shoving awful manuscripts into her hands. Dad, if you made it through this book without dropping it whenever you got creeped out, similar to how you leave the room during the scary parts in horror movies, I'm proud of you. And then to my brother, who will probably give me a weird look when I ask him if he wants to read this book.

To Alyse, for believing in me and my books and for pushing me to be a better writer.

To my wonderful clients, for showing interest in this book and believing in this story the same way I believe in yours.

Thank you to my amazing, supportive boyfriend for being my harshest critique partner and perhaps my biggest cheerleader. I don't think I could have finished this project without our coffee runs, my incoherent rants while papers were scattered all over our bedroom, and your encouraging hugs. Oh, and for making me drink water between cups of iced coffee.

Lastly, thank you to my fluffy writing assistant, Nova, for taking me out on walks to get me out of the house and for keeping my feet warm during late-night writing sprints.

about the author

Ashley grew up in Georgia, but, today, she lives in Colorado with her dog and spends her time devouring any book she can get her hands on, writing, and editing for her clients at Earley Editing, LLC.

Her love of reading and writing began at a young age, which led her to graduate with distinction from the University of Colorado Boulder, receiving a Bachelor of Arts in English with an emphasis in Creative Writing. She also enjoys snowboarding, exploring, annoying her dog, constantly eating chocolate, and sharing her writing adventures on Instagram.

Connect with her on TikTok, Instagram, and other platforms as @ashley_earley and on her website www.ashleyearley.com or reach out at www.earleyediting.com if you're interested in her editing services!